CODE RED

A SAM TAYLOR THRILLER

BEN BALDWIN

BLOODHOUND
BOOKS

For Ella & Megan,
Being your dad is the greatest job in the world.

I am not an adventurer by choice, but by fate.

— Vincent Van Gogh

ONE

THE TWO MEN sat in silence as they watched over the warehouse. Neither took their eyes off the large two-storey building, its steel frame illuminated by the orange streetlights that broke through the cold night air. Seated within the now freezing car, both men's breath had begun to steam as they waited. They had already been sitting for over two hours and now, as the late night became early morning, the first feeling of doubt began to creep into the vehicle.

Eventually, the man sitting in the driver's seat broke the silence. "I hate the cold, I bloody hate being cold."

The other man laughed dryly and pushed his hands further into his coat pockets.

"I'm deadly serious," the driver continued. "For one third of the year all I want to do is be somewhere other than here. I could hibernate from November to February."

The speaker eyed his companion, expecting a reply, but receiving no answer he resumed his vigilance. Outside the now frozen car, the snow had settled across the street and on the surrounding buildings. Somewhere, the sound of engines echoed in the darkness as the distant city passed on through the night.

More minutes went by and the driver stretched out his legs

under the steering wheel. Glancing to his right, he stared at his companion of the past two weeks, but only saw two blue eyes peering out of a face which had pulled the zip of the coat up over its chin. A black woollen hat covered the top part of the stubble-covered face. Even in the low light of the Amsterdam night, the deep-blue eyes glinted as they focused on a doorway into the deserted warehouse.

Officer Johannes Bos couldn't help himself and tapped his fingers nervously against the steering wheel. In his early thirties, the tall, blond detective was impatient for their evening's pursuit to reach its climax. In the last two weeks working with this new partner, they had never had a better chance of solving the case than this evening. They just needed the signal.

Bos looked to his left, down into the dark canal that ran through the industrial estate, out into the main dockyards of the Dutch capital. The fourth busiest in Europe, this dockyard with its never-ending trail of shipping in and out of the country, never slept. Yet in this small corner of the complex waterways that made up the city, nothing seemed to move in the snow-covered darkness.

"Cold night for a swim," Bos commented, peering out of the window at the dark waters. "I think they will freeze over again this year, my friend." He paused for a moment, thinking back to winters gone by. "Now *that* is something to see." He addressed his silent companion, but still hearing no answer, kept on talking. "We have these cafés, which specialise in serving customers on the frozen canals. They put tables and chairs out on the water with warm blankets for those brave enough to sit on the ice."

Both of them knew the words were covering a nervous energy as they waited for something to happen. Flecks of snow continued to fall all around the car, some now resting on the bonnet of the stationary vehicle, the heat of the engine now long gone as the dark sheet of metal was slowly covered in white.

Across from the lone vehicle, the warehouse stood menacing in the gloom. Both men had spent the previous afternoon looking over plans and satellite images of the rectangular building. At the front, opposite where they were parked, a wide glass frontage made up the main entrance. Bright light shone from the clear glass, lighting up the snow that fell close by in a pale glow. To the right stood empty lorry bays; to the left a canal ran parallel to the building, its ever-present depths a constant reminder of the city's unique waterways. To the rear, two fire doors were the only other exits from the building. A single wire fence surrounded the complex, making a car park for the now absent workers. On paper it was a simple task for the four armed tactical teams now hidden in various vantage points within the vicinity.

Bos unzipped his jacket and checked that the Walther P99 pistol was fully loaded before putting it back inside the hidden holster. If everything went well this evening, he hoped he wouldn't need it. If over twenty heavily armed tactical officers couldn't handle what was inside, what use was he going to be?

Out of the corner of his eye, he noticed his companion had been watching his every movement with the firearm, the blue eyes following each action as he removed the clip then pushed it back home.

"Last chance, I've got a spare in there," Bos told him, indicating the glovebox. "I'd even found you a Glock. But I forget that you English don't like to carry a firearm with you. You think it's not sporting to shoot your criminals," he continued, as the man shook his head and smiled at the offer. "Whatever happens next, you are to stay by the car. Remember you're not here, you're back at your hotel. I don't want to have to spend the next six months doing paperwork over why a foreign office official died on my watch."

The passenger raised an eyebrow and returned to watching the warehouse. Instead of arguing with his companion, he pulled out a pair of binoculars to study the now familiar building.

Breaking the silence, Bos's phone vibrated and a single message appeared on the screen. Both men peered down at the phone as it lay between them. Eight words, bright in the darkness of the car.

They passed the junction. Three occupants. Five minutes.

Bos looked up at his partner and nodded, then spoke into the wired microphone hanging down from one ear. "Target inbound, all teams be ready on my mark."

The static reverberated round the car as Bos finished speaking to the unseen tactical teams hidden nearby. Bos once more opened his jacket and removed his firearm, while his passenger returned to looking through his binoculars. Exactly four minutes later, the first distinct sounds of an approaching vehicle could be heard coming from behind them. Both men's eyes darted to the wing mirrors, looking for the telltale flash of headlamps. Barely moments passed before a pair of bright white lights appeared and each of them instinctively slouched into their seats to avoid being seen.

A large black Land Rover, its wheels crushing the crisp snow, drove past the parked car. The moment to strike crept nearer. The new arrival waited for a flimsy barrier to rise before driving through to the glass entrance of the main building. As the engine noise came to an abrupt stop, three figures exited the car. Long shadows spread across the as yet undisturbed snow from the reception lights. Looking through the binoculars, the English passenger could see as expected two male figures and a lone female entering the building.

Bos reached over and grabbed his companion's arm, pulling the binoculars down. "Remember, whatever happens, you stay here. You must not get involved. You're not supposed to be here."

The piercing blue eyes met the stern face of the Dutchman, and the Englishman gave a curt nod.

"Good. Leave it to us, we know what we're doing," Bos promised as he once more reached for the microphone hanging from his ear. Switching for the first time into his native language, he gave a succession of quick orders over the airwaves before checking the building a final time.

Speaking once again in English, he looked at his companion. "Off we go, then."

———

Sam Taylor watched as his friend gave the order to the waiting response teams situated around them. He heard from behind their own vehicle the grating sound of a van door opening, then saw a number of dark figures swarm past their position. Marking their progress across the virgin snow, his eyes were drawn to the footprints in the now broken white powder left behind in their wake. Refocusing, he returned his attention back to the lead officers. They had just reached the wire fence and were regrouping before making the last dash across the car park to the main entrance. He guessed the same process was being repeated at the other entrances to the warehouse.

Next to him, Bos was coordinating the movements, ensuring that they would all enter at the same time. Sam, a former captain in the military police, used to the nervous excitement felt at times like this, returned to staring through his binoculars. He had no intention of getting involved in the evening's events.

Across the road, the assault team was preparing to move on through into the main building. Sam watched as the lead officer crouching to the left waved one of his comrades with a small battering ram into position. The officer placed his hand to his ear and waited.

There was a pause where everything seemed unnaturally silent. Sam wondered if the falling snow had somehow frozen the scene in front of them. Still no order came through to the waiting team and Sam glanced to his left, wondering if Bos had lost his nerve. He needn't have worried. A second later, Bos uttered a firm directive and the man carrying the battering ram moved forward.

Only a heartbeat later they were inside, past the glass doorway and into the foyer. Breaking left, the team bypassed a seating area and then the reception desk. They eventually became lost to sight as they turned the corner towards the main warehouse.

The expectation was to find the three new arrivals and perhaps four to five basic night security guards. Break in, round them up, have everyone back in the station within the hour.

Sam would have guessed the first sounds in such a raid would have been gunshots, either fired as a warning or in defence. He was definitely not expecting to hear three explosions echoing over the snow. Still staring through the glass, all Sam could see now was grey smoke filtering through the foyer.

"What the hell was that?" Bos asked.

He tried to reach the teams over the radio, but the new sounds of automatic gunfire crackled out into the night sky.

Bos swallowed as the sound of the gunfire continued to echo. "I have to go see what's happening."

"We should both go."

"No!" Bos stared at his companion. "Remember, you're not supposed to be here. Stay put and if I'm not back in five minutes, call for help." He reached forward and tapped the car's built-in police radio.

The tall blond officer threw open the door and without another word, ran towards the gunfire. After a moment, Sam reached into the glovebox and pulled out the promised Glock 17. Checking first the clip and then the safety, he placed it on the seat next to him. Gazing out through the windscreen, he saw Bos reach the building, before making his way towards the continuing sound of gunfire. Looking at the digital clock in the centre of the car, Sam could see a minute had already passed since his friend had left the car. Deciding that was more than enough time on the sidelines, Sam picked up the Glock and opened the door, letting in the freezing air.

Ignoring the bitter cold, he began to move across the still-thickening snow towards the building. No need to call for backup.

The noise of the firefight inside would have attracted more than enough attention for the waiting Amsterdam police force to know something was amiss.

Reaching the fence, he slowed slightly and surveyed the building. He knew there were teams covering the rear and the right of the building, but had no idea what had happened to them. Sam paused to consider his next move, each exhale of breath condensing as it hit the night air. His attention was drawn to a light appearing from the left-hand side of the building where the canal ran parallel. It was gone within a moment, as if a door had opened then been quickly shut. Ignoring the gunfire from inside, he ran over to investigate.

Crossing the car park, running past the breached entrance, he reached the side of the building and pressed himself against the brickwork. Craning his neck around the corner, he saw a dark shape edging down the side of the building away from him. In the distance, floating in the water lay a single wooden boat moored up. Whoever it was had avoided the attention of the teams inside.

Without thinking, Sam edged round the corner of the wall and began to slowly follow the narrow footpath. Even in the limited light, Sam could see the outline of a woman. Her blonde hair was tied back, swaying as she walked. He moved forward down the path, which could only have been three feet in width, between the warehouse and waterway. More than once, he felt his foot slip in the snow as he tried to speed up, all the while trying not to sacrifice his stealth.

The woman had paused to bend down and untie the rope, which kept the little boat moored. As she did so, Sam stopped a few feet from her and raised his weapon. "I would appreciate it if you would stop what you are doing."

She neither jumped, nor seemed shocked by his arrival. Instead, she unwrapped the last coil of rope and, keeping it in one hand, stood to face him. Whether his attention had been taken by the unwrapping of the rope, or clouded by the darkness, he had entirely failed to notice that in the other hand she carried her own firearm. A firearm that now pointed directly towards him.

"I'm sure you would. But I would appreciate it if you'd let me carry on."

Sam steadied his hands, keeping the Glock pointed at her. She smiled at him and shrugged, her aim never wavering, as if the whole episode was nothing more than a slight annoyance. Even in the darkness he saw that she was incredibly beautiful, with a narrow, high face, blonde hair, full lips and what he thought were brown eyes.

For a moment, neither spoke. Inside the walls, the firing seemed be dying down.

"I think the party is nearly over in there." She indicated towards the warehouse.

Her English accent was perfect, her voice calm and relaxed as if it was just another walk through the city.

"We could go inside and see if we can liven it up again?" Sam suggested.

"Well, you turn around and I'll follow you."

"Like you followed Major Anderson to his hotel room?"

She shook her head and frowned. "I would have thought you had more imagination than that, Mr Taylor."

Sam was slightly taken aback that she knew his name. "Doesn't take much imagination when you have a dead body in front of you."

The firing suddenly stopped completely and voices could now be heard from inside. Somewhere, a siren sounded in the distance.

"Enough, it's over, you should come in with me. I can help you."

Her mouth began to form something when suddenly a voice shouted Sam's name behind him. While he never moved his eyes from her, his attention was broken just enough for her to fire two unreturned shots. His shoulder felt like it had been hit by a bus and he felt himself thrown backwards, into the canal. Spinning,

Sam's mind began to fog, the icy cold water swallowing him whole. The last thing he would remember from that night was a strange confusion that he did not even know her name.

TWO

THE NEW HEAD of Organised Crime, Johannes Bos, recently promoted and enjoying the perks of being a senior officer within the Amsterdam police force, sipped at his fresh coffee. Leaning back in his chair, he threw the last of the case reports back on the desk and stared out of his top-floor window. Outside, the early autumn sun shone down on the row of trees that lined the canal.

"Two weeks into the job and already acting like you own the place?"

Bos kicked the chair round to see the face of his deputy, Detective Ada Berger, peering round the door into their office.

"Head of department has to have some perks, does it not?"

The red-headed Berger rolled her eyes and opened the door to the office. Dressed as normal in one of her many dark suits and shirts, she took a seat at the desk opposite Bos. "I see you at least remembered to bring me one this time."

"Skinny chocolate latte with a caramel shot, chocolate sprinkles… and extra sugar, the biggest irony going."

The middle finger on Berger's hand made an appearance as she took her first sip.

"What's the plan for today then, boss?"

Bos sighed. The joys of leadership were limited to say the least, as the pile of case reports readily reminded him. With a team comprising himself, Berger and two other officers, the workload had soon increased to unmanageable levels.

"We should really take a look at where all those cars keep disappearing to, or there's that racket down in the dockyards. Then there's the dog that keeps shitting on my doorstep. I'd quite like to take that one down."

"Sounds like a case for Corsel and Hardenne. They'd like that," she said of the other two detectives that made up the small team.

Berger smiled. She had a pretty face with small bright eyes and a slightly husky voice. Since they'd started working together three years ago, he'd found himself enjoying her company more and more. They'd become close friends even outside of work.

"What about the Nile case?"

"What about it?"

"Vogt's been seen around the station this morning, looking for you."

Bos swore. "That little dwarf knows where to find me."

In truth, the Nile case was probably the most important open case, although everyone involved from Bos up to the commissioner had become exhausted by it. Eighteen months and they had still not been able to fully close the file. A file which had resulted in getting Bos the promotion, which now hung round his neck like a dead weight. It had even nearly killed his friend Sam Taylor only the year before.

"Did he say what he wanted me for?"

Berger placed the cup on the table. "I think he said he had another lead on our missing femme fatale."

It was Bos's turn to smile. "Bullshit, we've spent months searching for her. The last time anyone saw her, she was sailing away having shot our English friend. She'll be on a hot beach somewhere."

Bos pinched the bridge of his nose and rubbed his eyes in frustration. The unknown woman, along with the rest of her organisation, had plagued the team for nearly two years. The Nile operation was thought to be the world's largest black-market retailer. Dealing in everything from stolen yachts to weapons, its customers could gain access to anything their money could afford. The name itself was a symbol of the scale of the operations involved. The Nile was the longest river in the world and the largest online retailer on the dark web. Its rival, Amazon, while dominating legal online retailing, was second when it came to sourcing what the Nile operation could provide.

"Spoken to Taylor recently?" asked Berger.

"Not for a couple of months. Last I heard, he was in France."

Sam Taylor, the enigmatic Repatriation Officer, had made the only breakthrough the team had ever succeeded in finding on the case. Having been sent over to investigate the murder of a British Army major, he had managed to find a link between his death and the Nile's leadership. Two weeks of hunting had resulted in a tip-off about a high-level meeting in a disused warehouse. But that night had turned into a firestorm, resulting in the deaths of four officers and the near-death of Taylor himself.

"Wonder what he'd think of Vogt?" Berger asked.

Bos shrugged. "Probably would have punched the little bastard within a week of working with him."

One good thing had come out of the raid on the warehouse. While the woman had escaped, they'd been able to arrest two other big fish. Hans Franssen and Albert de Klerk had ended the night in a jail cell and spent the following eight months making themselves comfortable. It was known Franssen had controlled the Nile's cashflows and De Klerk handled the delivery side of the business. Yet that too had fallen through. The courts had failed to prove a solid case and both had been released a month ago. The frustration caused Bos's former manager to resign in disgust. It had, however, meant a promotion for Bos.

"Perhaps I should try to join Interpol," Berger mused, not for the first time.

"And work directly for that bastard Vogt?"

"Why not? He's always been nice to me. Plus he keeps offering to put in a word for me up at The Hague."

Bos ignored the attempted wind-up. Since the leadership of the Nile had been sourced to the city, they'd been overrun with representatives from Interpol, MI6 and the CIA. They had all come, made a scene, then left when they, like everyone else, had failed to make a breakthrough. Karl Vogt, however, was different. The German had spent months in the city, checking and rechecking every shred of evidence held on the elusive organisation. Many in the Dutch police force were now openly questioning the actual existence of the group. But not Vogt; he had never taken a backwards step.

The room fell into silence as Berger opened her laptop while Bos decided which of the files laid over his desk interested him the most. There was no sign of Vogt as the morning passed by. Both officers went about their business, coming and going from the room as they worked.

At lunchtime, Berger insisted they both left and went to the deli across the canal to fill up. Walking back carrying paper bags crammed with deeply filled sandwiches, their luck fell the moment they walked back into the station. A young uniformed officer stood waiting for them. Sweat had settled on his forehead.

"Mr Bos, sir," the young man spluttered. "I'm sorry to bother you."

"Spit it out."

"It's Agent Vogt, sir. He's looking for you. No, sorry, he's been looking for you, he needs you to meet him as soon as you can."

"Do you know what it's about?" Berger asked.

The young officer shook his head, fearful his answer might offend his superior.

"Fine, whatever. Do you at least know where he is?"

The officer did and twenty minutes later they were in a pool car making their way through the historic streets of Amsterdam. Berger drove, while Bos scrolled through his phone. Every now and then he stopped to look at the beautiful city he called home.

The innumerable cyclists, the tourists, even those whose intentions were purely to visit the Red Light District and coffeehouses with their varied offerings, all of them had made the city unique. He had lived here his entire life and loved every waterway that brought the city together.

It was not long before they saw where they were heading. Three police cars and a single ambulance, their flashing lights awaiting them. All three were parked up against the metal railings that ran alongside this stretch of the canal. Already, crowds of onlookers were trying to get close to the scene. Bos looked up to see the tall five-storey buildings, their rectangular windows full of curious eyes. Berger pulled up behind the first police car and they both clambered out to see what was happening. They were met by two uniformed officers who were taping off the rest of the road. Berger flashed her badge to one of the women, who was redirecting tourists in the opposite direction.

"What's happened?"

The officer raised an eyebrow, surprised they didn't know. "We've found a body."

"Whose?"

"We don't know; the Interpol agent is running things down there." She pointed behind her towards a canal barge moored to the wall. "He's in there."

Whether she meant the body or Vogt, Bos didn't know. They walked on through towards the waiting boat, its wooden hull freshly painted a deep blue with a white stripe running bow to stern. Walking towards the stern they saw two paramedics leaning against a trolley, ready to go. It would be a long wait if the forensics hadn't even arrived yet. They nodded a cordial greeting at the pair of them, then Bos leant forward and held onto the roof of the barge as he climbed aboard. Turning, he offered his hand to Berger, who dismissed it and made her own way over the side. Stepping aboard they saw the usual features of an Amsterdam barge, the rear steering controls embedded in a stand to one side.

Benches on either side of the deck, dark cushions offering respite from the wooden seat.

"Looks well kept," Berger commented as she looked around her.

"The flowers are fresh, certainly," said Bos, pointing to a line of bright flower baskets running along the roof of the boat.

"So's the body."

They turned to see a man stepping out of the cabin and into the afternoon sunshine. The balding middle-aged man stepped out onto the deck, the white shirt bulging from a belly overhanging its belt. A thick black beard ran round his face, which seemed friendly at first glance.

The newcomer could see the confusion in both their faces.

"Doctor Singh, pathologist." He reached out a chubby hand.

Neither Bos nor Berger moved to take it.

"You new here?" questioned Berger. "I know most of the pathologists in the city. One of the perks of the job."

Doctor Singh shrugged. "I'm agency working for Interpol. Apparently the city is short at the moment."

"Quite the introduction, straight into a murder."

Singh appeared bemused. "Who said it was murder? I've hardly had a chance to look properly myself. When I get her to the lab, I'll be able to tell you. But I'll tell you one thing, it was recent. She's still warm." He shifted his weight through the narrow doorway and squeezed past the two officers to make his way back on land. "Just make sure you don't touch her or disturb anything. Not until forensics have finished," the doctor warned. "I'll make sure the pol sends on my report if you want?"

Berger turned to stare at the retreating pathologist. "The pol?"

"Interpol. The fucker in there says they're running the show."

"On my turf? I don't think so," Bos vented.

The doctor waved his hand as he walked away.

"One last thing," Berger called after the doctor. "Why were you here so quickly?"

"The small bastard called me directly."

15

They watched as Singh waddled away, before they both bent and took the steps into the cabin. Stepping down, they found themselves in a cosy living area. Plush sofas lined both sides before giving way to a small kitchen complete with table and chairs. Circular windows gave the cabin plenty of light. Sitting in one of the chairs beyond the table was Agent Vogt. His short stubby legs were raised on one of the other wooden chairs. His curly brown hair was longer than the last time Bos had seen him. The rest of his features were unchanged: the same hooded dark eyes, gaunt cheeks and a strong narrow chin. What he lacked in stature, he made up for with presence. Bos had been in meetings where the short agent had said not a single word and yet still commanded the room.

"Vogt," Bos greeted him.

Agent Karl Vogt, his head resting back in his hands, nodded up at the pair of them. "Bos, Berger. Good to see you again."

"Take it she's in there?" Bos nodded to where a closed door led off to what he presumed was the bedroom.

"She is."

"What happened?"

"I don't know yet. No obvious sign of injury. No suicide note, no narcotics. Could well be natural causes." Vogt spoke in English, his German accent clipping the words.

Bos eyed the door, but didn't move. "Who found her?"

Vogt brought his hands down from his head and put them in his pockets. "Me, I got a tip-off this morning from one of my sources about someone matching her description living here. I did try to find you, but you were out getting coffee."

Bos ignored the jibe. "Why didn't you ring me?"

"I don't like phones. You know that."

"And the pathologist, where's he from? Said you were taking over?"

"I am. I've called the commissioner; it's agreed. Doctor Singh is an old colleague."

Berger sighed and squeezed past Bos to open the door into the bedroom. She walked in and left the two men alone. Vogt's hooded eyes watched her go into the room. "Remember not to touch anything," he warned.

"Yes, I know what I'm doing."

Vogt grunted and turned back to Bos. "How's the new job going?"

"Has its moments," Bos answered abruptly, then turned and followed Berger into the room.

The woman lay on the double bed, her head on a pillow. Blonde hair rested either side of the narrow face. Closed curtains cast a dark shade across the small room. A single wardrobe stood open with a few items of clothing within. There was nothing on either bedside cabinet. Bos joined Berger at the foot of the bed where the body was. Neither moved to check the woman's pulse.

"What do you think?" Berger asked.

"I don't know."

"How did he find her?"

"God knows, but you know as well as I do, he's got fingers everywhere."

"Not quite everywhere." Vogt had entered the room. They turned to look at the Interpol agent, who waved the comment away. "But that's not the question, is it?"

"What is the question, then?"

Vogt put his hands back into his pockets and sighed. "The real question should be, is it our missing Nile director?"

They all turned to stare back at the woman. She was dressed in a loose-fitting dress with a hooded jacket covering her torso. Her face looked peaceful in death, the decomposition not having started. Bos thought she could have been in a deep sleep.

"I don't know," he answered. "But I know someone who would."

THREE

HANNAH PEARCE, Senior Analyst within the Foreign Office's Repatriation Department, did not believe it. She simply refused to believe what she saw on the widescreen television, fixed on the wall within the London meeting room. Over the three years of working within the department she had supported the team in bringing home the deceased, the incarcerated and those that were missing. There had been brutal murders, kidnappings, corrupt police, and now she was expected to believe this.

"It's not true. You're having me on, Sam."

"I'm not, Hannah. When have I ever lied to you?"

"You case officers always do. You think you can take us analysts for fools."

The pretty brunette looked back at the screen, which projected Sam's laptop screen across sixty inches of high-definition glass. A coroner's report was pasted across it, typed rather than handwritten, to their relief. It outlined a brutal cause of death, which neither of them had either heard about or thankfully witnessed before. Each of the categories had been filled out in exact detail by an unknown physician in Kenya.

"It says there were witnesses."

"There were thousands of witnesses when Kennedy died, but I still think that was a cover-up."

Sam leant back in his chair and laughed at his colleague. They'd been going through cases all day and until now most had been the deaths of holidaymakers due to unremarkable natural causes.

"What's so unbelievable about it?"

Hannah pointed up to the screen. "Cause of death: hippo."

"Do you know how many people are killed by hippos every year?"

She shook her head in exasperation. "I could understand a shark attack and maybe even a crocodile attack in Florida."

"Or an alligator."

Hannah scowled at the case officer in front of her. Over the past couple of years, the pair had become close. The tall broad-shouldered former captain had always been one of her favourites. The chiselled face could portray kindness one moment and switch to firmness the next. She knew there was a steeliness to him, which she could never match. "Whatever, but there's no way a middle-aged man from Kent gets killed by a hippo."

"He does if he's drunk on safari. For the record, five hundred people are killed by hippos each year. But if you think *that's* mad, I know of someone who was killed at an illegal cockfight when his own bird stabbed him in the leg with the spur that he made the poor beast wear."

Hannah chuckled and played with the collar of her dress. "Did it win the fight?"

"No idea, but that's not my favourite. Best one I ever heard was of a man killed by a swan."

"No, a swan will only break your arm."

Sam was about to answer when there was a knock on the meeting room door and Jason Rose, their manager, came in. Jason was a tall, slightly overweight man whose family had left the warm Caribbean climate for the occasional dry weather of Exeter.

He liked to tell anyone who listened that his mother had never forgiven him for failing to inherit the family accent.

"Sorry to disturb, guys. We need to speak to Sam."

Hannah exchanged glances with Sam. "Yeah sure, I'll leave you to it."

"No, if Sam's happy she can stay. He'll only tell her when we're gone. Plus, she can be the office support on the case."

The voice came from outside the room, a firm Irish brogue that controlled the department on a daily basis. Emma Read, Head of the Repatriation Department, entered carrying a cardboard file, which she placed in front of her as she sat at the table. Jason stayed standing against the wall by the door.

"Ah, the annual safari death," she commented, looking at the screen. "Hippo this time? I can remember an elephant stampede once."

Sam winked at Hannah as he shut the laptop down and the screen went blank.

"I've had a call from Interpol in Amsterdam. There's an update on your shooter."

At the mention of Amsterdam, Sam could feel his shoulder beginning to ache. "Go on."

"They had a tip-off this morning about her whereabouts."

As she spoke, she pushed the file over to Sam, who flipped the cover and looked down. It was her. He knew straight away. He didn't even need a second glance – the deceased woman in the photo was the same woman who had tried to kill him that bitterly cold night. The memory of it came flooding back. The thudding pain in the shoulder. The cold grip of the icy water dragging him down. He had only been saved by the quick reactions of Johannes Bos diving in and somehow dragging him out. Later, the medical teams suggested that the cold water had helped save his life, but he had no idea how.

"They found her body in a canal boat in the city centre soon after we got the tip."

"How?" Jason spoke from the back of the room.

"We don't know; she's been taken for an autopsy as we speak."

Sam stared down at the face, with its narrow features, full lips, high eyebrows above a sharp nose. From the photograph she looked to be lying on a bed, her bright blonde shoulder-length hair spread across a white pillow. He wasn't sure how he felt. He still didn't even know her name.

"It of course doesn't help Interpol with their efforts at taking down the Nile, but it at least gives us some closure on the Anderson case."

"The major?" asked Hannah. "The one killed in the hotel?"

"Yes, it's how we were brought in on the case. Major Stuart Anderson was found murdered in a hotel room in Amsterdam around a year ago now. He was there for a NATO conference. Local police were struggling to find out what had happened, so we sent Sam over to see."

Picking up the photograph to look at it in a better light, Sam continued with the story. "I managed to establish our major was not all he seemed. Alongside visiting some of the… less family friendly attractions in the city, he was also there on other business." He stopped. There was something about the photo that bugged him.

"What business?" enquired Hannah.

"Major Anderson was a procurement officer for the British Army, specialising in personal ground-to-air rockets. The type that could take out an airliner. He was there to sell a batch to the Nile," Jason answered.

"How did you find out about that?"

"He liked to brag to the hookers he hired," Sam replied bluntly.

"Sam managed to find a couple of the girls he'd seen and one commented that she'd heard him arrange to meet someone to discuss business. After speaking with Interpol and knowing what Anderson had access to, we put two and two together."

"That's the official version. She had actually rifled his pockets while he was in the shower cleaning himself down. Saw the messages on his locked phone screen. But she didn't want to tell the police that, as she also found two hundred euros in his wallet."

"But she was willing to tell you?"

"I have my ways." He winked.

Emma sighed. "Sam provided the investigation team with a time and the police were able to find our Major Anderson. We watched as he entered the hotel fifteen minutes before the blonde woman you see below. She went in after him, then ten minutes later she was filmed exiting the building before disappearing completely."

Sam gave up on the photo; he couldn't put his finger on whatever it was. "During the time between Anderson entering the hotel and our deceased friend leaving, he had his throat cut. It looked like he opened the door, turned round and then she killed him. The room was covered in blood, a proper spray paint job. I felt sorry for the housekeepers."

"Room service found him about five or ten minutes after she'd left." Jason had seen Hannah's next question coming and headed her off. "He'd pre-emptively ordered a bottle of champagne and two glasses for the two of them. Instead, the bellboy found the body."

"Christ."

"From then on, no one had much more to go on; she disappeared. It was pretty desperate until a few days later, when we got a tip-off that the top Nile team would be at a warehouse later that night."

"Yet you ended up going for a swim? I know about that; the whole department does. Only you would get shot and nearly drown at the same time," Hannah joked.

Emma stepped in, her face grave. "They were betrayed; either the whole tip-off was a hoax or someone on the inside gave them away. The Nile was ready for them and nearly had enough firepower for the entire armed response team."

Jason now came to sit by Sam and picked up the photo. "She's a good-looking girl."

"*Was* a good-looking girl," commented Sam, drily.

The room fell into silence. Emma watched Sam, who stared back, meeting her eyes. Hannah, meanwhile, watched the both of them and thought how different but also how similar they both were. She knew both had been hand-picked by the former civil servant Sir Jeffrey Doyle to, in reality, run the department. Emma: cold, calculated, firm, kept the entire show going. Balanced political egos with practical needs. Sam: charismatic, resourceful, forceful, would ensure that the job was completed, regardless of political egos or unpractical needs. They complemented each other perfectly. She wondered jealously if there was any sexual chemistry between them.

"I take it neither Interpol nor the police have made any further developments on the Nile since?" Sam asked Emma.

"No. Interpol has taken over the case and restricted access to the corpse. Agent Vogt from the German branch is running the show."

"Never met him."

"He came onboard when you were in hospital."

Sam's shoulder was definitely aching now. Whether it was an imaginary or actual physical pain, his left shoulder was telling him something.

Hannah was studying the image while Sam flicked through the remainder of the file, showing the rest of the crime scene. There was an outside view of the boat as well as internal shots of both the bedroom and living area. Someone had photographed all of the contents within the rooms. There seemed to be nothing of interest.

"What was her role within the Nile?" Hannah asked the group.

Jason answered, "We don't really know. She wasn't the number one and two other senior directors were apprehended at the warehouse. However, they were released this year. As for the number one, we have absolutely no idea who that is. We had hoped she may have led us to him. Whoever it is has access to unbelievable resources."

"Looks like the investigation's back to square one," said Hannah despondently.

"Maybe, maybe not," said Sam. "They have the boat; that's a clue. It's clear she didn't live there. Look at the photos. There's nothing there. A woman like this would have a bit more than a couple of outfits. It's a safe house, is my best bet. Question is, *whose* safe house?"

"That's not our problem," Emma cut in. "We're only interested in bringing Major Anderson's killer to justice, and it's fair to say that's happened, so that's our case closed."

"But…" Sam knew there was something else, had seen it in her face when she'd sat down and passed him the file.

"But the Dutch police would like you to formally identify the body."

"I thought I already had?"

"They would like you to go in person. I've had both that Vogt agent and the commissioner ring me this afternoon."

Sam swore. He'd hoped he would never have to go back to that damned city. His mind also drifted back to the envelope he had hidden in his kitchen drawer. Was that related to what had happened?

"We'll pick up your caseload while you're away," Jason said, trying to sweeten the arrangement. "You can have Hannah as the case office support as well."

"Johannes?" Sam asked Emma.

"I don't know but I presume so, especially if he's heading up the Organised Crime Unit now."

"And we're not getting involved in the Nile case?"

Emma shook her head. "No, we are simply closing the Anderson case. It would be good for the family at least to get closure."

Sam knew he had to go, so he gave his consent. There was no other choice but to close the case.

"Great, I'll let them know you're on your way. Hannah, can you get him on a flight tonight?"

"No, it needs to be tomorrow. I'm seeing Sir Jeffrey tonight. Get me on the early flight from Heathrow. It won't make any difference – she's not going anywhere."

Emma reached over and pulled the photos together before handing the file over to Sam. "Did you want a flight back the same day?"

Sam paused for moment and thought about seeing Johannes Bos and then another face came into his mind. It would be good to see Ada Berger again. The red-headed officer might still be working on the case. She might even still be single.

"Hold off on booking a return for now, let's see what happens."

Emma and Jason stood to leave, wished him luck, then went on their way.

Hannah also stood to leave. "I'll get started on booking your flights."

"Thanks Hannah."

She paused at the door. "Are you okay?"

Sam's mind was still on the envelope in his kitchen, but he kept it to himself. "Yes, I'll be all right."

"And the swan?"

He laughed, remembering their earlier conversation. "A canoeist went too close to its nest, the bird attacked, he fell into the water and the swan kept forcing him under till he drowned."

"Bullshit."

"Google it."

Sam began to picture the struggle in the cold water and shuddered. He knew how the guy must have felt.

FOUR

WALKING THROUGH CENTRAL LONDON, away from the Foreign Office, Sam passed the crowds until he reached a side road just off Piccadilly Circus. Having bypassed the brightly coloured storefronts, he arrived at their usual venue just before six. He chuckled dryly to himself as he entered the small restaurant, squashed between two upmarket pizza chains, their tables half empty. Next to them, il Conte's already had a small queue of people waiting to get in.

A thickly-built man greeted him and ushered him to his table in the far corner. Taking his seat under a faded picture of a Mediterranean countryside scene, Sam checked his smartwatch to see where the old man had got to. The digital screen showed his unread emails and messages, but there was nothing from Sir Jeffrey.

"First again, Mr Taylor," the waiter greeted him.

"Nothing changes, Stefano, especially not him."

"No, no, Sir Jeffrey will always be Sir Jeffrey. Can I get you your drinks?"

Sam nodded and waited as Stefano went away to bring a pint of beer and a red wine to the chequered table. The doorbell chimed as a cold rush of air came into the room. Stefano went to answer it.

"Hello sir, please may I help you? Do you have a reservation with us?"

"Fuck off, Stefano, I've been coming here twenty years and you still pull that shit with me."

"We may have some space later if you come back?"

"That's why I don't tip, you miserable bastard. No customer service."

Sam looked at his old friend, who was now seated and had picked up the recently arrived glass of wine. The retired civil servant was pushing eighty but exuded the energy of a man far younger. He was carried by a slim frame, which had yet to concede any ground to the extra weight that plagued many of his age. Thick white hair was wavy on his head, which had been covered by a dark flat hat when he'd entered. Gold-rimmed spectacles sat on a large round nose, below which a well-groomed white goatee covered his chin. He was dressed this evening in a loose-fitting brown jacket over a white shirt and dark trousers.

"Best Italian food in London, hands down. Just a shame about the service."

Stefano walked over and made a show of handing over a menu to only Sir Jeffrey. "For you, sir." He turned to Sam. "Will you be having your usual? And what would your great-grandfather like to eat?"

"Two usuals please, Stefano. Don't worry. I'll help him cut it up."

"Fuck off the pair of you."

The Italian waiter left to take their orders to the kitchen.

Sam sat back and took a long look at his dinner partner. They had known each other for over twenty-five years, since Sam was a child. Sir Jeffrey, a friend of Sam's grandad, Gerry, had helped him to get a job in the Foreign Office after he had been forced out of the military. His own career had been far more interesting. A lifelong diplomat, Sir Jeffrey had travelled the world, meeting its politicians, monarchs, business leaders and everything in between. He was known to have crossed over the blurred line between international diplomacy and espionage on many an occasion. Sam had once tried to find out what he had received his knighthood for, but had only found a passing reference in the archives to 'services to the crown'.

"How's the family? Still in Yorkshire?" Sir Jeffrey asked, jibes forgotten.

"Yes, Mum and Dad still the same. Sister still married. Brother still unknown, well at least, not talking to me."

"And the office? Emma still queen bee?"

The term was used with endearment. Emma Read had been his protégé in the government well before Sam had left the army.

"Still the queen bee. She's sending me off again."

Sir Jeffrey twirled the wine in the glass as he listened. "Oh yes? Where to this time?"

"Amsterdam."

The wine stopped swirling in the glass. "Jesus. Same case?"

"Yes, the woman who shot me has been found dead today. Some Interpol agent called Vogt wants me to identify her." Sam continued describing the events of earlier. A few hours on, he still didn't quite know how he felt about everything, while at the back of his mind he wanted to take another look at the postcard in his kitchen.

By the time he'd finished retelling the day's events, two plates of steaming pasta carbonara had arrived and a second round of drinks was on its way.

"Did you say it was an Agent Vogt who asked for you?"

Sam confirmed the name before starting on the creamy pasta.

"I know of him. I've come across him on a couple of cases. He's very good. You'd like him."

"I would?"

"Yes, he's very clever, sees things others don't. Do you know he is a little person?"

"No?"

"Yes, and one of the best agents on the Continent."

They ate in silence for a few minutes, both taking a moment to look round the room. Sam's eye was caught by a family of four midway through their desserts. Two little girls, both with bright blonde hair, had retreated under the table with a pair of tablets to watch. He thought of his sister's kids and was glad he didn't have the hassle.

"So you're definitely going?" Sir Jeffrey asked.

"Yes. I don't see a reason why not. It will be good to see Johannes, at least."

"What about the Nile?"

Sam considered the question. Both he and Sir Jeffrey knew that going after a criminal organisation such as this one was out of the department's remit. But when he had been over there last year, he couldn't help but be dragged into the wider context. At the time it was clear that Major Anderson's death had been part of a bigger picture. However, since then his supply chain had come to a literal dead end, as had his killer. There was nothing left to do but confirm the woman's identity.

"No. Strict orders from Emma. I'm to confirm Anderson's killer is no longer available for trial, then come back. I'll be home in two days."

The older man raised an eyebrow and continued his way through the now nearly empty glass.

Stefano came and took the empty plates away. "The usual, Mr Taylor?"

"Yes please, Stefano."

Moments later, as though they had been prepared even before the order was taken, a single bowl of ice cream along with an Americano appeared on the table.

Sir Jeffrey took the coffee and admonished Sam. "Such a child, it's why I won't take you to a nice restaurant."

"Thank you for your compliment, sir," Stefano's voice echoed across the room.

Sam just grinned.

"So Emma says to keep out of the Nile operation?"

"Yes."

"Suppose she's right, you can't be doing everything."

They talked some more about the Nile case, both guessing the types of merchandise they were selling now. For all their size and scale, there was such little information known about them. No clear clients, no physical stock and no money trails. At times Sam had wondered if there was even an organisation at all.

"I'd be interested to know who the head man is."

"Or woman."

"True. We have the two that were caught when you got shot."

"Franssen did the finance and De Klerk was the supply chain."

Sir Jeffrey took out a pen and drew two dots on his napkin, writing 'F' then 'K' under them. A third dot joined them in a line, under which he wrote an 'S'.

"Then there's our deceased shooter."

He drew a fourth dot, this time above the three original markings. He connected each of the three to the fourth and placed a question mark over his work.

"So who is the ringmaster to this circus?"

"That I don't know."

Sir Jeffrey sat back and grabbed his coffee, deep in thought.

"I can see why Vogt is so keen to find out who's behind this."

Sam stared again at the napkin. "Why?"

"Whoever is heading up this organisation controls the biggest supply chain of black-market goods in the world. Think about it; he or she could be deciding which terrorist group to supply next. We already know they were in the market for ground-to-air rockets. What else can they get at?"

Sam didn't answer and Stefano brought over the bill. He knew the drill and gave it to Sir Jeffrey, who despite Sam's offer, continued his uninterrupted run of paying the cheque.

"I don't know why I bother, Stefano. One day I'll find somewhere more welcoming."

The Italian waiter just smiled and patted his customer on the shoulder.

Taking their coats, the pair of them made their way out of the small restaurant. Turning back as he went, Sam was not surprised to see a crisp twenty-pound tip on the table where they had been sitting.

By now, the night had grown cold as the two men walked to the nearest underground station. Autumn had well and truly set in, with the warmth of summer becoming a distant memory. Reaching the station, the pair were about to go their separate ways when Sir Jeffrey grabbed Sam's arm.

"One last thing, Sam. The Nile, an organisation that large operating out of one city. It has to have some sort of arrangement with the local authorities."

"You mean bribes?"

"Bribes, backhanders, people on the inside, bent police, whatever. But there has to be, there's no other explanation. So be careful; don't take any risks."

He looked into the older man's face and saw genuine concern. "Hey, you're turning into Emma, or she's turned into you. But yes, I'll be careful."

The old man smiled and glanced round the now quiet street. "Well, best be off. Once more unto the breach, dear friend." With that he turned away, waving an arm over his head as he walked into the night.

Sam watched him go, with a swell of affection for the old man who had done so much for him over the years. Taking the steps down into the station, he pulled out his headphones.

Arriving back at his Clapham flat, Sam went straight to the kitchen and pulled open the side drawer of random paperwork. He flicked through takeaway menus, letters and keys till he found the postcard with its row of traditional Dutch windmills. Without looking on the reverse, he threw it onto the side and opened the fridge. He needed another drink. Taking the tonic, he poured himself a large measure of Tarquin's Cornish gin from a blue bottle, its wax seal long since removed. After sprinkling a handful of junipers and dropping half a lime with some ice cubes, he left it to settle next to the postcard.

Leaving the kitchen, he began to pack for the trip. He played it safe and threw in enough outfits to last him a few days. After packing the usual travel essentials, he took the bag back out to the hallway. Taking the glass and the postcard from the kitchen, he fell back into the single sofa. After two long pulls of the icy liquid, he turned the card over.

From Amsterdam. Glad to know you're feeling better. See you soon. With love, X.

It had arrived in the summer and at the time he had presumed it had come from Ada Berger. He had become intimate with the attractive redhead during the days leading up to the shooting. Until that moment he had not heard from her beyond a sympathetic message after he'd arrived back in England.

But what if it *wasn't* from Ada? As soon as he had seen the photo this afternoon, his mind had wandered back to the postcard. Thinking about it now, why would Ada have written when all their communication had been over the phone? How would she even know his address? But then the same question could be asked about his shooter. How the hell would *she* have known where he lived? His shoulder ached and he untied the buttons of his collar to reach down and run his fingers over the scars. She'd hit him twice, either side of his collarbone. The doctors had told him he'd been lucky, the physio had told him that he would be back to normal before he knew it. They had both been right to an extent.

Nearly twelve months on, his mind was still conflicted. He was angry at himself for allowing her the chance to fire. He'd spent too many hours thinking over the moment, yet one question still plagued him. If she had been a man, would he have hesitated in pulling the trigger?

Sam took another drink of the gin and reread the thirteen words. He suddenly understood what she meant by writing to him. There was no concern in those words; she was mocking him. She knew where he lived, that he had recovered and that she would be seeing him soon. Was that a threat? Well, it had backfired. There'd be no reunion, more disappointingly no chance for revenge. He swallowed the remainder of the gin until all that was left was soggy fruit.

Standing, he took one last look at the words, his more logical mind picking up the subtle ways in which she had formed the letters. The curves on the 's' and flick on the final 'e'. These thoughts were quickly pushed to one side and he threw the card back on the sofa. The bitch, just like the case, was dead.

FIVE

JOHANNES BOS STOOD with his deputy Detective Ada Berger in the arrivals hall of Amsterdam airport, one of Europe's busiest transport hubs.

The two police officers were tired. Both had been seconded to Agent Vogt's most recent attempts at making a dent into the operations of the Nile. From the moment they had arrived at the small canal boat, Bos had known the case reports back on his desk would have to wait a while. Vogt had found a new energy with the discovery, and had every able-bodied law enforcement officer assigned to the team, exploring this new lead. He'd also demanded the presence of the arrival for whom they were waiting.

"Why do we need him to come over?" Bos had asked when the decision had been made the day before.

"Because he's the only one who can fully identify her as a member of the Nile."

"Then send him the photo and he can do it from London?"

"I want him to be sure, and so does your commissioner, so it's happening. I'd have thought you'd be happy to see him again. I thought the two of you were friends?"

Bos shrugged his shoulders. Sure, he would be happy to see

34

his friend again. Yet he'd be damned if he was going to let the German agent get his own way that easily. They'd been stood on the waterside, outside the boat where the body was currently being readied to be uplifted to the mortuary, where Doctor Singh was preparing to examine the corpse.

Vogt lit a cigar, which he puffed at in the early evening air while they waited for the body to be removed. They'd had to wait while Interpol's forensics had gone over the whole vessel. No one else had been allowed anywhere near the body.

"Are you and your team okay to begin questioning the local residents?" he asked Bos. "It would be useful if you could get any witnesses or CCTV of the area."

Bos had already called Corsel and Hardenne back to begin door-to-door enquiries. Berger, meanwhile, had made calls to the office to start investigations on the ownership of the vessel.

"Why can't we just compare the body to the CCTV we have of her following Anderson?" pushed Bos.

"I don't trust the quality of those tapes. It's not as if there are only a few young blonde women here in the Netherlands to choose from. Based on the CCTV alone, it would mean suspecting a third of the population. We get a firm identification and your friend gets to close his own case. I can't imagine the UK government's been happy that the murderer of one of their military officers has been at large, even if that officer was selling arms on the side."

Vogt puffed some more on the cigar. He was dressed in a sailors' pea jacket, which had clearly been tailored for him. With his dark curly hair and blunt facial features, Bos could easily have imagined him as a weathered old captain, standing on his ship's bridge during a brutal stormy night.

"Bring him in and get the body checked. I'd also like to meet him. I heard good things about him before I joined." Vogt paused as they turned to watch the paramedics carrying the body out of the cabin, the setting sun golden on the white sheet.

Bos looked on, feeling a spare part as the Interpol teams ran the show. He and Berger had been kept at arm's length and he was beginning to get annoyed. They'd not even seen the body since that first quick examination.

"It's probable we have a murderer on our hands," Vogt continued, lecturing the younger man. "I'd certainly feel better having an extra pair of eyes on the case."

The agent popped the cigar back into his mouth and patted Bos on the arm before turning to follow the corpse on its journey to the hospital. Bos had joined the rest of his team in beginning the investigation work of the local area and hadn't left until well after sunset. Now, as he and Berger waited in the arrivals terminal, he wondered if Dr Singh had found anything yet. He shivered at the thought of the overweight man pulling out intestines and other organs in search of a cause of death. Perhaps there was something to be said for a straightforward shot to the head.

"Coffee, boss?" Berger asked.

He gave her his phone. "Put it through the app and I'll get extra points."

Berger took the phone and flicked through the menus with her slim fingers.

"How do you know my password?"

"How many times have you sent me out to get your lunch?"

Bos hadn't been surprised by his colleague's willingness to join him that morning. He remembered the unspoken chemistry between her and Sam Taylor last time. While not knowing for certain, he was pretty sure it had gone beyond the unspoken, into something more physical.

The detective left to collect their drinks, passing him his phone back as she did. Looking up to the large clock held up from the roof by grey metal wires, Bos saw the time tick past ten. His eyes flicked to the arrivals board again and he saw that the nine-twenty from London had landed on time; he guessed his friend was making his way through customs.

Bos saw Sam Taylor before he had seen him. The tall, broad-shouldered Englishman hadn't changed. His light-brown hair was combed to one side. A chiselled friendly face with its single dimple making him look younger than his years, despite the stubble. He was dressed in a dark-green field jacket covering a black three-quarter zip jumper and shirt. Two brown suede boots stuck out from under a pair of dark trousers. He could have been wearing the same outfit as last year. Seconds later, the deep-blue eyes flicked up to see his friend smiling at him.

They paused, smiled at each other then embraced.

"Good to see you, Sam," Bos greeted his friend after they broke apart. "Good journey?"

"I've had worse. You on your own?"

The Dutch officer smiled knowingly. "No, I've brought a friend with me. She's just getting a coffee."

They moved away from the crowds back towards the exit, where they could now see the slim form of Ada Berger waiting for them, three cups in hand.

"I didn't think we'd be seeing you again, stranger," Berger greeted Sam.

"Can't say it's my first choice for a weekend getaway after last time. You should have seen the reviews I left online about the place. Shocking local hospitality, left me cold."

"Cold water, colder people," Berger replied.

"Still the same as Bos? Black Americano?"

"Indeed, thank you."

The three of them headed outside and walked towards the short-term parking bays.

"Warmer over here than in London," Sam commented, looking at the clear blue sky.

"We still have a few weeks before the real cold arrives," Bos confided.

"How's London?" Berger asked lightly. "Work treating you right?"

"Wet, too much rain these past few weeks. But nothing

changes there. Work is still the same, people going abroad and dying."

They reached the car and Sam dropped his bag in the boot before taking a seat in the back as Bos slid into the driver's seat. Berger took her usual place at his side.

"How's the case going? Cause of death?"

Berger answered, "Our physician didn't start last night, said he had a dinner to go to. Guess Vogt will have had him in early this morning to make up for it."

"He did, they started at seven this morning," Bos confirmed as he drove the car into the moving traffic of the roads leading out of the airport. "If it's okay with you, we'll head straight over to the morgue?"

"Sure."

Bos kept one eye on his friend in the rear-view mirror. The normally relaxed Englishman seemed on edge.

"I guess you've heard of Agent Vogt? He's going to be leading the case going forward and we've been seconded to him for the time being. I'm not sure where that leaves you?"

"I'm only here to close the Anderson case. Once I have identified my killer, I'll be able to go home."

Berger turned round in the chair. "So it's definitely her?"

"I think so. The picture's pretty conclusive."

"I think it's her."

Bos turned half an eye to his deputy.

"We've seen the Anderson case CCTV," she explained. "Vogt is just being difficult; he wants to drag Sam into the case after what happened last year. Knew we'd all made such a good team, he wanted us back together."

Bos wondered if by team Berger meant professionally, or something else.

"Well whatever, it's a good chance to see each other again," said Sam. "How's things been here? Congratulations on the promotion, by the way."

The Dutchman smiled sheepishly. "Thank you, although it was

unexpected. I think they were pleased about our Nile catch last year. The fact they got off wasn't held against me."

"He deserved it. Even if it's gone to his head," Berger teased.

"Everything else still the same?"

"Pretty much, same old faces causing trouble," said Berger.

"And Peter?"

Johannes and Peter had been married now for a few years, sharing an apartment in an upmarket area of the city. Peter, a successful investor, had been good company when Sam was last over.

"All good, sends his regards. We got a rescue, a boxer. Ugly thing, but he loves him."

They were coming into the more built-up areas of the city and the traffic became slower. Sam looked out of the rear windows, remembering the number of cyclists and cycle lanes the city had.

"And you, Ada?" Sam asked her.

"Oh you know, still the same, waiting for my own investment banker to come and whisk me away."

"She's wanting to transfer to Interpol with Vogt," Bos interrupted.

"And leave Bos to fend for himself? I don't know how he'd cope without seeing you every day."

Christ, the flirting's begun again, Bos thought to himself as he continued to weave through the tight traffic of the city centre.

"So, what's this Agent Vogt like?"

The two Dutch officers looked at each other.

"He's okay," Berger answered.

"He's a bastard," Bos answered.

Sam laughed in the rear of the car.

"He's very good," conceded Bos. "But he's hard work, too intense. He's clever but knows it and seems to enjoy making you feel uncertain."

"Did you know he was a dwarf?" Berger interrupted her boss. "Bet there's been a few short jokes bandied round Interpol over the years."

Bos laughed dryly. "Not to his face. The guy's practically taken over the German Interpol Agency. Made his name cracking a people-smuggling racket during the refugee crisis. There's a rumour he even got a personal thank you from the former German chancellor for his efforts."

"I heard about it; there were some pretty evil bastards involved in that. He did well to close them down," Sam said with genuine respect. "Hunted them down all the way back to Greece, didn't he?"

Bos nodded. "Yes, completely wiped them out. Wasn't long after that he was let loose on the Nile lot, but he's not had the same success so far."

They fell silent as they drove through the streets leading to the hospital with its basement mortuary. Bos's mind was already on what the afternoon had in store. As soon as Sam had finished confirming what they already knew, they'd have to get back to chasing dead ends. He dreaded to think what Vogt would have them doing next. Their enquiries the previous night with the neighbours of the canal boat had resulted in nothing. No one had seen anybody entering or leaving the vessel. Bos had not been surprised to hear that no one they'd spoken to had even known there was someone using it.

Bos's phone rang and he answered it.

A clipped accented voice came over the car speakers. "Bos, how are you getting on?"

"We've got Taylor and we're just coming round the corner."

Vogt grunted. "Good, I'll come up and meet you."

"Is there any update on the cause of death yet?"

"No, I keep chasing Singh."

"Will he let Sam in?"

"He hasn't got a choice in the matter," Vogt answered abruptly, then ended the call.

Before long, the three of them were heading towards the main entrance of the hospital. As they made their way through the parked cars, Bos could already see the small Interpol agent outside, waiting for them. He was still wearing his pea jacket but, perhaps in deference to the medical surroundings, he had forgone the cigar. Crossing the road, they walked over to the man leading the case.

"So you're Sam Taylor," said Vogt. "I've heard a lot about you. Welcome back to Amsterdam."

SIX

SAM REACHED out and took Agent Vogt's hand in a firm grip. Studying the face and dark eyes that looked up from under hooded brows, Sam guessed that the years of slights, jokes and all kind of insults had shaped this man into something to be respected. There was an aura to him, which spoke of authority.

"Agent Vogt." Sam spoke with reverence.

"Mr Taylor."

"Please, I prefer Sam."

Vogt pursed his lips and shrugged.

"Good, well thanks for coming. Appreciate it's probably not a case you'd want to get involved in after last time." He turned and led them into the hospital.

The reception area was full of the usual people to be found coming and going about their business. Doctors in lab coats, nurses in their uniforms, all mixed with patients in the open space. The Dutch healthcare system was regarded as one of the world's finest, its free universal system regularly rating highly across all scoring metrics used in the western world. Having experienced it first-hand, Sam knew why.

They followed the Interpol agent through the corridors and down a flight of stairs heading towards the basement. Sam watched the diminutive figure stalking the hallway. As they walked, Bos caught Sam's eye and raised his eyebrows in exasperation. Berger, meanwhile, brought up the rear.

"How are things in the Repatriation Department, Mr Taylor?" said Vogt as they took the stairs, ignoring Sam's request to use his forename. His clipped accent made the words sound merely a formality, rather than an expression of genuine interest.

"Our busy period has ended. Soon it'll be back to returning old people from their villas and retirement resorts," Sam replied.

Vogt barked a deep dry laugh. "Don't give me that. I know that's not all you guys get up to. I heard about the summer. You somehow managed to crack a national drug syndicate in a week after all the agencies in France had failed. That was good work."

It had been tough work, Sam acknowledged. A simple repatriation case of a deceased young woman had resulted in him being caught up in a deadly narcotics supply chain. What followed had involved breaking into a castle, escaping through a secret tunnel and then a shoot-out in a historic underground church. Perhaps a bit more than returning deceased pensioners home for a funeral.

They reached a plain waiting room with plastic seats dotted around a small table covered in magazines. Vogt left them as he went through a pair of double doors to see how much longer they'd have to wait for Singh. The remaining three each took an uncomfortable seat and settled down for the wait. Sam checked his phone before sending a brief update to the team back in London. He'd already decided to stay over that night and Hannah had found him a central hotel to sleep in.

Vogt returned and told them Singh was writing up his final comments but was confident he had an answer for them as to the cause of death. He took a chair opposite Sam and slouched back, his hands above his head. The time passed slowly and Sam watched as people came and went by the small seating area. Orderlies went along the white corridor pushing gurneys, a few cleaning staff started mopping the floor back towards the stairs, but there was no sign of Doctor Singh.

"What did you think about the release of the two Nile directors early this year?" Vogt asked Sam.

"Franssen and De Klerk? Bastards were lucky. If that warehouse had been full, there would have been a stronger case."

"They knew you were coming," Vogt commented. "The only thing they got wrong was the firepower. They didn't bring enough."

He was right, of course. The raid had failed because the Nile had been waiting for them, emptying the warehouse long before they had arrived. Added to the casualties on the assault teams and Sam's own near death, it had not been a good night.

The doors to the mortuary opened and a young nurse walked past, her face deep in a report. All four of them watched as she walked down the corridor in her blue hospital outfit. A black bob covered one side of her face, the sound of her heels echoing long after she had disappeared from sight.

"Probably better asking her for an update than that useless tub of lard in there," Vogt scoffed to no one in particular.

Five minutes later, his patience snapped. Having waited enough, he went to find the missing doctor.

"I think Singh's going to be getting a kicking," joked Berger.

Sure enough, moments later, Vogt's head peered through the doors. "Let's go, we can identify her now."

Sam followed the two local officers through the double doors, his stomach twisting. He was surprised how nervous he felt. The conflicting emotions of shame, anger and, strangely, regret all mixed together as he paced through the bright artificial lights, the sound of their steps now echoing down the empty corridor. As they reached the doors to the mortuary, they burst open towards them and out came the bulk of Doctor Singh, his large stomach stretching the seams of his shirt.

"Doctor," Vogt greeted him. "Going somewhere?"

Singh looked blankly back at the agent. "You've been chasing me all day for my report and now I'm going to print it off."

"You don't have a printer in your office?"

"Not unless Interpol are going to start paying more for their corpses?"

"Can we still see the body?"

Singh sighed and gave up. "Yes, she's still in there. You know which lab she's in, so I'll leave you to do the identifying while I get my report."

Vogt looked like he was going to argue, but after a pause he stepped aside for the larger man to pass.

Twisting back towards Vogt, they entered the mortuary office, comprised of a few desks around a counter facing towards three doorways into the different labs. Computer screens glared at the four newcomers as they walked in and Sam wondered which one Singh had used to write his report. Apart from the four of them, the place was deserted.

"Shall we go in?" asked Vogt.

Bos grunted a reply and turned to follow. Sam stayed where he was for a moment.

"You okay?" Berger had noticed his hesitation.

"Let's get this over with."

Vogt had stood by the first door, ready to open it inwards, his face triumphant. "My friends, our first step to finding the source of the Nile."

Stepping in, they found themselves in a typical mortuary. One wall was covered in drawers where the dead were kept cold. Around the other sides of the room lay surgical cabinets, tables, and a couple of wardrobes. They were all covered in an assortment of instruments, tools and other items belonging to the trade of the mortician. In the centre, under two large movable spotlights, lay a single table. It was empty.

Vogt had his back to them. Sam could see his shoulders had fallen, the ever-present confidence replaced by confusion.

"Looks like you have the wrong room, Vogt."

Vogt didn't reply and remained still in the middle of the room.

"Come on, let's check the other one," Bos continued, presuming the Interpol agent had mixed up his doors.

The curly-haired man turned around, his features a soft grey under the artificial lighting. "This was the right room."

"Well, Singh's probably put her away to wind you up," Berger asserted confidently, striding past him to begin looking in the drawers at the far end. "She'll be in here somewhere."

Berger began to open some of the cabinet doors to peer in and Bos went to help. Sam, meanwhile, had a wander round the lab, noticing how clean and tidy everything was. A surprise when he thought back to scruffily dressed Singh with his bulging clothes.

Berger closed the last of the doors. "Okay, she's not in any of these. Let's check the other two rooms."

There didn't seem to be panic in anyone's voices as they left the first room. Following all three back out into the office, Sam again felt something was out of place in the cluttered room. Only on entering the second lab to find the centre table empty did a sense of urgency creep in. Bos and Berger searched the cabinets a little quicker this time. Vogt had already left the second room to try the third and final room. Sam waited for the two Dutch officers and now running, they entered the final of the three rooms. Perched on a stool, Vogt was its only occupant.

"They're empty," he told the three of them as they rushed in. "Where the fuck is Singh?"

Bos took one look at Vogt and dashed off after the now distant Singh. Berger looked at Sam and then Vogt for a signal.

"The phones. Ring reception and get security looking for him, we can't let him leave," Sam advised, taking the initiative. Vogt appeared to be in shock.

"Could just be a mistake?" asked Berger.

The pair of them rushed back into the office space, half hoping to see the overweight doctor slouched on a chair. Berger went for the phone and dialled reception. She stopped and looked at Sam. "What about the woman?"

Sam didn't answer. A printer lay switched on under the desk, a stack of papers clearly visible. There was no mistake; Doctor Singh had lied about the printer and was now probably already outside the building.

"She's gone," Sam told her.

"But how?"

The door to the third laboratory opened and Vogt stepped out. He scratched his head and walked towards one of the other phones on the desk.

"The nurse," Sam guessed, speaking to Vogt.

"What?" Berger asked, confused.

Sam grabbed the detective's attention. "Singh said you saw the body earlier. When was that?"

Vogt stopped dialling. "I did, before you arrived. She was laid out in the first room. I stuck my head in, but didn't examine her. Then when I went in after we arrived, I only met him in the office. I didn't go into the lab."

"The black-haired nurse, then. Had to be."

Vogt nodded solemnly and began dialling again.

Berger just stared blankly at them both. "But she was dead. I saw her yesterday."

Sam sat back on one of the office chairs and ran his hands through his hair.

"Did you check her pulse?" he asked her.

She shook her head in confusion.

Vogt looked up from the phone. "I did. I found her. There was no pulse." They listened as he reported it and called in backup. Afterwards, he spoke to the room. "There's no point, of course. She's already gone."

Sam tried to piece together everything that had just happened. The woman who had damn near killed him had walked past him only minutes ago. How had he not recognised her? But then, why had she faked her own death?

He looked to Vogt. "Why?"

The dark eyes reflected Sam's own confusion back at him. "I

don't know."

Johannes Bos came crashing back into the room, breathing hard as he leant on the counter. "Security said they saw him get into a car with a woman before driving away. They're getting me the tape now. But why? What's he playing at? Why hide a body?"

He stopped when he saw all three faces staring blankly at him.

"There is a body, isn't there?"

Sam answered his friend. "She's gone, she walked straight past us in the waiting room."

Bos just stood there, his face in shock. "No!" he shouted. "I saw her, we saw her yesterday. She was dead." Pausing, he asked one final question. "How?"

They all turned to Vogt, expecting him to say something. He'd taken a seat and was now searching his pockets. Sam guessed that Vogt had known the moment he'd stepped into the first room what had happened. Their one lead into Nile had escaped; she had never been dead. The boat, the tip-off and certainly Singh, had all been leading to her miraculous recovery.

"Whatever has happened has happened and we can't change it." He withdrew another cigar and rolled it between his fingers. Sam sensed a cool undertone take over the German's voice as he exerted control over a deep anger. "I'm pretty certain Doctor Singh and his patient are well and truly gone from here. But that's not important. Our friend Mr Taylor has hit the nail on the head. What's important now is not how, but why? Why did she go to so much trouble to make us think she was dead?"

SEVEN

CHAOS NOW REIGNED. Teams of people from both Interpol and the local police forces descended on the hospital and the surrounding area. Bos and Berger tried to coordinate everything, but the tide of people was too strong. Vogt, meanwhile, kept to himself, sitting alone in the waiting area where they'd watched the disguised nurse saunter past. Left to his own devices, Sam wandered through the mortuary wondering what they had become caught up in.

Entering the first of the laboratories again, he carefully reviewed the scene. Starting with the chilled cabinets at the back of the room, he looked at the notices on each door detailing the inhabitant. All bar one were occupied with a neat handwritten note detailing each deceased individual. There were tags for inhabitants dying from natural causes, alongside a car accident, a drowning and one simply read 'gunshot.' The final one had a simple note with a single question mark untidily written. Was this Singh's handwriting?

Opening the door, he pulled out the shelving upon which a body would usually be stored. Leaning in, he pulled out his phone and turned on the torch function to look right to the back of the cabinet, but found nothing. Sighing, he pushed the shelf back into place and closed the door.

"Thinking of climbing in and having a rest?" The voice of Johannes Bos came from behind him.

"Maybe. I think soon it will be the only place to get any rest." He smiled and closed the door.

"Bet you weren't expecting this when you stepped off the plane this morning?"

Sam looked at his friend, the tall almost lanky frame with its long blond hair. He looked more gaunt than when they had last met the year before, as if the stresses of the new role had begun to take their toll. His grey eyes looked weary under the bright lights of the lab.

"Why's nothing ever simple in this case? It's like someone is out there just thinking how can they mess us around some more."

"What's happening upstairs?"

"We've sent teams to search the hospital and to patrol the area, but really what's the point?"

"They'll be long gone by now." Sam offered his unhelpful opinion.

"Whatever this was, it was certainly well-planned, so I can't see them not having some sort of escape route."

Bos stepped further into the room and ran his hand across the table in the centre. "Berger's upstairs now going through the CCTV, but we've just found all the cameras outside here have been unplugged. These guys are good, Sam. Really good."

Sam stepped towards Bos and sat with him against the table. He ran his hands through his hair, an unconscious action whenever his mind was overworked. "What's Vogt said?"

"Nothing, he's waiting for reports from his team before he wants us all to return to the office."

Sam asked the question that was most nagging him. "Do you think he actually saw her? He's the only person left who supposedly saw her in here and found her dead, yes?"

Bos thought about the question before answering. "Well, apart from Singh and some teams from Interpol. But who's to say they weren't working with Singh as well? I don't bloody know. Why would Vogt lie? But then he doesn't seem the type of person to be easily fooled, either."

"But is he the type of person to help someone else to be fooled?"

"No one else has hunted Nile as hard as he has over the last few months. It's been like an obsession for him."

Sam stared at the door, imagining Vogt outside in the seating area. "An obsession which has found what, exactly?"

"I don't see it, Sam. The dwarf's a little bastard, but he's too much of a bastard to be bent."

Starting at a row of waist-high cabinets, Sam knelt down and began opening them. The shiny metal doors clanked shut as he made his way along the rows.

"Fuck, fuck, fuck it," Bos said behind him. "We were betrayed at the warehouse that night and we found nothing." He slammed his fist on the table.

"Someone told me before I left England that for something this large, there had to be someone working for them in the authorities. Someone able to protect them, tip them off. But I didn't imagine they could do all this," Sam said as he searched each cabinet.

"But Vogt? Why does it have to be Vogt?" Bos kicked out at the table, sending it rolling across the room.

Sam paused in his search and looked back up at his usually calm friend. "Hey relax, it's only a theory. We don't need you to have a broken toe as well."

"I'm sorry, it's been a long couple of days." He looked for a moment genuinely embarrassed. "I never asked how you were feeling? Can't be easy for you, knowing she's out walking again."

"I'm okay. She didn't shoot me this time."

So far everything had been what he would have expected to see in a mortician's lab. They'd have to get one of the other members of staff to come and review the contents to see if there was anything out of place. Until he reached the last metal cabinet. Opening the door, Sam saw a large black rucksack with a sleeping bag next to it.

"Bos, I've found something."

Picking up the bag, he carried it over to the table and pushed it into place under the lights. Unzipping the main compartment, he pulled out a hoody, sweatpants, a T-shirt and women's underwear.

"Too small for Singh," Bos commented.

Searching further, Sam found a variety of food wrappers and a bottle of water. Turning the bag around, he opened up the front pockets, finding make-up alongside a torch, an inflatable pillow and a paperback novel. Sam flicked through the pages of the novel. Agatha Christie's *Death on the Nile*, an apt choice, though curious for an evening in the mortuary.

He bit his lip and rubbed the stubble on his chin. "This confirms for certain that she's alive. Until now, we were only guessing she was. Singh could have hidden the body somewhere else and that nurse was perhaps just walking past."

Bos raised an eyebrow.

"Okay, fair point, but at least we know now for certain." The Dutchman grinned and began repacking the bag. "Come on, let's show our findings to the Nile mole."

Vogt was still seated in the waiting area where they'd awaited the call to enter the mortuary. The German agent was in one of the plastic chairs, rolling his cigar between his two hands. He didn't look up as they arrived. "How's the search going?" he asked.

"We've got teams going through the hospital, but it's doubtful she's still here. There's uniforms on the surrounding streets to see if they swapped cars somewhere nearby."

"I wasn't asking you, Bos. Taylor's been searching the laboratory, has he not?" He still hadn't bothered to look up.

"He found this." Bos threw the bag on the chair next to Vogt, who took a single glance at it before returning to his unlit cigar.

"So she's not dead, then?" he asked in disappointment. "I was hoping you wouldn't have found anything like that in there. It would have meant there was still a chance."

"A chance of what?" Sam asked.

"That we, no sorry I, hadn't been played."

"Fucking hell, Vogt, get over yourself. She's gone and we'd better get after her."

Vogt looked at Sam and shrugged, before sliding off the chair. He paused and seemed about to say something else, but thought better of it. Instead, he slipped the cigar back into his pocket and walked past them.

They watched as the German agent walked down the long corridor to the stairs at the end. Just before he reached the doors, he turned back to them. "I want everyone back at the station for a briefing session at two. Get Berger to ring round."

With that, he was through the doors and out into the world of the living.

"Couldn't be bothered to arrange it himself?" asked Sam.

"If I told you he didn't have a phone, would you believe me?"

"I don't think anything about him would surprise me."

After a final check downstairs, they called a uniformed officer to stand guard over the area. Bos had reluctantly agreed to let the hospital continue to use the other two mortuaries. Death, unlike themselves, wouldn't pause its daily routines for the sake of a body that had escaped its clutches. The hospital director, a middle-aged woman, could only tell them that Doctor Singh had arrived after being called in by Vogt yesterday.

"He called yesterday to say we were to give the guy anything he needed."

Sam was intrigued. "Why didn't he use one of your team?"

The director shrugged her shoulders. "We're pretty short at the moment, plus it's not unusual for Interpol to have their own people take over. I think Vogt said he'd worked with him before."

"So it was all an Interpol job?" Sam asked Bos.

"Yes, we weren't allowed anywhere near her from the moment Vogt kicked us out of the boat."

Sam considered this for a moment and tried to think what difference it could make. There were political struggles between all law-enforcement agencies around the world. So to hear Interpol had pushed out the local police force wasn't a surprise on a case like this.

Arriving back at reception, Bos went to find Berger, leaving Sam to ring London.

"So the case isn't closed," Emma said, sighing on the other end of the phone.

"No, while she's not in custody we should be doing everything we can to help find her."

The sound of Emma's Irish laughter could be heard from the other end of the line. "Any excuse to get involved?"

He moved outside and looked around him to make sure he wasn't being overheard. "I spoke to Sir Jeff before I left."

"I know, he came to visit me this morning."

"He reckons that there has to be someone on the inside."

"I know."

Sam stopped to let a uniformed police officer walk past him into the main building.

"So now you're over there, what do you think?"

"He may be right. Regardless of what's happened today, the Nile's too well-embedded not to have any inside help. But today was something else; it's confused everything. There's no clear reason why this has happened."

"Shit," Emma said down the phone. "I don't like it when we're caught up in a game we can't understand."

"Based on our previous experience on this case, I don't think it'll be long before we find out what we've got ourselves into."

"I can't convince you to come home?"

"Not a chance. I'd convinced myself last night I was glad she was dead, but there was always unfinished business. I was pleased she was alive. In a way, I wasn't that surprised. I thought there was something strange about those photos they sent."

Again, Emma laughed. "I knew you'd plan on staying, so just

keep in touch. Is there anything else we can do for you while you're out there?"

Sam thought for a moment. "Yes, can you get Hannah to dig out the Major Anderson file?"

"If you want, but why, when we've been over all that?"

"Hannah's a fresh pair of eyes, for a start. It'll be good to see if we've missed anything. But I also want her to have a look at who else could still have access to some of the material he had. I'm guessing the Nile will have wanted to replace him. They will still have needed what he was selling. Perhaps we can find out who else has been to Amsterdam recently?"

"Who's to say they didn't try another country?"

"They may have, but I think that while the salesman changed, the supply chain is likely to have remained the same. So it's likely to be a Brit."

Emma said she'd have Hannah look into it, wished him well and hung up. Sam put the phone back in his pocket and waited for his friends to finish in the hospital. While waiting, he thought about everything he'd just spoken about. If they could find out who the new middleman was, perhaps that would offer some sort of lead. They had nothing else to go on still, after all this time.

Ten minutes later, Bos and Berger left the hospital to join him.

"Did you find anything?" Sam asked Berger.

She shook her head. "No, we found the tapes of Singh leaving and getting into a white car, which I'm pretty certain was being driven by our black-haired nurse. We have video of both of them in the reception areas, but as you know the mortuary cameras downstairs were down."

"*Was* it her?"

"I think so. I'll show you back at the office."

The three of them climbed into the car and set off to the central police station. Behind them, unnoticed, the engine of a dark-blue hatchback came to life. The driver didn't worry about keeping too close to the car in front. They knew where they were heading.

EIGHT

THE CENTRAL AMSTERDAM police headquarters was situated in a bland four-storey building just to the east of the city centre. For a city steeped in historical and modern architecture, it seemed this had slipped through the cracks. Like many buildings in the vicinity, its entrance opened to first a tram track and then one of the many tree-lined canals that were the city's trademarks. To the rear, a second canal meandered past the drab building.

They'd stopped for lunch on the way back from the hospital, where the three officers had gone over the day's events again in detail. None of them were keen to return to the station to be ordered around by Vogt for any longer than they had to.

"What's a German Interpol agent doing running a Dutch operation, anyway?" Sam asked the Dutch pairing.

Berger looked at Bos, who shrugged as he drank from his coffee. "I don't know, but it pisses a lot of people off."

"Bullshit, everyone knows." Bos gave his deputy a withering look before continuing. "Because like your friend in London, our superiors think that Nile has someone on the inside. They wanted an outsider to come in and flush them out."

"Yet you think that Vogt himself may be suspect," Sam probed.

The tall blond Dutchman put his cup down and frowned. "I

may have been a bit hasty on that. It was more I was pissed off with everything that had happened."

Berger laughed. "Vogt? That would be a twist. I'd quite like that; it would be something to watch. Especially after he purged so many people over the last year."

"Purged?"

"Forced people out, including our old boss."

Sam looked at Bos. "I thought he resigned after the acquittal of the two Nile directors?"

Bos gave the waitress some euros to settle the bill. "Again, there's the official version and then there's the Ada Berger version of events."

Sam noticed her foot had rubbed itself against him on more than a few occasions during lunch. She'd already dropped into a previous conversation that she was still single. Perhaps they could pick up from where they had left off.

"Hey, I just say it as it is. I'm not senior enough to have to worry about toeing the line. Vogt came in to clean up the mess following the fun you two had last winter. It's only because the great Bos here arrested Franssen and De Klerk last year that he kept his golden boy image… and his job."

Bos didn't reply, he just looked out of the window where the leaves on the trees had turned into a mix of bright oranges and yellows. Sam felt sorry for him. He could only imagine the pressure of the past few months. His friend may have got a promotion out of events, but it only meant the target had now moved to his back. And if Sir Jeffrey was right about a mole, who better than the newly promoted Head of Organised Crime? Sam pushed the thought from his head. Bos was his friend; he'd eaten at his house, met his husband. And if there was any remaining doubt, it had been Bos who had saved his life that night at the warehouse.

"There's nothing to say that there is a mole and that it's someone senior," Sam told them both. "It could be a variety of uniformed officers on the street. Who knows more than them about what happens here? I knew more about what happened in the damned army in the military police than any of its commanders."

Bos stood to pull on his coat. "Come on, let's go face the music. Look at it this way, Vogt's going to have to stand there and explain why someone he declared was dead walked straight past him. I wouldn't miss this for the world."

The three of them made their way back to the small Organised Crime office to dump their coats and Sam's baggage. Opening the door, they found Corsel and Hardenne. Corsel spoke first, standing to shake Sam's hand.

"Good to see you, Sam. Been a while."

Now on the other side of fifty with short grey hair and tanned face, Sam recalled how when he'd met him the year before, Corsel had been a committed lifelong sergeant, preferring to be in uniform on the streets he had grown up in. Now it seemed he'd had a significant change of heart.

"I needed something new for my final years. Margo wants to see the world when we retire, so I thought the extra euros wouldn't go amiss."

Sam clapped him on the shoulder. "It's good to see you and the promotion is well-deserved."

"Don't listen to him. He was the only one who was willing to join the team. We'd tried everyone before this old bastard," Hardenne piped up from the desk he'd been sitting on. "We even tried to recruit the canteen team first."

Standing even taller than Bos, Hardenne was the youngest member of the team. A recent addition himself when Sam had first met him, he looked like he'd been at the gym since the last time they'd met. Sam, himself well-built and standing six foot tall, could recognise the effort that must have gone in over the year. He had thick arms visible under his sleeves to rival Sam's own.

They grinned and shook hands. Sam was never quite sure what he thought of the younger man. He had suspected Hardenne had feelings beyond those of colleagues for Ada Berger and had detected a slight jealousy towards him the last time they'd met. Bos, he knew, also had his doubts about the man. He'd mentioned an overfondness for the city's café scene. Sam wondered if he'd broached the matter since becoming Hardenne's boss.

"What's happening at the hospital?" Corsel asked.

Bos grimaced as he slumped into his chair. "Nothing, we got nowhere. Whoever she is, she walked out of there without a misstep."

"Jesus, she's got some balls, hasn't she?" Hardenne remarked. "She's taken that smart-arse dwarf for a ride."

Berger chuckled. "You should have seen his face when we walked into an empty room. I'll never forget that."

Sam put his bag in a corner and perched on one of the desks nearest the window, which overlooked the rearward canal. He'd forgotten how much he'd liked watching the boats that trawled round the city with its little bridges and tree-lined waterways. Amsterdam always seemed to be buzzing, as if the constant movement of the water, along with never-ending cyclists, were the blood vessels of a living creature. He'd visited plenty of major cities, but he'd never quite found anywhere like here. Perhaps he would try Venice and see if its waterways had the same effect.

"He's not happy either way. I saw him storming in earlier, shutting himself in the conference room," Corsel commented.

"Don't worry, he'll have calmed down by the time we have to join him at two," said Bos. "How was your morning? Did you get any further with the canal boat?"

Hardenne shook his head. "No, the commissioner insisted we had support from homicide, but even then, we've got nowhere. The boat's registered under a false name, insured to somewhere in the south. We've found no CCTV footage of people using it and it's been moored there for over a year."

"She's not been hiding there for a year, we can be sure of that," asserted Bos. "Must have been a safe house, which became a useful spot for a body to be found."

Sam pictured the small space within the photos. The small

cabin was a clever idea if they wanted to make sure people were not able to examine the body too closely. The tight space limited numbers while the position of the bed meant that to have checked for a pulse, a person would have had to have crawled over it. He remembered Bos saying he'd not checked the body beyond standing over it, neither had Berger.

"She's good, isn't she?" Berger admitted. The room fell silent as they admitted the level of quality within the opposition.

"She made one error," Sam mused, still looking out of the window.

"She did?" asked Bos.

"We now have a clear photo of what she looks like. Until now you were relying on my description and grainy CCTV videos of her heading to the hotel."

"Didn't help us at the hospital when she walked straight past us," Berger noted drily.

"We weren't looking for her then. None of us was expecting to see her out walking, but now she's going to have to really disguise herself."

They left shortly afterwards to join the Interpol agent in the conference room. Seating was already at a premium as they entered the room full of officers. Sam recognised the commissioner seated with Vogt. He was disappointed to see the same overweight officer as before. Even from the other side of the room, Sam could hear his wheezing from the thousands of cigarettes consumed over the years. He looked up when they entered and called Bos over to sit with them.

"Duty calls," he muttered, as he went to join in their conversation.

The four of them went in the opposite direction, towards the back of the room, Sam and Corsel perching on the windowsill and Berger and Hardenne taking the final two seats. Looking round, Sam recognised a few faces and waved a greeting. After a few moments, the commissioner stood up and began to address the room.

"We all know why we are here, so I'll spare you the introductions. We've a few colleagues from across borders with us today, so I'll stick to English." Behind him, various maps were pinned to the wall around a large screen that had the image of the woman staring out at them. Sam saw Vogt had pushed his chair to one side and was once more leant back in his seat, arms folded across his chest.

Sam felt his phone vibrate in his pocket and on his smartwatch, but ignored it. He tried to concentrate on the conversation as the case was discussed. Another vibration and Sam couldn't help but twist his wrist to see the green message symbol ping up.

> Hello Sam, it was good to see you again today.

The words were bright on the small screen and he reread them twice. Looking closer, he could see it was from an unknown number. Taking his phone out, he flicked open the app, where he could see the sender was typing.

> We really should stop meeting like this

Around him, the meeting was still ongoing as various speakers gave their updates and opinions. It had to be her. He started to type, but stopped. She must have seen on her own screen.

> I didn't take you as shy

He hesitated again, unsure whether he should reply. To hell with it.

> I'm not the one who keeps leaving the conversation.

How had she got his number?

> Perhaps next time I can hang around, we could get lunch?

So there's going to be a next time?

> Always

About him, Sam heard Bos explaining how his team was working on planning the hunt. Christ, he wasn't supposed to be flirting with the actual fugitive.

I'm in a room full of police officers who are hunting for you. Tell me why I shouldn't pass them my phone.

> A room full of officers with handcuffs? Please do!

Somewhere in his mind, Sam's sense of humour was tickled. She replied again.

> But seriously, please don't. Let's just keep it between me and you for now. I need you to trust me.

That was pushing it, thought Sam, as he wondered what to put.

Last time I saw you, you shot me.

> No, last time I saw you I was dressed as a nurse.

Moments later.

> I kept the uniform, by the way

Of course she did, Sam thought, with a frisson of excitement. She certainly wasn't the shy type.

> I need to speak to you alone. Leave the meeting now.

His fingers hovered over the screen.

> No

Still in front of him, Berger turned round and raised her eyebrows. "Here we go again," she mouthed, but Sam had no idea to what topic of conversation she was referring.

> Sam, there's a blue Volkswagen Golf parked in the car park outside the station. Get to it now and sit in the driver's seat.

Minutes passed and he still hadn't replied. He decided to wait until he was back in the office to show the messages to the team, rather than raising it here. At the front of the room, Vogt was still unmoved, leaning back. Sam wondered if he was asleep. Bos was opposite, his arms folded as he tried to follow the conversations. It would be a shock to them all when he showed them.

> Come on, hurry up. What does Sir Jeffrey always say? Once more unto the breach, dear friends.

Sam stared at the Shakespearean quotation in surprise. How could she know that? He now had a choice to make, to stay or to leave. If he went down to the car, what then? She could kill him, but that could happen whenever. If you had the skills and the will you could kill someone prettily easily on the street. So, what if he didn't go? Perhaps they'd never find out what was happening. This could be their only chance. He felt a rush of excitement, the sense of danger as always taking a back seat when his curiosity was piqued.

Five minutes

Making his mind up, he made a show of rubbing his eyes and then his forehead. Corsel noticed first.

"Everything okay?"

"Migraine. I get them sometimes after travelling."

Berger heard them and turned round. "You okay, Sam?"

"I will be, just may need to get back to the hotel for a rest. Otherwise my head'll explode." Sam made the effort to force himself onward and stood up.

"I'll drive you if you like?" whispered Berger.

"I'll be okay, tell Bos I'll ring later. I just need to find a darkened room before I collapse."

Berger moved to follow him, but he pushed her down. "I'll be okay. Stay here."

His words caught the attention of everyone in the room and every pair of eyes looked towards him.

Vogt leant forward in his chair and looked at the Englishman. "Going somewhere, Mr Taylor?"

Sam couldn't be bothered explaining himself to either Vogt or the rest of the room.

"I just need to pop out."

The answer seemed to settle the question and the room's attention went back to the screen. Only Bos and Vogt continued to watch as he carefully made his way to the door. Bos stuck his thumb up questioningly, but Sam waved him away.

Moments later he was alone in the corridor. Conscious of time, he moved quickly back to Bos's office. Taking his bag, he pencilled a short note telling his friend to ring him that afternoon. Minutes later, he was walking out of the building and into the Amsterdam sunshine. Pausing for a moment to survey the scene, he tried to see if he was being watched, but nothing out of the ordinary moved on the quiet street.

"Bloody hell, what are you doing?" he muttered to himself as he turned towards the small car park at the side of the building.

There was only one blue Volkswagen parked in the bays and it seemed empty. Stepping cautiously forward, he kept looking around for the woman. There was no one else near the parked cars. Edging closer, he took a breath and moved to the driver's seat. He paused and looked round, his senses on edge, trying to spot anything out of the ordinary. Trying the handle, he wasn't surprised to find it unlocked. Throwing his bag onto the passenger seat, he slid in behind the wheel. Nothing happened. Minutes went by and he began to wonder if this hadn't been a prank, or a test of loyalty by the Europeans back inside.

Across the road, a tram rolled past and the noise of its metal wheels echoed round the vicinity. The noise was not quite enough to mask the sound of the door opening behind him. He went to turn to stare at his host but was stopped. The cold metal of a gun muzzle was pushed under the headrest into the nape of his neck.

"You made that far harder than it needed to be, Sam."

NINE

THE COLD MUZZLE made his hair stand on edge. Outside of the car, the world passed slowly on by. An old couple loped past, shopping bags in their hands. A young girl rode her bike alongside a man speaking on his phone. But no one would have noticed the two of them alone in the car.

"Have you nothing to say?"

Sam's eyes slowly moved upwards to the rear-view mirror and he saw for the first time in nearly a year the dark-brown eyes staring straight back at him.

"Hard to speak when you've a gun in your neck."

She raised an eyebrow. "Oh Sam, don't be like that. You must have known it wouldn't be straightforward. None of the best relationships are."

Still looking in the mirror, he could see the now familiar narrow face from the photo. A high forehead and strong chin. Two full lips broke into a smile.

"I'm glad you came, Sam. I really am."

"I'll reserve judgement for now, if that's okay with you?"

She shrugged and sat backwards, releasing the pressure of the gun against his neck.

"How do you know about Sir Jeffrey?" he demanded.

"Later, Sam."

"I want to know now."

There was a sigh from behind him.

"We'll come to questions later. Don't get any ideas; we both know one of these rounds would pass through the chair and go straight into your spine. So for now, no more questions."

He tried to twist round to get a better look at her, but she stopped him in his tracks. "No, not yet."

Sam took a breath. He knew he was going to have to play her game. He'd willingly walked into her trap, after all. The only question was, what could possibly be waiting for him at the end of it?

"So, where to? Perhaps there's a drive-through you'd like me to call at?"

She sat back and with one hand, kept the gun facing forwards while with the other, she released her blonde hair. The long golden threads landed on her shoulders. Sam could just about see she was wearing a black roll-neck jumper.

"Turn on the engine and follow the satnav. It'll take you where you need to go."

He did as he was told and, pressing the start button, brought the car to life. The screen to the right of him switched on, showing a preprogrammed route out of the city around eighty kilometres away to the south.

"When you're ready, put the transmission into reverse and let's get out of here."

The car moved out of the parking space and Sam guided it out to the exit, giving the station one last look. The once unwelcoming, dull building now looked a lot more appealing than it had done before.

His passenger noticed his gaze. "Surely you don't want to be back in there with that lot? I'm going to take you somewhere much more welcoming. Trust me, it doesn't take much to beat this view."

Pulling into traffic, Sam was careful to keep half an eye on his passenger behind him. He watched her eyes darting around, never stopping for a moment.

"Worried we might be being followed?"

"I'd be a fool if I wasn't," she replied. "Just keep driving and don't think of doing anything stupid. Break too hard, I shoot. Try to draw attention to us, I shoot. Just keep following the route and you'll be okay."

Sam gripped the steering wheel tightly, considering whether he could slam the brakes hard enough for her to drop the weapon.

"Any clues as to where you're taking me?" he asked.

"I'm not taking you anywhere."

"You're not?"

"I'm not the one driving."

As he approached a crossroads, the computerised voice of the satellite navigation told him to turn left.

"Turn right here, please," she said firmly.

"But it says I should go left."

"Do as you're told, Sam. Turn right."

The navigation application reset its route and told him to continue on, but again she overruled it and made him take a sharp turning over a small bridge. Two more of these directions followed and Sam was becoming bored.

"I've arranged no tail. So can we just get on with wherever it is you're wanting me to take us?"

"Who said I was worried about you setting a tail on us? There's worse things than your little police friends in this city, Mr Taylor."

She directed them away from the city centre and towards the suburban areas. Signs for the motorways that surrounded the city were passing by and he wondered which of the routes she was taking them on.

After ten more minutes, Sam watched as she made herself more comfortable in her seat, the gun still firmly gripped in her right hand. He felt her long limbs pressing against the back of his chair as she stretched.

"So, Mr Taylor, how are you? It feels like ages ago since we last spoke."

"I don't remember talking much last time we met."

The dark-brown eyes looked at him in the mirror. "What do you mean?"

"Last time we met, you tried to kill me."

She shook her head. "No, that's not right."

Sam paused before he replied, concentrating on a junction ahead of him as the monotonous voice of the navigation told him to head straight on. "You shot me."

"Yes, I shot you, but I didn't try to kill you."

Now Sam laughed. "What would you call it, then?"

"If I read your medical report correctly, I hit you either side of your collar bone. If I'd wanted to kill you, I'd have aimed for your head."

He didn't reply and silence fell in the car.

There was laughter behind him, a soft enticing sound. "Okay, I'm sorry for shooting you, Mr Taylor. I did check up on you though, afterwards, made sure you were on the mend."

"Another outing for your nurse's uniform?"

"Oh no, I had my contacts do that for me. I even sent you a get well card."

"So that *was* you! I did wonder. Nice to know you have some sympathy for those you leave to drown in canals."

Sam mused. He was in a car alone with the woman who had shot him the year before. Whom he had thought dead until a few hours ago. Not to mention the prime suspect in a murder case. Now he was letting her lead him to whatever she had planned next, at gunpoint.

"So what's happening, then? Why have you dragged me out here?"

They were merging onto the motorway, heading onto the main ring road out of the city. There were two possible routes he felt she might be taking him on, based on the destination he'd briefly seen on the map.

"No more questions, Sam. All will be explained when we arrive. For now, I get to ask the questions."

"That's not fair. I'm the one showing more faith by being here. You might at least humour me."

"I'm the one with the gun, so I ask the questions."

Sam laughed. "I don't even know your name."

"And you call yourself a detective? But to be fair, not many people know my name. Even those two foolish directors you arrested that night we met don't know who I really am. But I'll make you a deal. Do as you're told and at the end of it all I'll tell you my name."

He shrugged. This bed was entirely of his own making.

"Go on then, ask away."

"You and Officer Berger… are you still sleeping together?"

"Jesus. Is that where you want to start?"

She giggled and clapped her hands together, the firearm still held in her right. "She's very beautiful, I don't blame you. Let's see what I know about you, then you can fill in the gaps. Where shall I start? An ex-military police officer, you made it all the way to captain and served two tours in Afghanistan but were discharged soon after the second. Not by choice. You now live in London, alone. You're fluent in Spanish, thanks to your paternal grandfather, and in French due to university. You go running but don't like it. You work in the UK Foreign Office, in a department tasked with bringing people home from across the world whether they're dead, missing or locked up. You won't admit it, but you like your work and prefer it to the army. Your favourite drink is a dry gin and tonic with lime and juniper… and you're about to miss the exit."

Sam had been too engrossed in her words to notice the turn-off and had to make a sharp right-hand turn to get in the right lane.

"Anything else?"

"Your last assignment overseas was in France, where you picked up a slight injury to your face, which has left a small scar above your eyebrow. Although it hasn't hurt your looks in the slightest."

"I feel honoured that you've made such an effort to get to know me."

They were heading down the second possible route Sam had guessed they would take. It was slightly longer than the first, but for what reason, he couldn't guess.

"Oh, I agree. I'd love for someone to stalk me. But they'd be bored of it within a week. Tell me about your colleagues. It's Emma, isn't it, who runs things?"

"Yes, Emma is the head of department."

"Is she a good person to work for?"

Sam considered that for a moment. Yes, he guessed she was. Although at times cold and distant, he'd always liked her.

"I don't work for Emma, though. I work for Jason."

"Jason Ross?"

"Rose."

"Ah, my mistake."

"I'm glad to see you make them."

"And do you see many interesting cases?"

"A few. There was this major who was brutally murdered last year in Amsterdam. Had his throat cut in his hotel room. Left a wife and kids behind."

Even with the limited vision of the rear-view mirror, he could see his words had hurt her.

"You believe I did that and yet you still got in the car with me?"

That caught him out. Why *had* he got into a car with someone he thought was a cold-blooded murderer? In truth, in the spur of the moment and in the excitement of potentially finding his prey, he'd ceased to care that this woman was the main suspect in a murder case.

They drove along the Dutch motorway. Sam started to spend more time looking at the countryside around him rather than worrying about the silent woman sitting behind. They crossed wide flowing rivers, which over the centuries had made the region a centre of commerce for the whole of Europe. There were large open fields, which were fed by these waters. Many, Sam knew, would be full of flowers come spring. Tulips would be grown in their millions and transported around Europe. Before long, the navigation instructed him to leave the motorway and they began to travel on a road that ran parallel to one of the many rivers.

Sam looked down at the screen to his right and saw they were less than fifteen minutes from their destination. After they'd passed through a large village, that time dropped to only five. They were still following the river, but the road had narrowed, with the surrounding traffic limited to the odd passerby.

"Look out for the turning on the left, it's coming up." They were her first words since the comment about Anderson.

Sam turned down a single-track lane that cut through two grassy fields. Ahead, at the end of the road where he knew the river must've been, was the outline of a tall, oddly-shaped building. Pulling up outside, Sam chided himself for not recognising it as a windmill without its four sails. Dark bricks rose upwards, with small windows betraying three floors. At its peak, wooden panelling sat atop, with a large glass window now covering where the four sails would have driven the milling apparatus round. Gone were its days of milling wheat. Instead, what remained looked like a comfortable home.

He did as he was told, parking the car facing the water, with the building to the left of him. There was no chance he was going to let her have it all her own way. The car shuddered to a halt, tyres crunching on the gravel. They sat in silence for a moment, both waiting for the other to speak.

"I'll get out first, then you." She raised the gun and Sam could see it was a Walther. "Remember, I'll be watching you, so don't fuck with me."

He watched as she checked her surroundings before climbing out. Once she was out, she stepped a few paces away from the car then nodded at him. Sam was disappointed to see she had stepped far enough away to block any sudden rush by himself. Instead, he looked over at his bag, until now completely forgotten. From where she had situated herself, he knew she wouldn't be able to see him as he grabbed the top handle with his right hand. With his left hand, he opened the door and stepped out into the cold mid-afternoon air.

"Slowly, Sam. Take it slowly." The gun was trained on him, her hands steady.

Sam climbed out of the car, keeping his body twisted to hide his baggage. Looking over his shoulder, he judged the distance between them. He took a breath and went for it. Twisting forwards, using his momentum as a slingshot, he threw the heavy bag at his companion. She had not seen it coming. Her instincts kicked in and she raised her hands. That split-second decision gave Sam the chance he needed and he threw himself into her. He grabbed the hand with the Walther, then twisted her wrist harshly, forcing it out of her grip. Then he pushed her backwards to the ground and straddled her.

He turned the Walther round to face the fallen woman. "Now what did you say again? The person with the gun asks the questions?"

Lying in a heap on the ground, breathing hard, her face full of venom, the brown eyes glared back at him. Pleased with himself for finally getting the better of this woman, Sam was about to instruct her to stand. Instead, a familiar voice came from behind her, from the converted windmill.

"Let her up, Sam. Trust me, she'll be far more likely to talk inside than on the ground."

TEN

SAM GOT to his feet and stood, gun pointing directly at the sprawled woman below him. She stared back up at him, still fighting to get her breath back, her blonde hair dishevelled from the fall.

Leaning against the doorway of the converted windmill was agent Karl Vogt, a lit cigar clasped between his teeth.

"What the hell are you doing here?" snapped Sam, bringing the firearm up to point it at the Interpol agent.

"I can explain everything, but let's at least do it inside." His voice was calm, as if he was enjoying watching the pair of them.

"You're working with her?" Sam indicated the woman still on the ground. "She's one of them."

"You don't know anything, Taylor," she jeered.

"Shut it, or I'll return the favour you so kindly gave me last time we met."

"Sam, seriously, let's go inside and I can explain everything. She's with us."

"Us? Who's us?"

"Fucking hell, I didn't think this was going to be so difficult. Sir Jeffrey said you were clever." Vogt sighed. "Put the gun down, then let our mutual friend get to her feet and we can discuss it all inside."

Sam tried to process everything. The last time he'd seen Vogt, he'd watched Sam walking out of the briefing meeting about a missing woman. Now, he was next to this windmill, telling Sam to let the very woman they were supposed to be chasing after get up from the ground. He sighed then lowered the gun, yet kept the safety latch off.

"You go in first." He nodded at Vogt. "And you can get up and follow him." He turned to the woman.

She smiled and pulled her hair back, straightening it into place. "Can I have my gun back?"

"No."

She shrugged and climbed to her feet. Now he could see her fully, Sam saw she was dressed in a pair of tight black trousers under the black woollen roll-neck, all of which fitted her curves perfectly.

Sam followed her carefully into the converted building. Stepping through the doorway, he found himself in a homely hallway. To his right he looked into an empty sitting room, with deep sofas surrounding a fireplace. No sign of anything to suggest who lived here, no photos or ornaments cluttering the place.

Turning back into the hall, Sam walked past a spiral staircase into the kitchen. Overhanging beams made the room feel slightly claustrophobic, with the wide kitchen table surrounded by the oven, a fridge, then assorted worktops and cupboards. Stepping onto the flagstoned floor, Sam saw his hosts had taken seats around the table. Three green bottles of beer had been opened and Vogt, his cigar extinguished, held one out to Sam.

"Here, take a seat and we can talk."

Sam reached over and took the beer. He leant against one of the workstations, his right hand still holding the stolen firearm.

Vogt watched and raised an eyebrow. "Okay, so where do you want us to start?"

"What's her name?"

The woman at the table took a swig of beer and placed the bottle back on the table. "Natasja, my name is Natasja van Rossum."

Natasja sat back in her chair and folded her arms, waiting for Sam's next question.

"From the start. Tell me everything." Sam pointed at Natasja with the gun. "I want to know exactly who you are, what the Nile is, and why you're on first-name terms with an Interpol agent."

She looked at Vogt, who nodded his approval, before beginning her tale.

"I guess it starts with the source of the Nile."

Natasja took a sip of cold beer before she began her story. She seemed to be enjoying herself.

"The source of the Nile was a jeweller's in the city many years ago. Its owner was Albert Wever, one of the best diamond cutters in Europe. One day, he was approached just before closing by a sailor fresh from a trip to Africa. The man offered him more stones than Wever had ever seen – and for a fraction of the price."

"Blood diamonds?" Sam asked.

"Probably, but they could have been from anywhere. Wever didn't ask and in not doing so, started the Nile's single rule of compartmentalising information. If you don't need to know, you won't know. Instead, Wever took the offered stones, checked them out overnight and paid the man a fraction of what they would one day be worth after he'd finished with them. Two weeks later, another sailor appeared with more stones. Wever was soon dealing in the stuff. It wasn't as hard in those days to find buyers and so he began to grow his black-market side business more than his legal in-store work. These buyers began to ask Wever for other stuff and so he asked the sailor contacts. Within a few years, he had a network which spanned the entire world. Importers in Hamburg, buyers in Singapore, stock from America. It was all filtered through Amsterdam."

Sam considered her. "What type of other stuff was asked for?"

"Other luxury items such as watches, cars, yachts. Gold

became big for a time. I think Wever's first real red flag was when he was asked to source used low-currency dollars. There'd be cases full of the stuff. Then came the first request for weapons. That scared him for a bit but eventually, after a few reassurances, it became part of the routine. We even found a tank for someone once. One of the old Soviet ones. Don't get me wrong, it was a rich guy's toy rather than a revolutionary tool."

Listening to the creation of the elusive Nile, Sam thought of how he'd heard stories like this before. Someone had been in the right place at the right time.

"The trick was, Wever never had anything to do with it at first. It was a case of connecting the right people with the right shipping container. The original gig economy. No contracts and limited contact. As the organisation grew, he began to bring a few more people in to help. You've heard of Hans Franssen and Albert de Klerk?"

"Sure. The two Bos arrested last year, but were released."

She pulled a face. "Those two were brought in to deal with the finance and supply chains respectively. They also helped set up the dark web side of things, which suddenly made things seem more real in some ways. More official."

"What about you? Where do you fit into this?" Sam asked her.

"I was sales. I met Wever through my mother and he set me up as his replacement looking after his customers. By that time, he was getting older. Retirement was becoming increasingly attractive."

"I bet. Set himself up with nice illegal business, make a fortune, then sail away into the sunset?"

"Not quite," Vogt interjected. "Wever's dead."

Sam looked over at the Interpol agent, who until then had been drinking and playing quietly with his cigar.

"Your doing?" he asked.

"Perhaps. Let her finish."

Natasja continued. "After the dark web took off, we began to attract more and more unsavoury characters. For a time we managed to keep them at bay by agreeing to limited deals, but Wever in particular was getting edgy. He began to worry that he was simply funding terrorism."

"He confided in you, Franssen and De Klerk?"

"Just me. He called me over to his place to tell me he was going to stop, to turn himself in. By this time, he was well into his eighties. Franssen and De Klerk were putting more pressure on him to loosen the ropes, to let them go after the dangerous stuff."

"What happened?"

Vogt cleared his throat. "Two years ago, I found him sat in my garden in Munich. I've no idea how he found me, but there he was. Told me everything, offered to hand over the whole operation to me there and then."

Sam pulled a chair out from the table and sat down with the gun on his lap. "Why did he come all the way out just to see you?"

Vogt shrugged. "I've no idea; the guy was just there one day. He never told me why, but it wasn't long after the trafficking case made headlines. Perhaps he decided what I did on that case made me trustworthy. But there he was telling me about his entire career and that he wanted someone to help close it down. I didn't really believe him at first. I told him to come back the next day. During which time I did some digging around and decided on making him a deal."

"You told him to work for you?"

"I did. It was too good an opportunity to miss. You see, the thing about illegal operations is that if you close one down, people just find another one. Hence, there I was with the means to control the biggest supply chain of them all. I could decide which of the world's bad guys were going to get what they needed, how much of it and when."

"And it worked?"

"Perfectly for twelve months, during which time I met Natasja here. Wever introduced us and she acted as the go-between. I never met the other two. Wever didn't trust them."

Vogt stood and walked to the fridge to retrieve three more bottles of beer before handing two of them over.

"So, what went wrong? What happened to Wever?" Sam asked, wondering how the two of them had ended up having to fake Natasja's death.

"Allow me," said Natasja. "Last summer, a Polish group asked us to source personal ground-to-air rockets for them, the type a single person can use to bring down an airliner as it takes off."

"Jesus." The dots in Sam's mind began to join up and the face of Major Anderson began to become clearer in his head. He had been the British Army procurement officer for such weapons.

"Yes, and you can imagine how we felt about it. For a time we stalled, but this group were closer than we ever knew and we needed to do something."

"In the end, I approved the order," Vogt interrupted. "But only with the idea that we'd follow the rockets through to the group that ordered them."

"Risky business. What happened next?"

Natasja's bottle thudded to the table. "We were taken out."

"What?"

"Tell it properly, Natasja. He needs to know."

She stared at Vogt for a moment, before turning her doe eyes on Sam. "It started normally. We found a supplier, in this case through the British. Their Galahad ground-to-air rocket launcher ticked all the boxes. We tapped up an old contact, your Major Anderson, and flew him over. That's where it all went wrong. I met him a couple of times, did the usual negotiating routines. Then on the final night, we'd agreed to meet at his hotel for the final numbers. We needed to be sure there was no one to overhear. It's what we did with every client.

"I met him beforehand then followed him back to the hotel, giving him a fifteen-minute head start to make sure there was no one following us. But when I got there, he was dead. I walked in and there he was on the floor, blood everywhere. I panicked and fled the hotel through one of the service doors. I went to the only place I knew was safe. I went to Wever."

Her voice faltered for a moment. "I went to Wever for help as I knew something bad was happening. I got to his house in the suburbs, but he was at the bottom of the steps. They would say he fell, an eighty-year-old man, but I knew he'd been pushed. What with Anderson's murder framing me and now this, I knew we were under attack. Someone was trying to muscle in. The advantage of the Nile meant that the leadership was detached, but it was also a negative. It meant someone could come in and cut off the head."

"So what did you do then?"

"I had to leave Wever where he was. We tipped off our friends in the police and they looked after him. But I needed to disappear. I rang Vogt, who told me to use one of the safe houses we'd set up."

"The same boat they 'found' you in yesterday?"

"Was that really only yesterday? Yes, I hid out there until he arrived and we tried to piece together what was going on. At the time we didn't know who we could trust, or even who we were up against. So we had to wait it out. They found Wever's and Anderson's bodies. We didn't know whether Franssen or De Klerk were involved, so we kept quiet then waited."

"Then you came along and managed to find a link between Natasja and Anderson," Vogt added.

Natasja continued. "At that point, we knew we needed to make a choice before we lost any chance of continuing to run the Nile. We took the decision to make a fresh start. Instead of waiting, we'd take off the head of the snake. Then we'd try to pick up whoever was trying to take over. I arranged a meeting with De Klerk and Franssen at one of our warehouses, then I tipped off the police that it was about to happen."

Sam pictured Bos's face the day he'd come running in to tell him that they'd finally had a tip-off. He thought of the planning that had gone into their raid on the warehouse, the excitement of the breakthrough.

"I rang it in and then planned on escaping as you and your friends made your entrance. You'd pick up the other two directors and hopefully anyone else who was trying to kill us."

"I don't remember it going down quite like that."

"No, we were betrayed again."

"Betrayed?" Sam laughed. "It was your plan that went up in smoke."

"We were betrayed. Someone in your team, in the Amsterdam police, told them we were coming."

ELEVEN

THE WHOLE STORY SEEMED CRAZY, and there were too many questions she'd failed to answer.

"You said you have people in the Amsterdam police. How do you know it wasn't one of *them* who let it slip?"

"It wasn't them, trust me," she said.

"The person who betrayed us over the raid is still working in the force," Vogt added.

Sam looked at them both, not really sure what he thought. "So, who is it, then?"

The Interpol agent shook his head. "Later, let her finish."

They turned to Natasja, who reluctantly continued. "We arrived as planned at the warehouse, the three of us together as you saw. But the moment we entered the main part of the building, I was jumped by a group of thugs I'd never seen before. They left the other two, Franssen and De Klerk. It seemed they knew what was happening. Instead of it just being us, there were fifteen armed men all waiting for the police to enter."

"But why? Why not just get rid of you and leave the place? Why start a shoot-out?"

This time, Vogt answered. "They were making a statement.

New owners, new management. They'd guessed Wever was working with me and they wanted to bring me down with them."

"Big statement. Where's your proof?"

As Vogt reached into his jacket pocket, Sam raised his gun.

The German rolled his eyes and pulled out a photograph. "They were going to hide this on Natasja's corpse. Well, that's what they told her."

Sam unfolded the paper and saw a photograph of Vogt and an older man he guessed was Wever. They were sitting in a café somewhere. Wever was facing the camera, whereas Vogt's back was turned. His small frame, however, left little doubt that it was him.

"They hoped to suggest you as the mole?"

"Or at least cast some doubt over me. I thought it was more a message – *we know what you're doing* – rather than an attempt to discredit me. Enough of the right people knew what I was doing with Wever by that point. At best, it would have helped hide their real inside man."

Sam handed the photograph back. "So, they'd been planning on moving in for weeks. What happened then?" The last question was directed at Natasja.

"The explosions happened first, as three tripwires near the entrance blew. Then the shooting kicked off. The guards that had me weren't the sharpest and I managed to escape when they realised the police had more firepower than expected. I'd moored the boat that morning and knew about the side entrance, so that bit was easy. If you hadn't shown up, I'd have been gone into the night."

"Forgive me for not apologising," said Sam drily. "I think it's fair to say I ended up the worst off of the two of us that night."

Natasja ignored him. "After that, I had to go into hiding. Everyone I had known either disowned me or went missing. Within days, I was on the outside without even a window to look in. I thought that was it. Even Vogt told me to move on."

She stood and moved round the table to sit on a cabinet to look out of the window. The late-afternoon sun illuminated her strong face in its glare. Sam felt a slight pang of pity for her.

"So… why the past few days? Why all this acting? If, as you said, you were out of the Nile, this hasn't helped anyone. Nothing's changed."

Vogt pointed his now empty bottle at Sam. "It's brought you back."

"This whole episode was just for me? When you could have just called me?"

"We needed a reason to get you back inside the police investigation."

By now, the Dutchwoman was beginning to look bored. She crossed her legs and rested the palms of her hands on the edge of the woodwork.

"The Galahad rockets. After Anderson was killed, the contact they had lined up to replace him fell through and they were unable to find a replacement. It seems they'd been trying to get hold of some for months, but nothing was happening."

Sam nodded. "That was because the Ministry of Defence came down on the whole supply chain after what happened with Anderson. No one was getting their hands on them. I've seen the Galahad launcher in action and it's terrifying to even imagine it in the wrong hands."

Vogt nodded. "Glad you agree. Those rocket launchers can be used to bring down a helicopter or a low-flying commercial airplane coming in to land."

"But they've now found someone willing to arrange a few missing shipments," Natasja told him.

"Bullshit, there's no way. The MoD wouldn't make that mistake again."

Natasja shrugged. "I got a call from an old contact. Obviously not a regular, as he didn't know I was on the outside. Must have seen the merchandise and wanted to check what to do with it. Called me on my old number and asked if it was still the usual route."

"What did you say?"

"I tried to bluff my way through, but he soon twigged and hung up. I rang Vogt straight away."

"Still doesn't explain why you needed me. Why didn't you contact the Ministry of Defence? They could have located your missing rockets."

"We have and they can't. They say nothing's missing and to stop bringing up old history."

"So why the worry? If they say nothing's missing, surely there's nothing to worry about?"

"After everything Natasja's told you, do you really believe that? Or feel comfortable enough to risk it?"

Sam was getting frustrated now. "So, again, why did you need *me* back here?"

Vogt and Natasja looked at each other.

"We need to find the rockets, we need to find the Nile… and the best way to do that is through the mole in the Organised Crime Unit: Johannes Bos."

Sam stared at the Interpol agent in disbelief. "Bos? A mole?"

"Yes, Johannes Bos is the Nile's mole," Vogt told him.

Sam gave a nervous yelp of laughter. "I don't believe it; he thinks it's you!"

"I'm sure he'd like you to think that." Vogt's dark eyes stared up at him.

"Come off it, what proof do you have?" Sam looked at Natasja. "Did *she* tell you?"

"Fuck off, Taylor. This has nothing to do with me."

"Natasja knows nothing about it. Bos was installed behind her and Wever's back. He's Franssen's man."

"I don't know how much you've been drinking, but Johannes Bos is not working for the Nile. I know him; he saved my life. I met his husband, visited his house, petted his dogs."

"I'm sorry, Sam, but it's the truth. Think about it. He stopped you going into the trap that night, and he himself held back. He manages to 'get' two of the main Nile men and gets promoted out of it. Trust me, I don't want it to be true either. But his husband proves it. The husband used to work for Franssen when he started out in investments. They were at the same company before it was taken over. Took me a long time, but I managed to find the link. The two of them were good friends."

Sam felt his temper rising. "I've sat here and listened to this bullshit and this is the best you can come up with?"

Vogt slapped the table. "Look, Sam, you're the only one who could come into the team and be able to help us with this. Everyone else is compromised – too close to it all and, most importantly, to Bos."

Vogt had needed a reason to bring him back and what better reason than to identify the woman who had shot him? After all, apart from Vogt, who else had ever seen her?

"So you faked her death just to bring me over here without raising suspicions. How did you do it? I'm guessing the good doctor Singh was on the inside?"

"He was, he helped to drug her enough to get her to the hospital. It was an Interpol masterclass. The two paramedics were also working for us. After we got her away from the boat, it was very easy to just wait for you to show up."

"When you arrived at the hospital you went in first to give the warning? Let me guess, you wanted us to see her walking out?"

"I thought that uniform suited me." Natasja grinned.

"Jesus. I'm sorry, Vogt, I just don't get it. What are you wanting me to do? You've already been told there's no missing rockets by my government. And I don't believe you about Bos, I just don't."

Vogt sighed and stood up from the table. "I need two things from you. I need you to find out who could have replaced Anderson in having access to the Galahads."

Sam remembered asking for Hannah to do the same, but kept it quiet for now. "I can try, but it won't help if there's nothing missing."

"That's not up to you to corroborate. But you were really

brought here to watch Bos, find out what that bastard's really doing. He's up to his eyeballs in the Nile and I want him finished."

Sam swore and ran his free hand through his hair. "I need to think about it. That's a lot of information you've just thrown out there. Including accusing a friend of mine of being corrupt."

Stepping back into the hallway, he left the pair of them in the kitchen and went outside. The temperature was plummeting as the late-autumn sun began to drop towards the horizon. Four oystercatchers flew in circles over the water, their black and white feathers bright in the late sunshine. The car was still parked up outside the converted windmill and he realised the keys were still in his pocket. Perhaps he should just drive off and leave them there. Get on the first plane home.

"Fuck." He spat the word aloud to the empty scene. Only the river still moved in the silence. Could Bos really be a traitor? He couldn't see it, but he knew the agent inside was convinced. Then there was the woman, Natasja van Rossum, if that was her real name. Last year she'd been the prime suspect for a brutal murder. There was something not right in her story; he'd need to think about that.

"I knew you'd come back."

Sam turned to see Natasja had followed him out, her black jumper now covered by a thick cream-coloured coat, which she had tied tightly round her waist.

"You did?" he replied coldly.

"Of course, it's like that silly *Henry V* line your friend Sir Jeffrey uses. 'Once more unto the breach.' Shakespeare summed up every Englishman's point of view. You just can't help but drag yourselves into trouble. It's like it's bred into you at birth."

"And is that a bad thing?"

She shrugged. "Perhaps, I guess it all depends on whether you make it out alive."

"Yeah, well perhaps this time I might decide not to get involved?"

She shook her head and came to stand next to him as they both gazed at the slowly passing water. "No, I already know you'll do it. So does Vogt. I was thinking more about last year and how you managed to link Anderson to me. You could have just come over, taken the body and gone home, but you had to get involved. Do you ever think that if you hadn't, you wouldn't have got hurt?"

Sam ignored her question.

"Fair enough, I'm sorry about Bos."

"Why are you sorry? He's not your friend; he may not even be guilty."

"He is, Vogt's right."

"Not about this he isn't. How do you know I'll help you?"

"Your friend Sir Jeffrey told us. Vogt rang him a few nights ago. Seems they know each other."

Of course they do, Sam thought bitterly. Sir Jeffrey was about as retired from international events as Sam was from drinking. He turned to the woman next to him.

"And you? Why are you here? You don't strike me as someone here to do the right thing. You spent years on the black market and now you're all cleaned up? Spare me."

She shrugged and put her hands in her pockets. "I'm just here for revenge. If I find the bastards responsible first, I'll shoot them rather than let Vogt have his way."

She spoke the words calmly, almost relishing them. For the first time that day, he believed every word.

"Like you shot me?"

Natasja closed her eyes in exasperation and turned away from him. Sam watched as her right hand came out of the coat pocket holding the Walther he'd left on the table. He felt a sliver of panic as she raised it, then aimed at a single wooden post nearby. She fired four shots, each of them finding their mark. From where they were standing, it was a show of expert marksmanship. As the echo of the shots faded into the distance, she turned back to him.

"No, not like I shot you. Now, can you get over yourself, go back in there and tell him you're in so we can fuck off back to the city? It's getting late and I'm hungry."

Sam watched as she walked away from him, hands back inside her pockets, her steps crunching on the gravel. As he began to follow her back inside, he remembered the final lines of the Shakespearean verse. The desperate English King was rallying his men for one final push against the walls.

He let out a grim laugh. "'The game's afoot: Follow your spirit, and upon this charge cry *God for Harry, England, and Saint George!'*"

For better or for worse, Sam was going to follow the woman who had shot him and left him for dead in Amsterdam's cold waters.

TWELVE

THEY RETURNED to the table to discuss what would happen next. Only now did Sam tell them both about his quest to find who had replaced Anderson. He still had his doubts about the missing weaponry, but thought it best to check out the new man as a precaution. Bos, on the other hand, was a different problem.

"He's not the mole. I agree there must be one, but it's not Bos. Why can't it be one of Natasja's old insiders? She said it herself. Same system, new management."

"It's not one of my old contacts, I promise you."

"Enough," Vogt said, ending the argument before it could begin. "We have to start trusting each other. Just stay close to him. See what he's doing. We know this deal will be a big one for Nile and they'll be nervous about Natasja's sudden appearance then disappearance. From the call Natasja received, we found out the shipment must be on the water, so time's getting tight. If they think Natasja's back on the scene, they'll become agitated and will want to know everything we're doing to find her."

"So the deception wasn't just for me?"

"It had other benefits."

"Gives our Nile friends something else to think about. I can imagine they'd be quite keen to have a chat with our female friend as well."

Natasja chuckled. "Hmm, good luck with that. This is my city."

Sam looked at Vogt. "So what do you want me to do? You're in charge of the operation, after all."

"Tomorrow, I want you to go with Bos and speak to Franssen and De Klerk. They are the only two people we know for certain are involved in the Nile and who know Natasja. It would make sense to speak to them, plus I want Bos to be in the same room as his paymasters. Let him sweat."

"I keep telling you, it's not him–"

"I also want to give Bos a reason to think you may just have a real grudge against Natasja. If he thinks you're not too keen on bringing her in alive, he might be more willing to trust you a bit more." Vogt rubbed his chin. "You already have a motive. It would seem entirely normal if you wanted revenge."

"I'm more than happy to shoot her, perhaps in the leg?" Sam's eyes twinkled.

Natasja raised her middle finger.

The Interpol agent stood and walked over to one of the cabinets, pulling open a drawer. Reaching inside, he pulled out a magazine clip. From where Sam was sitting, he could see the outline of the dull metal bullets.

"Here." Vogt threw the magazine at Sam. "Tell me what you notice."

Sam caught the clip in the air and looked at it. Dropping it from hand to hand, he looked it over.

"Glock?"

"Yes, I know you like your Glocks. What else?"

"You tell me."

"They are blanks. Tomorrow I'm going to give you a Glock when you're in the station. I'll make a scene of it. When you get a moment, you need to swap the ammunition around."

"Why?"

"Because tomorrow, when you're visiting my old colleagues, I'm going to try and kill them," Natasja said calmly.

Vogt glared at her. "She's going to make it *look* like she's tried to kill them and you're going to fire these at her."

Sam looked at the pair of them in turn. He had to admit, he was impressed.

"How are you going to do that?" he asked the Dutchwoman, an eyebrow cocked.

"That's on a need-to-know basis."

"Christ, spare me the flirting." Vogt sighed. "It would be best if you didn't know, though. The surprise will be genuine then."

Natasja would take Sam back to his hotel, while Vogt made his own way back. As he waited for Natasja to drive them into the city, Sam checked his phone to see messages from both Berger and Bos. He remembered how easily he had lied to both of them as he left. Now he had to think of a reason why he had not spoken to them for nearly the entire afternoon. Deciding to stick with the migraine story, he apologised and said he had been asleep. Bos replied, telling him not to worry and saying he'd get him from his hotel in the morning. Berger didn't reply. Sam still couldn't see Bos as anything other than the friend who'd saved his life. Whatever Vogt thought, Sam was not going to write him off just yet.

"You coming, then?" Natasja had come back into the room.

Exiting the building, they found Vogt finishing his cigar in the evening air. He turned to stare at the pair of them. "See you tomorrow."

Sam nodded at the Interpol agent and climbed into the car. Natasja followed him and took the driver's seat.

"So, shall we catch a film, go for dinner or shall we just go back to your place?"

He shook his head and laughed. "Just drive."

Natasja grinned and set off back towards the city. Looking behind them in the wing mirror, Sam watched as Vogt turned away to finish his cigar, overlooking the cold river. As they drove,

Sam's mind went over everything that had happened. It was hard to process that his day had started with the early morning dash to the airport and had led to being here now with the woman he had thought was his attempted assassin, and then dead. Neither of which turned out to be true.

By the time either of them spoke again, they were back on the motorway.

It was Natasja who broke the silence. "So, how are you feeling now?"

"I honestly don't know."

"About the Nile?"

"About it all; it's a lot to take in."

She eyed him as she drove. "I know you don't trust me."

He didn't reply.

"I *know* you don't trust me, but please believe me when I tell you, the Nile is a serious organisation. Even if they don't have these rockets, the other merchandise they have is worth worrying about."

"You didn't seem to care before your boss Wever got cold feet."

Natasja paused before replying. "Maybe not, but he did, and he always cared what happened to the things he sold."

Sam listened, but he still had his reservations about her, especially regarding her own relationship to the Nile.

"What I'm really trying to say is... don't underestimate what they can do. These new guys, they're brutal. When they had me in the warehouse that night, the way they talked about killing. It was coarse; they dehumanised it and they enjoyed it."

Sam returned to watching out of the window. He didn't like the Nile and what it stood for, but he had yet to see its supposed brutality first-hand, just the aftermath. Major Anderson's blood-stained corpse on the hotel-room floor, walls covered in dark blood. He may have been a crooked military officer, but he had also been a husband and a father. For nearly a year, Sam had thought the woman next to him responsible, until this afternoon.

"I'm sorry about Bos."

"You are?" Sam asked, surprised.

"He's your friend, isn't he? Can't be easy to see him as the enemy."

"He's not the enemy. I may have agreed to help you hunt down the Nile guys, but I've not accepted Vogt's judgement on Bos."

Natasja shrugged. "To be honest, I don't care who it is. That's yours and Vogt's problem."

"Don't let him hear you saying that."

"We all have our secrets, Sam."

"I'm not sure I want to know yours," Sam lied. "So, what've you been doing since that night at the warehouse?"

Her eyes flicked briefly from the road to him. "Honestly? Hiding. At first I wanted revenge – to find out who was responsible for what had happened – but I soon had to give up. There were a few close moments where they nearly found me, but as I told you this is my city and it wasn't hard for me to disappear. If it wasn't for that misplaced call, I think Vogt would have had me emigrate and put it all behind me."

They talked some more, her sharing stories about the city. She asked him about his time in the army and why he left.

"I upset a general. Found his son up to his neck in an illegal racket in the forces. Nearly embarrassed the army, so they packed me off."

"That's why I don't like authority. You do the right thing and all you get is trouble."

"Made it worse that some of the ringleaders were old friends."

This time Natasja didn't reply. Instead, she watched the traffic as she came off the city's ring road. After a while, she began the conversation again.

"What about this Sir Jeffrey?"

"An old family friend who's looked after me for a long time. He knew my grandfather Gerry when they were in the navy together. What he's got up to over the years is a common topic of office gossip. He's had fingers in so many pies I've lost count."

"Fingers in pies?" Natasja asked.

With the English fluency levels across the Netherlands he regularly forgot it wasn't the first language.

"It means he's involved in a lot of things. By the time he retired, he had contacts across the world. Generally, he knows what's going on in most places."

"I'd like to meet him."

"He'd bloody love you."

"He would?"

"Yes, you're resourceful, clever, confident, arrogant and charismatic. He'd eat you up. Plus, he loves an attractive woman," he told her truthfully.

"You think I'm attractive?" Natasja said coyly.

Sam didn't rise to the bait, instead watching the city pass by. He began to recognise a few local landmarks.

"I'll park round the corner so you can get out."

She pulled up by the kerb and he turned to look at her. Her features seemed different to what he remembered of them from the year before. He didn't know what to say.

Stopping to get his bag from the back seat, he bent down through the passenger window and smiled, his eyes creasing at the corners. "Make sure you miss me next time you're shooting." He touched his forehead in a small salute.

Natasja winked and set off back into the Amsterdam night. Sam watched until the blue Volkswagen was lost to the sea of traffic. He sighed and turned towards the hotel.

A modern hotel built into one of the more traditional buildings, its four storeys were topped by a green copper-roofed tower. Entering the foyer, he admired the dark brown and black aesthetics made golden by the lighting. A young girl greeted him and checked him in, giving him a room overlooking the main road from the second floor.

Entering the room, he fought the urge to simply fall asleep on the bed and threw his bag on the luggage rack in the corner. Instead of the bed, he fell into the desk chair and grabbed the room service menu. Ordering a pizza and a couple of beers, he picked up his mobile.

Hannah answered on the third chime. "Hello, stranger. I hear you're hunting a zombie."

Sam chuckled. "Very good. Have you been working on that all day?"

"To be honest, no, it was my boyfriend's joke."

Sam ignored the part about the boyfriend before the jealousy kicked in. "Well, it needs work. Did Emma ask you to look into Anderson's replacement?"

"She did, but I've not been able to get anywhere so far. The Ministry of Defence is not keen on us asking about that department after last year."

"Get Emma to pull rank if you need to. I need to know who's over there now, please."

"Sure thing, boss. Anything else?"

"There is, but I need you to exercise complete caution. I can't have it coming back to either me or the department."

"Interesting."

Sam sighed and looked out of the window at the main road. The hotel was situated just off the main S100 thoroughfare, with streetlights hanging from wires dipping over the street.

"I want you to investigate one Albert Wever, in particular his death, which was the same day as Anderson's. Anything you can get me without the local police knowing who you work for. Think you can do it?"

"I could try someone at the embassy. Can I ask Jason or Emma to try to call in favours?"

"Yes, but same rules apply."

He could tell even over the phone she was desperate to know why. Time to make her wonder even more, he decided, remembering the stab of jealousy from when she'd mentioned her boyfriend.

"Also, same request for Natasja van Rossum, although I have no date of birth or death to go on. To be honest, I'm not convinced it's a real name."

"Why can't you ask the locals to do it?"

"I don't want them to know."

There was a pause at the end of the line as Hannah debated what to say next. Sam began to wonder where his pizza was.

"Fine, be like that, but you better tell me why when you're back."

"I will."

Another pause. "How are you doing being back there? Shame about the woman."

"Yeah, all good. God knows where she's gone."

There was a knock on the door.

"Right, dinner's here, bugger off back to the boyfriend and let me eat."

Sam hung up the phone and stood up. Stretching his back, he rubbed his cheeks before walking towards the door. Sooner or later, he would have to admit to himself that he had a soft spot for Hannah Pearce. The short brunette was the best-looking girl in the Foreign Office. Whoever that boyfriend was, Sam envied him. Yet opening the door, the image of the analyst was driven out of his mind.

"Room service," announced the sultry voice of Ada Berger.

THIRTEEN

HANS FRANSSEN still felt uncomfortable attending these new Nile meetings. Ever since the new management had come in last year, there was always that sense of being on the edge. Now, as he drove through the quiet streets of the Dutch capital, he wondered why they were being called in that evening. It wasn't the first time. The new guys enjoyed keeping them all on their toes. It was their attempt at letting everyone know who was in charge. Times like this, he missed the old man. At least Wever never made them come out in the middle of the night.

The dark-grey Audi pulled off the main road of the Zeeburgereiland and onto the side road that ran alongside the deep waterway of the Amsterdam to Rhine canal. It had become a feature of the new regime to have their meetings in the new warehouses they kept just outside the city. Franssen had long decided it was their way of showing off the scale of their operation. Like Franssen needed to be told. He'd helped Wever back in the old days, when payments were simple cash transactions. Now the clients wanted to pay everything in Bitcoin or some other new method. The days of the paper dollar were long gone.

Arriving at the warehouse, he slowed at the security gate.

Looking at the drab building, Franssen had to give the new guys credit. They had moved away from the big industrial estates and into these run-down boatyards. The boatyards had proved a good location for keeping unfriendly eyes out of their business. The main building was clad in dark-blue-painted wood, nothing special to an outsider. Surrounded by broken down boats half covered in tarpaulins, the base was hidden to all but the most observant. This new set-up even allowed the business to transport stock directly from the water into the warehouse.

Two men came out of the booth to check the vehicle. Franssen watched as their breath misted in the cold air. Wever had never gone to these lengths. He'd relied on his relationships with the people of the city. *His* city, he liked to say. Franssen had to blink as a bright torchbeam was flashed in his face. While he couldn't see anything, he knew the pair of them were armed to the teeth. He'd seen the payments for the state-of-the-art automatic rifles held by each of the guards. The new guys had brought their own people with them, all of them Polish like the boss.

"Name."

"Fuck off; don't play that with me."

They looked at each other and then at him.

"Name."

"Franssen, you prick."

They waved him through the now opening gate.

"Pricks."

Franssen drove on through, looking up at the darkened building. Every time he came to these places at night, it reminded him of the evening he'd been arrested. The subsequent months inside had been tough. Even with the promises from the Nile of his release, the fear had always been there. The day he had finally been released, he had walked out a free man to find the new head parked outside the courthouse. He'd driven both De Klerk and Franssen to an upmarket restaurant, treated them both to as much alcohol and food as they could take. Then at the end of the evening, he'd taken them both by the hands and asked them to come back to work. They'd both known it hadn't been a question.

Now here Franssen was, still in the Nile and still making sure the money kept moving. Yet things had changed. Under Wever, everything had been run on a shoestring. As few people as possible was the rule. Now? There were people everywhere, all of them part of the inner circle. The operation had become something else entirely.

Parking the Audi, he saw De Klerk's car already between two stored sail-boats. Their wooden hulls rested on stilts as the paint peeled away. He turned off the engine and paused for a moment, letting the tension leave him as he readied himself. There was no way out, he knew that. Not under this management. Best keep his head down and go along with it. He had, after all, given them their greatest asset. Well, their greatest asset outside of the watertight financial operation he'd built over the years.

Franssen left the car and walked over to the main entrance, where two more guards stood around the reception desk. This time neither attempted to stop him. Instead, one of them called out in a deep voice.

"They are in the warehouse office."

"Thanks, I'll head on through."

"Best hurry up. They are all waiting."

Fuck them, Franssen thought as he walked through reception and the double doors that led further into the building. He subconsciously increased his pace. Entering the main warehouse, he found himself surrounded by the varied stock of the Nile. If the outside looked like a run-down shack, inside was something else. Bright lights shone over the warehouse, covering every inch. There were crates of weapons piled high, rare sports cars stolen from across Europe and, shining white in the distance, two sports yachts. Franssen was always impressed with the range of stock that had found its way through them over the years. The docks of Amsterdam never failed to deliver. To his left were newly arrived crates with French writing printed on them. He recognised the warnings on the sides to be for landmines and shuddered.

Walking further in, he stepped past the only area of the warehouse he truly found interesting. A thick metal cage stood to one side, a robust metal padlock chained around it. Within were boxes of rare jewellery, many of Wever's own later designs as he filled his time practising his old profession. Next to these were various watches, which were next to impossible for most people to buy. Green leather boxes piled high next to bright blue. Franssen's own professional interest was kept in the cage next door, where the boxes of used currency were stored ready to be shipped out. Not normally involved in sourcing, Franssen had played his part in getting hold of the various dollars, euros and pound notes. Their value, however, paled next to what Franssen had already given the organisation. Not everyone could provide a direct link into the Organised Crime Unit.

The cabin was situated at the far end of the warehouse. Perched on metal frames, it gave the occupants a clear view. Franssen's feet clanged on the metal steps as he made his slow progress to the awaiting door. Opening it, he stepped into a brightly lit office, with a white wooden table placed in its centre. Around it were seven expectant faces, all of which looked up at him as he entered.

"Hans, my friend. Glad you could make it. Take a seat."

The invitation came from the man at the head of the table. In any other situation, the middle-aged man would have looked more likely to be found on a golf course than here. He was slightly overweight, with cheeks that were turning pink from regular alcohol intake. The face would once have had rather sharp features, but had now turned plump. Receding grey hair was kept trim atop a high forehead. Jakub Dudka waved Hans Franssen towards an empty seat on the right-hand side of the table.

Franssen moved to the indicated seat, his back now to the window that overlooked the warehouse floor. Once seated, he looked down the length of the table. De Klerk was on the other side, at the furthest end from Jakub Dudka. Franssen thought he looked ill. The usually clean-shaven, well-dressed De Klerk looked worn out.

The rest of the table was made up of men far younger than either himself or De Klerk. Young Poles brought over by Dudka to run his organisation. From the little Franssen had learnt over the past months, he'd found out they had all come from the same small village in the eastern part of the country. They were all small fry, expendable pieces in the new order of the Nile's organisation. All except the man seated to the side of Jakub, his younger brother Marcel.

In their mother tongue, the name Marcel meant 'little warrior'. Marcel Dudka was not little, but he was a warrior. The slim, pale Marcel was his brother's enforcer, the brother who did the dirty work when it was needed. Whenever they were in the same room, Franssen's eyes were always drawn towards him. The younger Dudka brother was thin, so thin his face was gaunt, the skin pulled tight across his skull. But what made the man really stand out from the crowd was his paleness. The only colour came from his short dark hair and dark-green eyes, which seemed to never blink.

Franssen wasn't ashamed to say he feared both of the Dudka brothers. Jakub would smile at you one moment and have Marcel break your neck the next. The brains and the brawn. It showed itself in other ways, too. Jakub could talk for hours, about any subject he chose. Yet sometimes Franssen wondered if Marcel was a mute.

"I'm sorry to have brought you all here this evening. I know you've all got better things to be getting on with," Jakub told the assembly. "But we have some problems, which we need to resolve between us."

"The woman?" a voice from the table spoke out.

Jakub nodded. "Our old friend Natasja van Rossum."

The room went silent. They all knew her and who she once

was. Most had spent the best part of the last year trying to find her.

"Some of you may know she was found dead yesterday."

Franssen knew, and with his source in the Organised Crime Unit, he also knew the rest of what Jakub would be saying.

"Don't get too excited," he told a couple of the attendees who had cracked out smiles.

Whatever else could be said about Jakub Dudka, he enjoyed an audience.

"Earlier today, Natasja van Rossum somehow managed to come back from the dead and escape out of hospital."

Murmurs rippled across the table as those who were hearing it for the first time processed the news. Franssen kept his thoughts to himself.

"We don't yet know the full details. In particular, why she has chosen now to make such a move. It could be, and I stress only *could* be, to do with the Galahad deal."

More murmurs. Franssen watched the different faces react to the news. In particular, his eye caught both of the Dudka brothers watching out for De Klerk's reaction. Turning in his seat, he saw his old colleague looking distinctly sickly. The goddamn Galahad deal. It was always the bloody Galahads. Ever since Wever had refused to do the deal, things had gone wrong.

It had been the first time Franssen had met the Dudkas. They had been acting on behalf of some group back in Poland who wanted to make a statement. Wever had known it was a step too far and had refused at first, but then out of the blue he'd had a change of mind. The deal was back on. De Klerk had made the arrangements, found Major Anderson and flown him over. Natasja had taken over then, showing Anderson the sights of the city as she finalised the deal. Yet things were moving fast. The Dudkas were no longer just eyeing the Galahads, they were after the whole operation. De Klerk was first, he'd been frustrated with Wever for years and when the Dudkas approached him, he had no qualms about signing on.

Franssen's own emotions had been mixed. He had liked Wever, but had seen the end a long time coming. The old man's reign was drifting to a close and so he had sided with the new guys, too. It had been too easy. The old man's strategy of keeping everything and everyone at arm's length had finally caught up with him. Between himself and De Klerk, they had managed to either close down those too loyal to Wever, or realign those less committed to the cause. Dudka's next move had been to gatecrash the Galahad deal. De Klerk set up the meeting with Anderson, but the major got cold feet and threatened to pull out unless the price increased. It was not the move to make with the Dudkas.

Instead, it had become Marcel's moment to step up. In the space of twenty-four hours, the younger Dudka had solved all of their problems and left them as the masters of Nile. First, he had gone after the elderly Wever. Franssen had heard the younger Dudka had broken the old man's neck, then dropped him down the stairs. When the police found him, they had mistaken it as an accident. An old man alone falls down the stairs. Marcel had then found evidence that the old man had been working with Interpol. The Nile had been breached.

The next problem had been Natasja, who would never have betrayed Wever. Marcel had wanted to kill her as well, but the elder Dudka had decided otherwise. Jakub had suggested taking down two birds with one stone. If Anderson couldn't be reasoned with, perhaps his successor could? If Natasja could be implicated in his death as well? Marcel had once again arranged it all. The pale-faced killer made short work of Anderson and it had only been Natasja's escape that had foiled the plan.

"If it is the Galahads, we need to be ready," Jakub said, interrupting Franssen's thoughts. "We know she can be a real bitch and so we need to be ready. I want everyone we have out looking for her again."

One of the more confident members spoke up. "But Jakub, we've been looking for her all year and found nothing."

That was true. After Anderson's death, all their efforts went into finding Natasja. Instead, Natasja had tried to set them up with the police raiding their warehouse, but Franssen's asset had proved their worth. It had become a double bluff. Using the information provided by his informer, they turned the tables back onto Natasja. He and De Klerk played along, pretended that they were unaware of what was really happening, and went to the faked meeting. Yet their preparations had not been enough and in the ensuing firefight she'd escaped. A stretch in prison for them and months of searching for her had followed.

"But this time she's shown herself and must have done so for a reason. It will have taken some effort, after all." Jakub looked at Franssen. "Have the police come up with a reason for it all?"

"They're as confused as we are."

"Fucking hell, why now?"

No one answered the eldest Dudka.

"It has to be the Galahads." Marcel spoke quietly.

Jakub stared at his brother, but didn't reply.

Franssen watched on and began to realise why De Klerk was looking so stressed. The Galahads had been a chain round all their necks, but especially his. He had been the one who had been most vocal about bypassing Anderson with the new man. When the new man had been unwilling to cooperate and the rockets failed to appear, he'd found himself to be very unpopular. De Klerk needed this latest source to work more than anyone.

"So, where are they?" Jakub stared at De Klerk.

De Klerk stuttered and then cleared his throat. "My contact is arriving in the city tomorrow and I'll meet him to finalise everything."

"Is that it?"

De Klerk blushed. "They are on the water. I know they are on the water."

The two brothers looked at each other, the older, middle-aged Jakub and pale, slim Marcel. Franssen felt a twinge of concern for his old colleague. This deal had failed twice now and he couldn't imagine De Klerk surviving another one.

"Then meet him as soon as you can. I want to know everything. If it helps, me and Marcel can join you when you see him."

De Klerk paled at the thought and mumbled something that none of them could catch.

Jakub turned to Franssen. "Are we ready to pay him?"

"Yes, we've every option covered. I think we'd prefer euros if possible?"

Jakub gave a curt nod. "And the police? We need to find Natasja before she can meddle."

"I'll keep talking to them."

"And Hans."

"Yes?"

"Tell your contact, if the police could take her out first it would help us all out. I think it would be best for everyone if she wasn't taken in alive. Well, not this time!"

The rest of the room took the cue, and all laughed at the poor joke. Franssen tried to give his most confident smile in response. At the end of the table, Marcel Dudka let out a sly smile. The Nile was prepared.

FOURTEEN

ADA BERGER STOOD in the doorway of Sam's hotel room, a smile etched across her face. In her hands she held a large room service tray, which Sam noticed held double the amount of food he'd ordered.

"Are you going to let me in, or shall we let it go cold?"

Sam recovered from the surprise and stepped back inside, letting her in after him. "Moonlighting as a butler now?"

"I may have to, unless Bos starts paying me more. Come on, sit down, I'm starving."

She walked into the room and placed the tray on the still-made bed. Taking her suit jacket off, she looked round the hotel room. Sam noticed the black holster fastened to her belt.

"Looks like they've spruced up the place since we were last here."

"You don't visit other men here when I'm away?"

"Well, the establishment's management has started to recognise me."

Returning to the desk chair, Sam pointed to the covered room service plates. "That how you managed to get another one of those?"

"No, my detective badge did that. I asked at reception what

room you were staying in and they told me you had just ordered room service. So I told them to double it."

"I'm not sure what London will say about that."

She shrugged and threw him a bottled beer, then passed him the plate. "Surely that's what expenses are for?"

Sam chuckled and twisted the bottle open.

"So how's the head?" she asked as she pulled a slice of pizza from the plate.

"Better, I slept it off."

Berger lay back on the bed against the pillows. "You just wanted to get out of that meeting."

"No, I didn't. Well, maybe. Was it that bad?"

"Christ, yes! They had us in there for nearly the whole afternoon. Only that bastard Vogt escaped. Someone called him to return to Interpol headquarters back at The Hague. Did you know he doesn't carry a phone? The poor reception girl had to come up and get him." She sighed and took a long slug from the beer bottle. "I've honestly no idea what's happening. We've got uniform out on the streets, there are teams trawling through hours of CCTV footage and everything else you would expect. But it's a waste of time."

"It is?"

Berger gave him a withering look. "You saw what happened at the hospital; she's too good for us. It was a well-planned operation. We should give up trying to find out what happened or where she went. We should be looking into *why*."

She looked at Sam, expecting him to agree with her. Realising he'd finished chewing the latest slice, he couldn't avoid replying.

"Why what?"

"Why she's suddenly decided to do this. Why now? What's she after? It's a crazy move and what's it actually achieved? You can't help but wonder. Must be to do with the Nile. They must be after something. She has to be still working for them."

Sam remembered the outside world didn't know Natasja was on the run from the Nile as much as from the police.

"You're probably right, but there's no point worrying about it. Let Vogt worry about all that; it's what he's paid to do. He'll no doubt have us all chasing shadows in the morning. Did you want another one?" He indicated the two remaining beer bottles on the tray.

"You're right there, he's already said we all have to be in tomorrow to be given our assignments. Even you!"

Standing up, he picked up one of the bottles and leant over his bed to pass it over. Berger reached up and took it. As she did so, their hands touched for a moment. They looked at each other. Sam moved away first, sitting back in his chair, taking the remaining green bottle for himself.

They drank in silence for a moment, tension palpable between them. Sam found himself surprised to be thinking of a pair of dark-brown eyes rather than the woman in front of him. He decided to try to start his assigned mission from earlier in the day.

"How's Bos dealing with it all?"

Berger looked at him, surprised by the change of direction. She sat up, a tone of disappointment in her reply. "He's okay, well least I think he's okay. He had to rush off after work and we didn't get much chance to talk. He's like the rest of us, just pissed off to be back to where we were last year."

Sam debated where to go next. "How's he been since taking the new job?"

"Yeah, okay, it suits him and he deserves it. He's done a good job wherever he's been. Just a shame he's inherited the Nile crap."

"I worry about him. Must have been a tough year."

"It has been, for all of us. But Bos has been all right. You've met Peter, haven't you? Well, they're still together, although I think Peter lost his job earlier in the year so money must have been tight for a while."

"Shit, I didn't know that."

"He doesn't talk about what happens outside of work much, but I think things have settled down."

"And you? How are you?" he asked, more softly, leaning towards her slightly.

She smiled and shrugged. "You know me, still waiting for my rich man to take me away." She scoffed.

"Really? I'd have thought you'd have had them queuing for miles. I was worried you'd be all loved up."

"Oh no, that's not happening anytime soon."

"Are you *really* wanting to join Interpol?"

"Maybe." She moved closer towards him, along the edge of the bed. "Could be something a bit… different."

He'd forgotten how husky her voice could be. The small eyes were dark under their long lashes. She was very close now to where he sat.

"Working for Vogt?"

"Jealous?"

She leaned forward, placed her elbow on his knee and rested her head in her hand.

"Maybe, of you not him. I bet he's a good person to work with."

She scowled. "And you? Still skulking round the world bringing back bodies?"

"I sometimes help the live ones as well."

Ada Berger's patience had finally worn out and she stood up over the Englishman where he sat in his chair. Stepping forward, she sat on his lap, her legs either side of his.

"God, you do like to talk."

Placing her hands round his head, she kissed him firmly on the mouth and he gave in and reciprocated before standing up and carrying her to the bed.

Berger left rather than staying the night. Lying in bed, he watched her search for her discarded clothing. The glare of the streetlights shone through the curtains, illuminating her naked silhouette as she moved. Sam watched her pale limbs stretch out to pull on her clothes. Once dressed, she turned and kissed him before heading out into the Amsterdam night.

———

Sam awoke the next morning to see a message from Bos that he'd pick him up from outside the hotel before heading to the station. Sam could have walked, but was glad of the chance to see Bos after the previous day. He briefly considered getting up and going for a run through the quiet early morning streets. But the extra sleep seemed more appealing after the strain of the previous day. Lying there, he once again tried to make sense of everything, but the memory of Ada Berger made thinking difficult. Forcing himself up, he took a shower and tried to clear his mind under the hot water.

Later that morning, he knew Vogt would have him go with Bos to visit Franssen and De Klerk. Somehow, during those visits, he was supposed to find out how Bos was working for them. No, he reminded himself. *If* Bos was working for them. His instincts still told him Vogt was wrong. Then there were the Galahads. Again, he wasn't fully convinced they were a real threat, but it wouldn't hurt for Hannah to look into it.

The analyst was also looking into the Nile itself, the deceased Wever and the very much alive Natasja van Rossum. Regardless of whether Vogt trusted the elusive Dutchwoman, Sam was convinced there was something she wasn't telling them. Charismatic, alluring and attractive she may be, but she had also been involved in running one of the largest criminal networks in the world. Just because Wever had suffered a crisis of conscience, it was no guarantee his protégé had been a true convert.

Leaving the shower, he quickly dressed, changing into another shirt and three-quarter jumper combination. It took a moment to find his boots from where he'd kicked them off while otherwise occupied with his visitor. The boots were the last vestiges of Sam's old life in the military, the hard suede leather the perfect tool for breaking up or even finishing fights. He never quite felt comfortable without them. Fully dressed, he grabbed the dark-green field jacket with its clip of blank ammunition zipped away and put it over his shoulder. Checking he had his phone and watch, he was out of the door and heading for breakfast.

A continental breakfast and two large black coffees later, Sam was out on the main road waiting for Bos to pick him up. The air was cold that morning, with an autumnal breeze blowing in from the sea. Sam shoved his hands in his pockets and shivered. The memory of the freezing water engulfing him came back unbidden into his mind. It didn't bode well for the rest of the day.

At that moment, Bos pulled up in front of him and brought the car to a stop. Sam opened the passenger door and slid in.

"Good morning, Sam, feeling better?"

"Yes, a lot better, thanks. How are you? Did you get a good night's sleep?"

"I'm okay. Peter sends his regards by the way. Tells me you're to drop by before you go home."

Vogt, Sam knew, would have jumped at the chance to look around Bos's house. He felt guilty for even thinking it.

Bos moved the car into the Amsterdam traffic, with the usual balancing act of avoiding the other commuters making their way on foot, bike, car or bus. Sam looked across at his friend. The thick blond hair was a bit longer than last year, and perhaps there were a few bags beginning to grow under the eyes, but apart from that there were no physical changes in his friend. If the past year had been tough balancing the needs of the Nile and the police force, it wasn't showing.

"Have you any preference of what you want to do today?" Bos asked him.

Fully aware that Vogt had already decided where they were heading, Sam bypassed the question. "I don't mind. Guess we'll need to go back over the old associates and see if any of them has seen her?"

"Agreed, although it does feel like we are going over old ground. What do you think of Vogt then, after yesterday?"

"Impressive, but I can see why he puts people out."

Bos laughed. "You can say that again. You should have heard the comments when he left the room. Our people will be glad to see the back of him."

They crossed one of the numerous city bridges, black iron railings on either side. Sam looked over and saw one of the tourist boats making its way along the canal, ready for the day's customers.

Bos cleared his throat. "So, are you and Berger still a thing?"

Sam grinned but didn't reply. Instead, the conversation moved on to Bos's home life and how Peter was getting on.

Leaving the car and walking into the station, they headed up towards the conference room. Entering, they found half a dozen officers milling around. Sittting together in one corner were the Organised Crime officers. Berger, Corsel and Hardenne were talking lazily together as Bos and Sam joined them.

"Working banker's hours, you two?" Berger greeted them.

"Glad to see you're on top form today, Detective Berger," Bos said sarcastically.

"Ignore her, boss. She's not had that sugar concoction she injects into her veins," Hardenne joked.

"How do you stay so thin drinking that every day?" asked Corsel, whose own waist had expanded since his sergeant days of walking the streets.

"Good genes," she told him.

The door to the conference room flew open and Vogt strolled in, heading to the front of the room. Hands in his pockets, his dark curly brown hair combed back, Sam watched the man he'd last seen standing in the setting sun's rays by the river smoking a cigar glare at the faces in the room. When Vogt's eyes met his, Sam returned the stare icily. He wasn't going to let the short bastard think he could push him around. It was too early in the day for that.

FIFTEEN

AGENT VOGT SPENT the next thirty minutes lecturing the assembled officers. He went through the latest updates, outlining the lack of progress made by those who'd been working overnight. Watching on, it was clear to Sam that each of the assembled officers respected his authority, no matter their opinion of the man.

"Any questions?"

Sam realised the lecture was coming to an end and made an effort to look interested. No one spoke and Vogt raised his eyebrows.

"Anyone got anything interesting to add? Anything at all?"

Again, no one spoke and he dismissed them from the room. "Bos, Taylor, stay here please. I need to talk to you."

"Fucking hell, why us?" Bos whispered as they waited for Vogt to walk over.

"Probably wants us to go out and solve the case. You know, make him look good."

Bos stifled a laugh as they watched Vogt take a seat opposite them.

"Sorry to keep you."

"No you're not, don't pull that one."

"No, you're right, I'm not, Detective Bos. But take it as a compliment. I need you and Taylor here. I've not made this official, as it may be seen as borderline inappropriate as they were only found not guilty a few months back."

Bos and Sam looked at each and then at Vogt.

"Franssen and De Klerk?" Bos whispered.

Vogt nodded.

"I should have guessed. What do you want us to do with those bastards?"

"I want you to visit them, tell them about the woman and find out if they've seen her."

Bos looked uncertainly at Vogt. "You what? When do you want us to do that?"

"Now."

"Fucking hell, are you sure? If we go over there accusing them of all sorts, they'll have our badges."

"We are not accusing them." Vogt spoke calmly. "We are simply going to warn them that a mutual friend has resurfaced."

"And why can't one of the others do it?"

Good question, thought Sam. *Over to you, Vogt.*

Without missing a beat, Vogt replied, "You and Taylor made the breakthrough last time. Having a senior officer such as yourself will smooth any disgruntled feelings about being spoken to again. Plus, Taylor here has never met them. I suspect he'd like to."

"Don't look at me, I'm just a tourist," warned Sam.

Vogt's patience began to break. "Don't you play games with me, either of you. I don't need your shit with everything else going on. You are going to visit those two bastards and you're going now."

The Interpol agent stood up and moved to leave, then stopped. "Oh and Taylor, I've agreed it with the commissioner, you're to visit the armoury and get yourself a firearm. This time let's make it official, so Bos here doesn't have to sneak one out for you again."

With that final order, he left.

"Fuck me, he's a bastard," Bos muttered. "Nice of him to give you a weapon this time, though. Saves me getting into trouble."

"Hmm." Sam was wondering when he'd be able to switch the magazine with the blanks in his coat pocket.

Bos tapped the table and swore again. "Bastard. Look, Sam, I need a favour."

Sam turned to look at his companion. Bos looked worried.

"Just let me ring Corsel to come in."

A few moments later, the middle-aged Corsel came in. The detective appeared confused and looked from Sam to Bos.

"What's Vogt got you doing this morning?" Bos asked him.

Corsel shrugged. "I'm on the traffic cameras, trying to find the car they left the hospital in."

"Not anymore. I want you to go with Sam and visit De Klerk this morning."

Sam looked round in surprise. "What? Vogt wanted both of us, specifically."

"I can't, I'm sorry but I need to be somewhere this morning."

Sam stared at the Dutch detective in disbelief. "If Vogt finds out, he won't be happy. Where are you going?"

"It's personal."

"I think you should really reconsider and come with us."

"Just trust me, I need to be somewhere. It's important." He looked at his watch. "Come on, I'll take you to the armoury and Corsel can get a car ready."

The Head of Organised Crime stood and led Sam out of the room without giving him a chance to respond. In the end, Bos didn't give Sam a chance to speak to Vogt. He took him to the downstairs armoury and waited for the armourer to bring him a well-oiled Glock 17 and holster, which he fastened to his belt under the dark-green field jacket, all the time shrugging off Sam's questions.

Then Bos escorted Sam back upstairs to the waiting Corsel, parked on the side of the road in a white police car.

"Look, Sam, I'm really sorry about this. I didn't realise he'd be sending us round the city. I thought I'd be here all morning and could sneak out. But I'll explain later," Bos told him as he watched Sam open the passenger door. "I'll ring you when I'm done and come meet you so we can see Franssen together."

Sam could only nod a reply as Corsel started the engine and pulled away. He made a quick decision, pulled out his phone and messaged the unknown number Natasja had been using the day before.

> En route to De Klerk. Bos unable to join – no reason why. Please tell Vogt.

How she was supposed to tell Vogt anything when he didn't have a phone, he didn't know. But he guessed they must have developed some way of communicating with each other.

"You look worried."

Sam looked up from his phone and turned towards Corsel. The detective was looking at him, his weathered, friendly face full of concern.

"I'm always worried, comes with the job."

Corsel laughed. "I should have stayed a sergeant; life was far easier."

"I'll come to that in a minute, but what's happening with Bos? Has he been doing this a lot recently, just disappearing like that?"

"The boss? A bit, keeps saying he's got appointments in the middle of the day. Doesn't really make much of a difference; he's usually back after an hour or so."

Sam wished he hadn't asked the question. The answer made him feel sick.

Corsel must have realised Sam hadn't liked the answer. "I wouldn't worry about him. I've known Bos for years and he's always kept his personal life to himself. It was years before we even knew about Peter. Now he's the boss, I guess it's even harder for him to share things with us."

"Do you like having him as your boss?"

"He's all right, I've had worse. He lets us get on with things, gives us the space to make our own decisions. If it wasn't for the Nile case, we'd be one of the more successful departments."

"And what do you think to it all? The Nile stuff and everything that's gone on?"

Corsel considered the question before answering. "I think whoever's behind this operation is both very clever and very dangerous. Look at what they did last year to those armed response units; they pretty much slaughtered them. And what they did to you, shot you down and left you for dead." He added the latter part as almost an afterthought.

They joined the heavy traffic of the S100 Nassaukade, heading back towards Sam's hotel. Sam always enjoyed driving in a marked police vehicle, watching the nervous glances of other drivers as they concentrated on not drawing attention to themselves. One woman driving an SUV kept looking down at them, Sam could see, even from below white-knuckled hands tightly gripping the steering wheel. If only she knew neither of the officers could have cared less about her driving abilities.

"Don't hold that against them. Whoever shot me was pretty amateur. I was so close, I don't know how she missed," joked Sam as he thought about the expert show of marksmanship the day before.

Corsel chuckled. "So I heard. Good job Bos was up for a swim to drag you out."

"One thing I don't understand. Why've you turned to the dark side and given up being a sergeant? I'd have never thought you'd leave uniform for the suits."

"Don't get me wrong, I loved been a sergeant. But I'd done it for nearly thirty years. I'd seen everything, learnt everything and done it all. I was getting tired and then a vacancy came up so I went for it."

"Any regrets?"

"Plenty, but overall I'm enjoying it. Few years of this and then

I'm retiring to the country. The wife's always wanted to live in a windmill and I've wanted to live next to a river full of fish to catch." He stopped abruptly, as if he'd said too much.

As Sam turned to look at him, an image came into his mind of where they'd met Vogt the day before.

"Sounds nice. I hope it happens for you."

Corsel shrugged it away and concentrated on the traffic ahead. They'd passed the hotel and were about to come off the ring road back into the city. De Klerk lived in one of the more upmarket parts of the city just off the Vondelpark, one of the largest of the city's parks. Sam had already spotted signs for the Rijksmuseum, the Stedelijk Museum and the Van Gogh Museum. In different circumstances, he would have spent hours exploring the cultural hotspots of the Dutch capital.

"Ever met De Klerk?" Sam asked Corsel.

"Nope, he was arrested while I was still in uniform. I followed the trial, we all did. When the case collapsed over a lack of evidence, we were told specifically to leave the pair of them alone. Bloody joke, if they ask me, the murdering bastard." Corsel spat the final words out. He must have realised he had spoken too harshly.

"Sorry Sam, just I knew some of the officers injured the night De Klerk was arrested."

"Don't worry, you should have seen how I was feeling about seeing the woman who I'd last seen firing a gun at me. Can't say I was happy."

Corsel laughed again. "Bet you weren't happy, especially when you found out she had walked right past you."

"I was too busy admiring a good-looking woman to realise we had history."

"Femme fatales, every man's weakness."

"Emphasis on the fatale."

"She's some woman, isn't she?"

Sam raised an eyebrow.

"Well she is, isn't she? She managed to escape the Nile, escape the police, and now she's got us all running round after her again. She's managed to have everyone fooled."

Sam studied his companion. The kindly Corsel had said something just then that triggered a switch in his mind. But it would have to wait as Corsel announced their arrival. The car pulled into a leafy residential street. Dark red-brick buildings dwarfed the car. Sam read the small street sign, Van Eeghenstraat Street. To one side a line of high-windowed townhouses looked out onto the dark tarmac. Opposite, between the road and the park, stood large detached houses, each with their own gated driveways.

Corsel had parked in front of one of the three-storey buildings. The front of the house was hidden by thick green bushes, a few tall trees surrounded the property. Peering through the gates, Sam could see a deep-red door under a covered porch. A curved balcony had been fitted to the first floor, leading to what Sam guessed was a sitting room.

"I really like the architecture in this city," Sam commented.

"It's a beautiful city, although I suggest you lower your ambitions if you're planning on moving here. That house must be worth millions of euros."

"How does he afford it? No, sorry, what's the official reason for being able to afford a house like that? Other than being involved in an illegal crime syndicate?"

Corsel unclipped his seatbelt. "Inheritance – checks out, although it's old money and it stinks of shit."

"Stinks of shit?"

"Dirty money, but beyond our means to prove."

"Then let's go and see the rich bastard."

Sam climbed out of the car and walked round to join Corsel outside of the gated house. The gate was unlocked and the pair of them walked through onto the gravel driveway. Both men admired the new silver Mercedes AMG GT parked up outside the house.

"Looks like it could do with a clean," Sam commented on the immaculate vehicle.

"Don't think I could be seen driving it."

"Me neither. I'd be ashamed."

They stepped up to the door and Corsel rang the electronic doorbell.

"Smile for the camera, Sam."

Sam looked at the doorbell camera with its blue light and wondered who was at the other end. Moments later, the door was pulled open and De Klerk emerged. The man that stepped out would once have been extremely handsome. Thick black hair, now turning grey, was neatly trimmed and styled. The face, tanned and sharp, was pointed with a strong jawline. But beyond the designer shirt and shined shoes, Sam could see the face looked strained. Large bags had formed under the eyes and the cheeks were becoming gaunt. Whether it was the long-term effects from his time inside, or something more recent, De Klerk looked a tormented man.

SIXTEEN

"AND WHAT THE fuck can I do for you two gentlemen?" De Klerk addressed the pair on his doorstep.

"Albert de Klerk?" Corsel asked, brandishing his badge.

"Oh for fuck's sake, not again. Haven't you guys had enough embarrassment chasing innocent men this year?"

Corsel continued on. "Mr de Klerk, I'm Detective Corsel and this is my associate, Mr Taylor from the British Foreign Office. May we come in?"

"No."

"I'd appreciate it if we could come in and talk to you about a private matter."

"I'd appreciate it if you didn't," De Klerk replied.

Sam, not known to have the best of patience when dealing with such people, decided to step in.

"We can continue this discussion outside, Mr de Klerk, but we have reason to believe your life is in danger. And while I don't mind enjoying the fresh air, you may feel a bit safer inside."

De Klerk's face paled slightly as he moved his stare to the Englishman. Sam's handsome face could turn stern at a moment's notice. The two piercing deep-blue eyes stared flatly into the Nile man's face.

"My life's in danger?" he asked sarcastically. "From whom?"

"We can discuss it further inside," Corsel insisted.

Their host glared at the pair of them and, realising defeat, resignedly beckoned them in. Following through the dark-red door, Corsel whispered into Sam's ear, "Bit of a push to say his life's in danger?"

Shrugging, Sam replied, "I didn't say who from, plus who knows what our mystery woman's after?"

"I can't get used to you detectives."

They followed De Klerk through the house, its interior decorated in whites and greys with a black tiled floor. Finally, they entered a kitchen with black units fitted around the walls. He indicated for them to sit at the large kitchen table with its shiny surface.

"Can I get you two gentleman anything?" De Klerk's tone was a little more friendly now he was playing host.

Both men declined the refreshment, but took a seat at the table, while De Klerk remained standing. Sam looked out of the wide bi-folding glass doors onto a pristine garden. White stone tiles ran out and round one side, providing a seating area covered in black furniture. A patio heater stood tall in the centre, while across the other side of the lush grass a hot tub was situated under a wooden canopy. Sam noticed a wrought-iron gate embedded in the greenery at the far end, which he guessed led out into the park.

"So, who's going to kill me?" De Klerk asked the pair of them.

"Your old acquaintance, the woman you were with the night you were arrested," Sam answered, his tone neutral.

"Right, the woman who I told you I didn't know and had only met that night to discuss purchasing some property?"

Corsel raised his hand. "Please, you don't have to tell us your alibis again. You won that round."

De Klerk studied the older detective. "So, what is it?"

"Do you know she was found dead two days ago?" asked Sam.

"And risen the next. I know what's happened, Mr Taylor. It's all over the news. I saw her face on the television last night and in the morning papers. The unknown ghost!"

"She's certainly not a ghost, Mr de Klerk."

"So you say, but you still don't know who the hell she is."

But you do, you slimy bastard. Sam knew both Franssen and De Klerk had stuck to the story of not knowing their companion that night. Their stories had revolved around being invited to view a potential property for purchasing, coincidentally interrupting an armed gang. They had only been saved by the unexpected arrival of the armed response units. Both men's defence had revolved around never having even heard of the Nile. No prosecution had been able to prove otherwise and the lying bastards had walked.

"Not yet, but we will," said Corsel coolly.

De Klerk looked at Sam. "Excuse me, but I don't seem to know you."

"I am attached to the investigation. I'm here representing my government in the investigation into the murder of a Major Stuart Anderson." Sam knew from Natasja the day before that De Klerk had known Anderson. "We believe this mystery woman was involved in his death in the days prior to her meeting you." He spoke the words coldly. This man may have escaped the noose before, but life was full of second chances.

"That was a terrible business. I heard all about it last year. That poor man, killed in his hotel room. You don't still think I had anything to do with that? I've told you I'd never met the woman before that night."

"No, we are here for something else, Mr de Klerk. As we say, we have reason to believe that you may be in danger."

"And why do you think that?"

Corsel was looking at Sam with the look of a man who had seen this problem coming. Sam couldn't have cared less.

"We found a file in the location where we thought we'd found this mystery woman's body," he lied, smoothly. "Within this file were, amongst other things, your home address, photos of your house and a photo taken from that gate at the end of your garden. It would seem she'd been watching you for a while and we wanted to let you know."

If De Klerk had been looking strained before, he now looked genuinely ill. Even if De Klerk found out the truth and made a complaint, what could Vogt do to him for lying? Sam wasn't officially working for anyone on the investigation. If De Klerk didn't like being lied to, well, he could complain all he liked.

"Jesus, here? She's been *here*? When? How?"

"All in good time, sir. We'll make sure you have all the facts before we leave. But we need to know some things from you now, in order to try to keep you safe." Sam was very good at laying it on when needed. It was amazing what the use of a few 'sirs' would do. It had been his bread and butter back in the military. Senior officers were always a few exaggerated sirs away from being fobbed off.

De Klerk nodded and came to sit at the table with them. "Oh my God, she's after me."

"Why would she be after you, sir?"

Now at the table, De Klerk looked at his hands nervously as he tried to compose himself. "I don't know, I really don't know. Perhaps she blames me."

"Blames you for what?"

"I guess... the sale falling through on that warehouse."

"But why would she want you now?"

"You tell me!"

"I don't know, sir. Is there something that may have triggered it? Have you perhaps seen her recently?"

Sam was enjoying this. He was the only one in the room that knew everything. De Klerk, on hearing the news about the imaginary folder, would have thought it was revenge for his betrayal. They both knew Natasja had plenty of reasons for wanting him dead, it was just that De Klerk couldn't show it.

"I don't think so. I've not seen her since that night. Perhaps she's planning on blackmailing me for something. Did it say anything else in the file?"

In different circumstances it could have been comical watching De Klerk trying to fish for more information without giving himself away.

"I'm sorry, I can't disclose any more, but I would advise that there were handwritten notes outlining distances between these windows and that gate."

"Oh, Jesus."

Corsel quietly caught Sam's eye, a smile hidden. "I know it's a lot to take in, Mr de Klerk, but we're here to help you."

"A lot to take in? I've a crazy bitch trying to kill me. What are your people doing about this?"

The last question was put to Corsel, who didn't answer.

Sam stepped in again. "Sir, I appreciate this is a bit of a shock to you, but we need to try to understand why there's a file full of photos and details of your house in the possession of a suspected murderer," said Sam, watching the indecision in the man's face. This new information about being a prime target for a woman he knew very well could easily kill him, had left him shaken. If he went to the police, the Nile would kill him. If he relied on the Nile's protection, there was no guarantee the two Dudka brothers would care to lift a finger.

"When did you last see her?" Sam pushed the point.

"I told you, last year."

"Have you seen anything suspicious recently? Anyone hanging around outside, or strange vehicles?"

"No."

"Where were you last night after she escaped?"

"I was here all night. What's that got to do with anything?"

"It was the first night she'd been at large again since we found her and I wanted to make sure you were not followed. We would have checked any CCTV footage."

"Oh Jesus, this isn't happening, not now."

De Klerk had put his head in his hands.

"I'm sorry, sir, is there something else we need to be aware of?"

"No God damn it, Mr Taylor. I've had enough of people like you asking about my business."

The room fell quiet as each man processed what they had heard.

"Mr de Klerk," said Sam, "we need to talk about your protection. I can see this has come as a bit of a shock to you."

"What else did the file say? Was I the only person in it? Were there others named? Other houses?"

"I'm afraid I can't share that with you, sir, but I will say it was a very complete dossier and we will be making further enquiries."

De Klerk's face betrayed his intense thought process. Sam could guess he was wondering if Franssen was also in the same danger. Perhaps even the unknown heads of the Nile operation.

"Is this why she staged her death? To… what… draw me out? Perhaps to draw attention away from what else she's planned?"

"We don't know the reasons behind what's happened just yet. It's too early to jump to any conclusions right now. What matters right now is your safety. If possible, I'd like to talk to you about providing you with police protection."

"Protection?"

Time to really twist the knife, decided Sam.

"Yes, we believe this threat to be genuine and so I'd like to ask you to come with us into police custody for your own good. It would just be for a short time, a few days at most."

Just enough days for your Galahad deal to fall through.

De Klerk blanched. "I can't do that. I have business to attend to! I'm not going back into any custody of yours."

"Then do you have friends you can stay with outside of the city?"

"I'm not leaving this house, Mr Taylor."

"Then would you be open to having an officer staying here inside the house with you?"

Corsel could not help himself; he let out a sly smile at their host's deep discomfort.

De Klerk looked at Sam like he had come from a different planet. "Absolutely not. Mr Taylor, I thank you for coming here today, but I'm afraid after what you people have put me through this last year, I'd rather not have anything from the police. She's had all year to kill me and I suspect this is some form of distraction from whatever game she is playing with you."

Sam tapped his fingers on the table, judging he had taken the lie as far as it could go. He looked at Corsel, who had been enjoying the whole exchange.

"Very well. Detective Corsel, please can you ask those units to stand down. We will leave Mr de Klerk here to his own devices."

"Thank you. Now if you don't mind, I'd like you to leave."

Sam and the Dutch detective did as they were asked and headed for the exit. De Klerk followed behind and Sam noticed him squeezing his fists nervously as he walked.

As they reached the doorway, Sam turned towards him. "You will tell us if you see her again, won't you?"

"Yes, yes of course."

"Thank you for your help and please keep safe."

Sam stretched out a hand towards their host, but was ignored in favour of a brief wave and a quick shutting of the door.

"What did you get from that? Apart from a formal complaint at some point?" Corsel asked him.

Sam turned and walked down the gravel driveway. "He can't do anything to me; let him complain. As for why, we both know he still works for the Nile. Let them think our mystery woman's coming after them for a while. He knows full well he can't have any protection from us without alienating his employers. Let's see if *they're* willing to protect him."

Corsel fell in behind Sam and followed the younger man until they were back in the car. "What now?"

"Let's go and find out where Bos is before we see Franssen."

Back inside the house, Albert de Klerk's mind was racing in circles trying to process what he had just been told. It had to be the Galahads; there was no other reason for her reappearing. Franssen, God *damn* Franssen. Why hadn't his asset told them about the file?

It was not until forty minutes and two glasses of whisky later, that De Klerk found out he had been lied to.

"There's no file, Albert," Franssen told him patiently over the phone.

"How do you know?"

"I spoke with our asset and they assured me the Englishman was lying. They say he's very clever and likes to play games like this. Just ignore it. They're clearly getting desperate."

"Did you tell the Dudkas?"

"No, I'll leave that to you. It may make them want to watch the Englishman a bit more. But until then, please stop worrying."

"That's easy for you to say, Hans. You don't have to get these fucking rockets," De Klerk snapped down the line.

Franssen ignored his friend's curtness. "When are you seeing your contact?"

"Later, he's travelling into the city later today."

"Are you seeing him at the usual spots?"

"Yes. I'll see him at one of the museums, I'll get a price out of him for you. You'll then pay him and he'll tell us the container number."

Franssen paused for a moment, considering the latest news. "The shipment's docked, then?"

"The ship's in the harbour and we just need to know which container."

Franssen tried to reassure his old friend. "You see, in two days' time, this will all be over and we can concentrate on finding her again."

In two days it would be over, the Nile would have the container number, then the Galahads they had searched for these many months. It would all be over, in just two days.

SEVENTEEN

BOS HAD NOT RETURNED to the station by the time Sam and Corsel walked into the office. Hardenne was still out in the city on errands for Vogt, so only Berger remained, working through various reports on a laptop.

She lifted her head as the pair walked in. "How was our old friend?"

"Wasn't too keen to help us out," Sam admitted, as he walked over to Bos's desk. Shuffling round the crowded surface full of reports and stationery, he slid into the vacant chair.

"Too bad, wasted morning then?"

"Not at all," said Corsel. "Sam here convinced our host he was about to be assassinated by our mystery woman at any moment."

"You what?"

"Don't worry about it," said Sam. "At the very least it will have given our friends something to think about."

"So, what now?"

Sam looked at his phone to see if Natasja had replied, but the screen was empty. Even Hannah, usually so prompt with any challenge, hadn't updated him on her searches into either Wever or the new Galahad sources.

"We wait for Bos to get back, then head off to see Franssen.

He's based on the other side of the city, if I remember correctly. So we can grab a bite to eat on the way."

After half an hour Bos came through the door, finding them debating the merits of the attempts at cracking down on alcohol and antisocial behaviour in the city.

"Might stop a few of your countrymen coming over for their stag weekends and filling our cells up," Bos interrupted.

"There'll always be enough people around to fill those drunk cells, regardless of any new public orders," Sam told him.

The tall, blond-haired Bos remained standing at the door and smiled at them all. "Good morning?"

"Yeah, I told De Klerk someone's going to kill him and Corsel threatened to steal his car."

"I did. A nice big Mercedes would look good outside my house."

Berger shook her head. "You lot do talk a load of shit. How's your morning been, Bos? Did you get what you needed to do done?"

Bos smiled. "Hopefully, it's nearly there. A couple more days and we'll see."

Sam looked at him quizzically. "Going to tell us where you went?"

"Maybe later. Are we going to see Franssen now?"

"We are indeed, so don't sit down. I'm bloody hungry."

Bos needed to grab a few things and Berger asked if she could come along with them both. Sam left the pair of them, claiming to need the toilet, but instead looking for Vogt. Giving up and asking one of the passing officers if they'd seen him, he was told the Interpol agent was out.

Frustrated, Sam slipped into an empty meeting room then pulled out both the Glock and the blank ammunition clip from the day before. Pressing the release catch, he removed the existing magazine and replaced it with the blanks. He looked at the clip he'd just removed, counting all the rounds were in place, then slipped it into his pocket. Next, he checked over the Glock 17 he'd been given. It seemed nearly new, the black metal had no visible marks and the cocking system moved into place smoothly.

Sam made the firearm safe and switched on the safety before placing it back in the holster. Back in the military, he'd spent his life around firearms. Now fully integrated into civilian life, the very sight of one had become strange, almost uncomfortable.

Sam quickly texted a note to Natasja that Bos was back. He knew she'd be getting ready to make her appearance. Arriving back at the office, he found his companions ready to go. They said their goodbyes to Corsel and headed downstairs.

"What are we doing, then?" Berger asked. "We can get the tram from Elandsgracht straight to Weesperplein, right next to where Franssen lives. Or shall we walk it? I know a good café right on the Herengracht canal?"

After lunch, Bos forced them all on again, following the Herengracht waterway on foot. Sam liked how much effort had gone into keeping nature within the cosmopolitan areas. Trees grew along nearly every street they walked down or passed by, their remaining leaves turning orange and yellow.

Crossing the wide Amstel River that split the city, they turned into the street where Franssen lived. Situated like De Klerk's home in one of the affluent areas of Amsterdam, Sam spotted the building in an instant. The entire street was made up of dark brick townhouses, all dotted with long lines of windows looking out onto the murky green water. Franssen's house was the darkest, standing out from the rest of the street, built with bricks painted black. The five-storey windows were arched with cream-coloured paint, contrasting sharply against the brickwork.

Embedded into each of the building's roofs were the old wooden hoisting beams that once lifted the cargo into the narrow buildings up from the canal boats now standing empty. Only one of the building's hoists still had its rope crane left over from days gone by. Sam tried to imagine the street in its heyday, the cargo from all over the world being hoisted up into the buildings.

As the three of them stood outside the glass doorway, Sam

began to wonder when Natasja would appear, and what he should do when she did.

"Top-floor apartment, covers the entire building with an open balcony. Near enough in the centre of the city. How much do you think it's worth?" Bos asked Sam.

"Minimum, a few million euros?"

"I checked the place out earlier in the year. He bought it for just over three point five million a couple of years ago."

"How?" Sam asked, thinking about the same question they'd asked of De Klerk.

"Investments. The guy was a shit-hot investor once upon a time. Started as a young whizz kid, made his way up in the world of finance and then one day he walked out."

"Why?"

"I don't know. Well, I mean, we know he went on to join the Nile. But what made him leave, I don't really know."

Bos pressed his thumb to the metal intercom system. A noise buzzed for a moment and a voice came over the static. Sam could see the light of a camera come on as Franssen spoke.

"Hello? Who are you?"

"Mr Franssen, my name is Johannes Bos and I'm the head of the Organised Crime Unit within the Amsterdam police. I'm here with two of my associates. Please may we come in? We have a few things to discuss with you."

There was a pause for a moment, but unlike his colleague De Klerk, Franssen was quick to let them in.

The door buzzed open as the lock came undone and he spoke over the intercom. "Come on in, straight through to the lifts on your left. Fifth floor."

All three of them looked at each other, waiting to see who'd go first. In the end Berger stepped in first, then Bos. Following behind, Sam looked at the Head of Organised Crime and thought back to Vogt's certainty of his guilt. If the German was correct, Johannes Bos was entering the home of one of his paymasters.

They stepped into an elevator, which Sam noted needed a key

to work unless bypassed by someone up above. Within moments, the two metal doors were reversing to let them out into a small landing, where a single door led away. A silver number five had been screwed into the thick painted wood and as Berger moved forward to knock, it opened.

Standing in the doorway, dressed in a three-piece suit complete with shirt, tie and gold chain hanging across one of the waistcoat pockets, was Hans Franssen. Sam guessed him to be in his mid-sixties, with his clipped silver hair and a pale face. The eyes looked slightly watery, as if from decades of staring at screens and printouts. Franssen was even taller than Bos, but painfully slim.

"Thank you for inviting us in, Mr Franssen. I appreciate that after the year you've had we may not be the people you would wish to see in your home. This is my deputy, Detective Ada Berger and this is Sam Taylor, who's with us from the British Foreign Office."

Franssen shook both Sam and Ada's hands, gripping Sam's a moment longer than expected. Sam felt the watery eyes studying his face with interest.

"Come on in. I've prepared fresh coffee for us in the sitting room. We may as well enjoy the last of the year's sunshine while we can."

Franssen moved away from the entrance and pushed open a pair of glass double doors, which led into the main body of the apartment. Everywhere was painted or decorated in very light browns and creams, supplemented by dark furniture. Sam guessed the room had probably been professionally designed and decorated by someone other than Franssen. To the right of where they stood, a corridor ran out of the main room and Sam could see what looked like a small tree growing out of a centrepiece. To the left, a kitchen area was situated around a marble island with rows of wine bottles fitted below.

They moved past numerous pillars. The floor was illuminated by natural light, which flooded through the arched windows.

Franssen led them out of the main room, through a glass door and into a sitting room, which faced out onto the balcony. Sam looked out past the balcony's furniture to see straight onto the roof of the adjoining building.

"Please, take a seat." Their host indicated a group of low armchairs around a single coffee table. A cafetière was placed in the middle, surrounded by four cups.

"How did you know we were coming, Mr Franssen?" asked Sam, glancing at the prepared table.

Franssen didn't miss a beat. "De Klerk. You can probably guess he rang me after your visit, Mr Taylor. He was quite distressed, as you can certainly imagine. I was making myself an afternoon beverage and you arrived in good time."

"You were quick to get out four cups for us?"

Franssen looked at him in a bemused, slightly confused way. But Bos saved him from having to answer. "I'm sorry about my friend, Mr Franssen. He can be a bit direct. Thank you for the refreshments."

He looked at his companions and indicated for them to take a seat.

Franssen took the remaining seat for himself and began pouring the black liquid into the china cups. At the fourth cup, Berger reached out, stopping their host.

"Not for me, thank you. Too strong for my liking."

"Of course. I'm sorry, would you like anything else?"

Berger refused and Franssen leant back in his chair. Crossing his long slim legs, he looked at his guests.

"So, what is it? Where do you want to start? Are you here to tell me she's going to kill me, or are you just wanting me to tell you when I last saw her?"

Bos gave Sam a withering glare, then turned to back to Franssen. "I take it Mr de Klerk has briefed you on the situation?"

Franssen smiled at them. "He has. Our mystery sales agent, your mystery corpse and your mystery shooter." The last words were directed at Sam.

"The one and only," he replied coldly.

"I'll save you all some time. I've not seen this missing woman since she tried to sell me a warehouse last year. I don't believe she's trying to kill me, regardless of whether you're here to tell me you found a dossier with pictures of me in my bedroom. Let me tell you now, I do not want any protection."

Sam watched the older man carefully, his every movement fascinating. "I'm sorry to hear that, Mr Franssen, but I should warn you it was very thorough. I do believe that you may be in danger."

"If that's the case, Mr Taylor, I'd like to see this file immediately."

"I think Mr Franssen has made it clear he does not want our help with any protection," Bos interrupted.

"Of course, my apologies," muttered Sam. So Franssen knew he had lied this morning. His heart dropped. It meant someone within the investigation team had told him there had never been a file. Sam should have known when he saw the freshly prepared coffee and the four cups. The bastard had not had the time to have prepared that. Only someone in the station could have told their host that he was having three guests. So Vogt had been right in his assumption. There was a traitor within.

EIGHTEEN

BOS TRIED TO PUSH ON. "Mr Franssen, we're here about the missing woman. I know you've said you haven't seen her since last year, but we need your help. We're trying to establish why she may have wanted to go to such extreme lengths in the last couple of days."

"And why should I know?" Franssen asked.

Berger saw the danger and jumped in. "Just for clarity, Mr Franssen, we're not accusing you of anything but we are speaking with the small number of people we know have had dealings with her, in however small a capacity. We're just trying to find a reason for all of this."

Franssen smiled at Berger warmly. "Of course, Detective Berger, but I must tell you what I told all of your colleagues last year. I met that woman once, the night she drove us to that bloody warehouse. Prior to that, I had only dealt with an intermediary."

"Who you also didn't know?" Sam added sarcastically, deciding he didn't like this man. Whether it was the cut of the suit or the joyless décor of the apartment, everything the man said felt false.

"You're right, but a man like me has many business opportunities. I have to say, a midnight viewing of property that had not yet come to market, arranged by people I didn't know, is not one of the strangest things I've ever done. In fact, it felt completely normal, until the shooting started."

Franssen knew that after the one failed prosecution, these officers had very little they could throw at him. The stark contrast between him and De Klerk this morning was due to more than the knowledge that the death threats were false. Franssen was a different kettle of fish.

"Which is why we are here. I'm sure a man with your experience may have some ideas of why our female friend has acted like she has?" asked Sam innocently.

"I'm afraid, my friend, that is your job and not mine." Franssen sat back, a sly smile on his face. "But perhaps you can find her before she tries to assassinate me?"

The bullet missed Hans Franssen's head by a matter of inches. The first any of them knew about it was the shattering of both the balcony glass and the inside door behind their host. For a moment, all four of them sat frozen to their chairs, before the three officers sprang into action. Bos, the closest to Franssen, tackled him to the floor. Sam and Berger jumped from their chairs and crouched behind, searching the neighbouring rooftop, guns drawn.

Kneeling on the roof opposite, her rifle resting on a parapet, Sam could just see Natasja looking through the scope of the rifle, her blonde hair blowing in the wind. Twisting round, he saw Bos crouching down, pulling Franssen further inside the building. Two more rounds followed and hit somewhere above their heads on the wall behind them.

"I think you should play the lottery tonight, Sam," Berger shouted from behind her chair. "No one can say you lied now!"

Sam grinned and pulled out the Glock with its blank ammunition. "I'm just glad she didn't hit me this time."

Looking again over the edge of the chair, he tried to estimate the distance between them and Natasja. Franssen's balcony was only around five metres wide before it connected with the next building. A small hedge separated the two rooftops and Natasja had situated herself at the furthest end of the building. An impossible shot for a small handheld firearm.

"You two get back in here now," Bos shouted from further inside the apartment.

Time to act the part, he told himself, and shouted over to Berger, "Give me some cover. I'm going to get her."

"You what?"

"Just fire some blind rounds."

Berger shook her head in disbelief, but did as she was told. Leaning out slightly, she raised her weapon and fired a few rounds towards Natasja. Sam used the diversion and ran forward through the wreckage of the glass door before landing in front of the dividing hedge.

The firing from both women had stopped. Sam paused to catch his breath. Turning back, he saw Berger looking after him nervously. He raised five fingers and began to count down, lowering a finger on each second. As he dropped the final finger, Berger began to open fire again and Sam vaulted the hedge to land on the next rooftop. Jumping to his feet, he began to run while at the same time firing the blanks blindly at where Natasja had last been seen. He half expected to hear the thud of returned rounds, but as he got closer he saw Natasja had broken cover and was now running across the rooftops.

"Keep going. I'll call for help and head downstairs," he heard Berger shout from behind.

Looking up, he saw Natasja had made it to the next building. Sam had reached her first hiding spot and found she had left the rifle behind. Running on past, he leapt onto the next rooftop and finally saw her planned escape route. The hoist he had noticed earlier, with its crane to the street. Reaching it, she grabbed one of the ropes and began to abseil downwards, seemingly with ease.

Sam had a choice. He could stop and walk back towards Bos without any shame. He'd chased the would-be assassin across three rooftops and no one would blame him for not following her down a hundred-year-old rope hoist. But then he thought of Berger heading down in the lift.

Swearing, he followed the Dutchwoman in grabbing the rough rope. Trying not to look down, he twisted round and planted his foot against the brickwork before beginning to make his way towards the ground. He couldn't say he was scared of heights, but those minutes of hanging over the street below felt like an age. His mind jumped back to the despised obstacle courses of his officer training, the drill sergeants forcing the new recruits through the sapping barriers in every weather imaginable. Eventually, he had covered the top two floors and felt his legs grow steadier as his confidence built. By the third floor he began to speed up, the rough rope in his hands providing a firm grip, despite blistering his palms.

Sam was just reaching the first floor when he grew overconfident. Climbing down slightly too far in one go, he felt his feet slip against the brickwork. Next, the rope which had felt so firm in his hands betrayed him and he fell to the pavement in a heap. Rolling to one side, the breath knocked out of him, he looked round for Natasja. She had set off up the street and was about to cross the small bridge to the other side of the canal.

Standing unsteadily, he began the chase, sturdy boots pounding the ground. By now she had crossed the bridge and was heading towards the next waterway. Behind, Sam could hear Berger calling after him. Somewhere in the distance there were sirens making their way towards them.

Sam crossed the bridge, then dodged a braking car as he made his way over the next road. Ahead, he saw the first blue lights flashing towards them. Natasja, running directly away following the road from the bridge, saw them too and made a hard right down one of the side streets alongside the next waterway. Sam followed, but as he did so, he saw the blue lights up in the distance separate. There were two cars approaching. The first vehicle kept coming towards him, but the second had turned off, following the city's grid system. They were going to head her off.

Sam reached the next waterway, where he had last seen Natasja running. The street he had entered was quieter and he could just about still see her ahead of him. She was still running towards where he was now sure the police car would soon appear. He was about to shout a warning, then realised she was on the other side of the canal. He had somehow taken the wrong turn. The next crossing was too far away.

Looking at the canal, an idea crept into his mind. Along both sides of the waterway, boats were moored to the walls. Ahead of him, a single canal boat was making its slow journey towards him. Quickly judging the distances between them, he took a breath.

Breaking his stride, he made a sharp turn and climbed onto the roof of a deep-red canal boat. The travelling boat was now level with him and Sam leapt forwards to land on its roof. Ignoring the shouts of alarm from the shocked captain, he waved his arms to regain his balance. He paused for a moment, realising the gap between his vessel and the next moored boat was a lot further than he'd counted on. The sirens were drawing closer. He had no idea where Berger was. He had to jump.

Crouching down, he threw himself forward. It was more of a dive than a leap and he landed hard against the side of the stationary boat. Flailing around, he tried to find something to hold onto as his feet fell into the canal below, the cold water pouring over into his boots, soaking his feet. Scraping his feet along the side of the boat, he tried again to find something to climb up. He felt his hands slip from the roof and his whole body began to slide inexorably into the water below.

A pair of hands frantically reached over the roof's surface and grabbed his tightly. As his torso made its way onto the wooden beams of the canal boat, Sam twisted himself upright.

"Christ, you make a racket, don't you?"

He grabbed her wrist and pulled the two of them back onto dry land, looking around desperately to find a way out before the patrol car pulled round the corner.

"What are you doing?"

"The police, they're following. They'll be coming round that corner any minute." He spotted an alleyway between two buildings. "Quick, in there now." Sam dragged her forward into the narrow alleyway.

"What are you doing? It's a dead end."

A large dumpster was fitted to the back wall. Its plastic blue lid leant upwards against the brickwork.

"Get in."

"You have to be joking. I've got my own route out."

"You don't. I told you, there's a patrol car coming round that corner at any moment. Get in, or I'll throw you in." He took a step towards her.

She glared at him, the dark-brown eyes full of menace. "I should have shot you earlier."

Still grumbling and shaking her head, Natasja climbed into the green plastic container. "It fucking stinks!"

"Life's a bitch. I'll text you when you're clear."

Sam pushed the lid down and returned to the street. As he stepped back out into the sunshine, Berger came round one corner of the street and a patrol car approached from the other direction. The Dutch detective was breathing hard.

"Lost you, sorry. Where is she?"

"I don't know. I got caught coming over the canal and I lost her. I checked the alleyway but it's empty." Sam watched as two uniformed officers climbed out of the now parked car.

"Any luck?" Berger asked them.

"No, but she may have gone down another street, entered one of these buildings or even one of the boats."

"She didn't, I would have seen her. She must have taken a different side street."

Sam held up his hands in a gesture of apology.

"Fucking hell, not again." Berger slammed her hand against the nearest door. She stared at Sam's dripping boots and trousers.

"Don't ask. My shortcut didn't quite work."

Berger shook her head in bewilderment. "You English are mad."

Sam's mind wandered back to Bos, probably still alone with Franssen, and what they could be discussing.

"We've got more people on their way to continue the search," the officer told Berger.

"I wouldn't bother," she told him wearily.

"We should try the next street, or she may have doubled back under the bridge then gone the other way," Sam suggested.

"Probably," agreed Berger. "We need to get back to Bos and Franssen. Can you two continue the search?"

The two officers agreed and headed off to look around the area. Berger and Sam started a much slower walk back to the luxury penthouse apartment.

"We got lucky, didn't we? She could have killed any of us."

Sam eyed her carefully. He reached out and put his arm round her shoulders. "I wouldn't worry about it; she wasn't after us. If she wanted us dead, she wouldn't have started with Franssen."

"I wonder what she'll do now?"

"Who knows? De Klerk may want to reassess the offer of protection."

What Sam was really interested in was what the Nile would do in response. Natasja had not only faked her own death, she had now gone after one of its own. He thought back to the nervous De Klerk and the impending Galahad deal.

"I don't know why it is, but whenever you come to town everything just goes mad," Berger told him, resting her head on him as they walked.

"You saying life's boring without me?"

"Let's just say having you around makes it more... interesting."

Sam paused to take his boots off and poured a trail of murky water onto the floor. "I really hate having wet feet."

"Stop falling into canals then."

She had a point, Sam thought, as he wrung out his socks and stuffed his bare feet back into his wet boots.

Arriving back at Franssen's apartment they walked further apart, both conscious of the marked police car outside the building.

"I wonder how he's feeling now?" Sam mused, remembering their host's cocky attitude earlier.

"Well, at least he doesn't need a fake folder to tell him he's on a hit list. Perhaps he'll be a little friendlier."

"Maybe. You go ahead. I just need to ring London," he told her as they reached the entrance that had now been jammed open by one of the officers.

Berger patted his arm, then left to take the elevator to the top floor. He watched her enter through the double doors, then took out his phone.

> You should be able to get out now. Police are looking in the other direction.

> Fuck you, Sam Taylor

Sam grinned to himself. About time he'd got a bit of payback.

NINETEEN

AFTER THE INITIAL shock of the attempt on his life had worn off, Hans Franssen began his verbal assault on Johannes Bos. The detective had dragged their host away into the depths of the house. They had crawled over the broken glass of the smashed internal doors, slashing their trousers and cutting their hands.

Yet when Sam and Ada arrived back at the scene, they found Bos on the receiving end of Franssen's anger. "You and your officers have put my life in danger," Franssen lectured him from the dark-brown sofa he was sitting on. "That woman has been out of my life for a whole year and then you show up. She must have followed you."

"I'm sure she didn't need us to find out where you lived, Mr Franssen. Personally, I think you should count yourself lucky that we were here when it happened. Otherwise, I'm pretty sure she would have finished the job."

Franssen saw Sam and Berger had arrived back. "Catch her, did you?"

"No, she escaped again."

"Fucking useless."

"You're more than welcome to go after her if you'd like," Sam offered.

Franssen glared at him. "What will you be doing about this?"

"We'll continue our search. She must be somewhere."

"How intuitive of you."

They all turned as the doors behind them opened and in stepped Karl Vogt. The Interpol agent was once again in his dark-blue sailors' pea jacket, his face grim under his curled hair.

"And who the hell is this?" Franssen demanded.

Vogt ignored the jibe, pushing past Sam and Berger to stand in front of Hans Franssen. Sam watched as the agent looked up and down, taking him in. Franssen seemed to physically recede from the smaller man. The anger that was driving his abuse of the officers diminished with every moment.

Eventually, it was Vogt who broke the silence. "Hans Franssen, Agent Vogt of Interpol." Franssen gave a curt nod and Vogt continued. "How are you feeling? Do you need medical attention?"

"Nothing a good whisky can't solve."

"Good, it's not every day you can say you survived an assassination attempt. Good job my officers were here to help." Franssen did not offer a retort.

"As I'm sure you're aware, your assailant was the very same woman we have been hunting for. A very resourceful and dangerous person."

Sam, Berger and Bos may as well have been in another room, as neither of the two men paid them any attention.

"Yes, well, she showed that today."

"I'm glad we agree." Vogt took a moment to look around the room before continuing. "My officers will need to spend some time going over the crime scene. Is that okay?"

Franssen was about to speak, but Vogt continued. "They will be finished later today. Next, we need to discuss your own safety. We have to presume she will be back at some point to finish the job."

Sam had to hide a smile. Franssen now had the same dilemma as De Klerk had this morning. Accept police protection and risk the wrath of the Nile, or risk Natasja's revenge. Only this time, Franssen had clear evidence of the threat posed.

"We can arrange for an officer to be stationed in the house, or we can have you put into protective custody?"

Franssen, like De Klerk, refused.

Vogt sighed and walked over to the window, looking down onto the street. "Then there's only one question I need you to answer, Mr Franssen. Why has our missing person decided to come to kill you? And why now?"

"How the hell am I supposed to know? The woman's crazy."

"Why *wouldn't* you know?"

"I've told you everything I know about that woman."

"But have you told me everything about the organisation she works for?"

Their host jumped to his feet and stepped towards Vogt, who calmly turned round to stare right back up at him.

"What did you say, Agent Vogt?"

Vogt spoke each of his words slowly, as if to a child. "I asked if you've told me everything you know about the organisation the woman who attempted to kill you in your own home earlier today works for?"

The thin-framed Franssen flushed. "You people have dragged me through hell over the last year and you come here asking me that? Give me one good reason not to have my lawyer come here and have her sue your short arse back into The Hague?"

"Please feel free to do so. The very worst that could happen is I'm taken off the case and sent back to Germany. I'd be delighted to be home before Christmas. You, however, would prove that you still have something to hide."

"How does that work out?"

Sam stepped in. "If you didn't have anything to hide, you wouldn't need a lawyer."

Franssen swivelled round, caught between Sam and Vogt.

"Perhaps this organisation has hired her to kill you?" Sam continued, knowing full well the opposite was true.

Franssen didn't answer.

"There's a chance she will return again, Mr Franssen. She has been suspected of both murder and attempted murder since this investigation began," Vogt chipped in.

"I think we have reached as far as this conversation is going to go, Mr Vogt. You may leave your men to do their investigation, but I will not be sitting around to listen to your baseless ramblings. I will be in my office if you need me, arranging a replacement window!"

With that, he turned back towards Sam and began walking out of the main living room. As he came level, the pair locked eyes. Sam stared back without blinking and Franssen broke away.

Instead, he looked at Bos. "Detective Bos, thank you for your help today. I believe you may have helped save my life."

Then to the surprise of everyone, including Bos, he reached out and shook the detective's hand. Franssen walked away, leaving the four officers alone in the pillar-lined room.

Vogt looked at them all and raised his eyebrows. "Well, this is a fucking screw-up."

Already, a team from the station was arriving to begin going over the crime scene. The spent bullet was still to be recovered and a team would need to collect the leftover rifle from the neighbouring rooftop.

The diminutive agent stared at the three of them, about to say something else, but thinking better of it. He looked down at his watch then back up to them.

"You three had better head off. Bos, you and Berger go back to the station and close off anything you wish before calling it a day." He looked down at Sam's sodden boots and trousers. "And you should go and get dried out. Probably worth checking in with London, as well. They'll be wondering what you're doing with yourself."

The three of them did not need an excuse to get out of Franssen's apartment. They'd left the room for the elevator almost before Vogt had finished speaking. Bos commandeered a recently arrived pool car and drove them away from the crime scene. Sam sat in the back with his feet squelching in his boots. All three were tired and the atmosphere was sour. Conversation was limited and Sam was glad when they arrived at the hotel.

"Got any plans for tonight?" Bos asked.

"Zilch."

"I'd invite you for dinner, but Peter's dragging me somewhere."

"You don't have to worry about me. I can look after myself."

"Berger, do you fancy looking after our guest?"

Berger pulled a face at them. "Don't bother looking at me, I'm not babysitting. I already have plans this evening with my friends."

"Honestly, I'll be fine. Just let me know what's happening tomorrow, or if anything changes. I'll just probably go for a run or something."

"Maybe if you practise a bit more you might be able to catch her next time," teased Berger.

"And with that I'm leaving. Also, I didn't see you breaking any running records this afternoon."

Stepping out of the car, he turned and watched as they disappeared into traffic. He wondered if he'd see Berger again this evening as he walked into the hotel lobby. Pulling out his phone, he texted Hannah to see how she was getting on. By the time he had exited the lift and was walking down to his hotel room, he felt his phone vibrate. Hannah's reply shone brightly on the screen.

Ring me when you can

Entering the hotel room, he started a call to Hannah and sat the phone on the desk on speaker, then flung himself onto the bed. As he heard the call being answered, he shouted out to the room.

"Next time Emma tries sending me off somewhere, I'm telling her to piss off."

"Point taken and noted." Emma's Irish brogue came over the phone.

Sam swore and sat up. "Jesus, you're everywhere."

"Just in the office. Take it you've had one of those days?"

"Nearly ended up back in a canal."

"Don't think I want to know. How's the case going? Any luck finding the missing woman?"

Sam gave a summary of events. As he finished up with the second disappearance in two days, the two women sighed.

"So, our old friend is back to her old tricks," Emma surmised. "Which makes what you asked Hannah to look up for you even more interesting."

"Anderson's replacement?"

Emma nodded. "We've spent pretty much all day calling in favours, but we have some news, which you need to know."

Hannah picked up the story and Sam listened closely. "When our missing friend killed Major Anderson, the Ministry of Defence went into lockdown trying to make sure no other equipment went missing."

"Probably a good thing," remarked Sam.

"You'd think so, wouldn't you? Anyway, his replacement was another major, Major Matthew Harmison. But he was found dead earlier this year."

Sam raised his hand to stop her. "Found dead?"

"The police say he killed himself," replied Emma. "His wife found him hanging in his garage. I had to ring through to the local police force to get a full report."

Sam thought back to the conversation with Vogt and Natasja. What had they said about the delay in getting the latest Galahad shipment? Something about the next deal falling through? Maybe the next source hadn't been willing to cooperate and had found themselves on the wrong side of the Nile too.

"Are they certain it was suicide?" he asked Emma.

"What makes you ask that?"

"You know, predecessor gets killed, only logical to rule it out."

The Head of the Repatriation Office replied. "Funny you should ask, the detective I spoke to wasn't so certain. For one, his wife was pregnant and he was looking forward to starting a family. Second, no suicide note was found anywhere in the house. It's rare for a suicide not to leave anything, especially as he was about to become a father. The detective did say it was just a feeling, but he was never convinced that it was suicide. But the local military leadership came down on them and forced it through."

"Makes sense. They didn't want any more questions, after what had happened with the old guy." Sam began to untie his wet boots. "So, the next guy?"

"Captain James Broad, a career soldier but had missed his chance at promotions." Hannah continued reading from her notes. "Took over towards the end of the summer. He's the only one we can find that may have any way of making a couple of Galahad rocket launchers disappear."

Sam had managed to get one of his boots off and threw it to the floor.

Without looking up, he asked, "So what do you think? Any chance he could be the new seller?"

There was a pause.

"What?"

"The MoD reported again today that no Galahad launchers or rockets are missing. They even put in a complaint with my superiors for bringing up the subject and wasting their time again," Emma told him.

"But?" Sam asked.

"But bearing in mind Anderson's killer has just resurfaced and is back at large in Amsterdam, it's not the best news that Captain Broad is in the Netherlands right now."

"What? Where?" Sam threw the remaining boot to the floor and leant closer to the phone.

Hannah took the question. "He's been posted to a NATO working group and has been in The Hague for the past month."

"Jesus," Sam said, thinking how easy it would have been for the Nile to have found Captain Broad. "So what have you done? Have you told anyone he might be in danger, or had anyone investigate him?"

Again, the two women hesitated before Emma answered, "I spoke with his commanding officer who basically shut me down. Told me Broad was an excellent officer and more than trustworthy. I asked if I could speak with him myself, but was told he'd just left."

Straight into the lion's den. Broad would be in the city at the very same time Vogt suspected the Nile was completing a deal for the Galahad rockets. Sam was no longer on the fence. He had to agree with Vogt; this was really happening.

"Fucking hell, talk about timing."

"Do you think the events of the past few days are all linked to Broad?" Emma asked.

"Yes, but probably not in the way we originally thought. When we saw De Klerk this morning, it was obvious he had been under some stress recently, which this would explain. He's the supply chain man, so would know about Broad. Franssen is a cold one, but he's the finance man so he'll just be concerned about getting the money. It's the leadership we need to be thinking about."

"The woman?" Hannah asked.

Sam hesitated, but Emma cut in. "After today's shooting, we can't be sure on that anymore. Who knows what her relationship to the whole mess is?"

Sam relaxed, knowing he didn't have to explain things to them. "So, what do you want me to do? Can't say I'm any closer to finding Anderson's killer."

"That's up to you. You're on the ground. Do what you think best."

"I need to speak to Vogt. He's the only person who's got any

strategy here. Perhaps this information will make a difference."
Although, how he was to reach Vogt was another question.

"What about Johannes Bos? Is he not able to help?" asked
Emma.

"Yeah, maybe. What about the other things I asked for?
Anything on Wever or Van Rossum?"

"Sorry Sam, I've not had the time to do it without the local
authorities knowing where it's coming from. I'll have something
for you tomorrow."

He bit his lip, thinking back to his conversation with Corsel
that morning. "Get what you can for me, but also see if you can
find out which officers were involved in investigating Wever's
death, please."

"Any point in asking why you're having my team search this
for you?" Emma asked forlornly.

"It's one team, remember, Emma." Sam smiled. "And no, not
yet, but trust me, it may be the only link we get."

Sam pre-empted any further questioning, brought the call to a
close and fell back onto the bed again. His feet were still wet and
cold.

TWENTY

LYING down looking up at the painted ceiling, Sam once again reminded himself not to come back to this city. It had nearly killed him the year before and was now driving him crazy as he found himself caught between Vogt, Natasja and the Nile. Now, after hearing the news from London, he finally accepted there was a job to do.

Whatever else Vogt and Natasja were trying to do here, Sam had three tasks in his mind. The first was to find the Galahads before they could do any harm. They were the British Government's responsibility, so they were his responsibility. Then there was the actual killer of Major Anderson. Whoever it was, was out there – and their arrest was Sam's case. Finally, there was the mole. Whoever that bastard was had betrayed him last year and was doing so again.

He needed to speak to Vogt; *his* people could look after Broad. Follow him until he met with De Klerk, before dragging them both in. The other two challenges would have to wait. Sliding down to the floor, he picked up the phone and opened his messages from Natasja. He quickly typed.

> Urgent – need to speak to both of you. Galahad deal on. New seller in town. Repeat: new seller in town.

The message flew off into the ether and Sam waited. As he did so, he changed his damp trousers and pulled on a pair of running shoes from his bag. The boots would need to dry out. There was still no answer, so he headed downstairs. The hotel lobby was quiet with only the odd group or individual dotted around, minding their own business. With still no answer, he went to the hotel bar and ordered a gin and tonic followed by the house curry.

Looking down at the phone, he flirted with ringing the number, but decided against it. She'd get in touch with Vogt before coming back to him. By the time the food arrived, he'd started on a second gin and tonic.

Moments after finishing his meal, Natasja's message filled the phone screen, displaying an address at Oudezijds Achterburgwal, followed by another message.

> 8pm. Stand by the tree with a red bike fastened to it. Make sure you're not followed.

Sam quickly typed the address into his phone's maps application and swore loudly.

The barman paused from sorting bottles to stare at him. "Everything all right, sir?"

The phone told him it would take just over an hour to walk there and he worked out he would arrive in time if he left immediately. Quickly sending back an affirmative, he turned in his seat and went to grab his coat from the room. A further message from Natasja reminded him to make sure he wasn't followed.

Stepping out into the evening air, a fresh breeze blew into his face. Looking down both sides of the street, he couldn't see anyone watching out for him. No cars parked up or figures loitering near the hotel. Checking the route on his phone, Sam headed off into the Amsterdam night. As he walked, he kept watching his surroundings, checking that the faces around him were continually changing as he walked forcefully through the crowded streets. Every so often, he took a leaf from Natasja's book and took a different turning to what was marked on the phone map.

Deciding he had time, and as a final check for a tail, he pulled into a coffee house and took a coffee to take away. The hot cup made his fingers sore in the chilly night. He stood in the doorway for a moment and surveyed the scene again. The city's nightlife buzzed all around him. The port city made an appealing tourist destination and Sam looked on jealously at the people around him, all enjoying their time, free from the pressures of finding a criminal organisation.

Setting off again, he wondered about the Nile in all its forms. Arms dealers, murderers, smugglers, thieves. All this effort put into finding them and they still didn't know who was sitting at the top. Then there was Captain Broad. He more than anything was Sam's responsibility. Sam felt a twinge of anger thinking of his own comrades happily selling weaponry to strangers. It had happened before, including on his watch. The memory of those days – the successes, the failures, old friends lost forever – all of it made his stomach twist. Broad was crossing a line. A Galahad could cause serious damage in the wrong hands.

At the final bridge, Sam looked along the dark canal. The crisp orange and yellow streetlights began to be replaced by the neon red of the district's offerings. Following the street, Sam passed the first of the adult establishments, a brightly lit shop with steps leading downwards. A sign next to it advertised DVDs, toys, dolls, lingerie and other pleasures. The crowds were different here. Tourists seemed more numerous, while the locals were limited to individuals making their way round the streets. He walked past a strip club, its neon signs advertising naked girls and hourly sex shows. Sam eyed the group of burly bouncers, well-equipped to deal with any trouble.

Continuing through the busy streets, Sam tried to keep his eyes away from the numerous windows, but found himself failing hopelessly. There was too much to look at in these streets. Men and women were all out enjoying themselves and flirting with the temptations around them. One dark-haired girl caught Sam's eye even as he tried to look away. Her curves were perfectly exhibited in a dark-green one-piece and she smiled mischievously at him. A finger beckoned him towards her. He smiled politely, shook his head and continued on.

The phone vibrated in his hand to tell him he was approaching his destination. Slowing his walk, he noticed the tree with its single red bicycle fastened to the thin trunk. Groaning internally, he saw the tree was right in front of a row of three glass windows, all occupied by young women. Accepting his fate, he walked forward to stand under the branches and directly outside the third window.

Sam turned away from the occupied window with its red light bathing the area and looked out onto the street. He tried to concentrate on the two boats moored to the water's edge as he waited for his next instruction.

A knock on the window interrupted his thoughts and he turned round out of instinct. The glass window was set a few steps up from the pavement, so that when he turned round he found himself at eye level with a pair of nylon-covered legs. Following them upwards, his eyes wandered past dark skin covered by only the smallest of underwear until he was staring into a pair of dark eyes. The face broke into a wide suggestive smile and beckoned him inwards.

"You coming in?" the voice called out to him.

Sam stuttered and shook his head apologetically, then turned back around to stare at the street. He looked at his smartwatch and saw the minute hand had passed the hour mark. Where the hell were they? Another knock came from the window behind him and he tried to ignore it. Turning round again, he raised his hand to apologise. Checking his watch, he saw five minutes had nearly passed.

Behind him the knocking had restarted and he guessed his continued presence was blocking the lady's trade for the evening. He was about to cross the road when he heard the window behind him open.

"Where the hell are you going?" a familiar voice called out.

This time turning, he found himself at eye level with a new pair of legs and looking up he saw Natasja. Unlike the previous occupant, she was fully dressed.

"What the hell are you doing in there?"

"Just shut up and come in quickly."

Sam took the steps up into the cubicle. Closing the door behind him, he pulled the curtain, blocking out the streetlights. Moving forward, he stepped out into an open room that had been closed off by the cubicle's rear door. Entering, he saw a bedroom furnished in dark red. The walls were red, the carpet was a darker red, the furniture was red, as was all of the bed-linen. The only things not in red were the various mirrors located around the room and up on the ceiling. For such a small room, Sam was surprised to see a bed, a shower, a sink and a few cabinets fitted comfortably into the space.

The cubicle's previous occupant was nowhere to be seen. Instead, sitting on the bed, leaning against the headrest, was Vogt. Natasja had already taken a red leather chair in one of the corners. The only other remaining seat was the leather chaise longue at the foot of the bed. Sam remained standing.

"Why here, of all places?"

"We needed to make sure you weren't being followed and we needed somewhere safe," Natasja told him. "I told you, this is my city and I have lots of friends round here. My people were watching out for you from the moment you walked down this street. Misty has helped me out many times over the years."

"You should have accepted Misty's invitation, you may have upset her," Vogt joked.

"Anyway, if I remember rightly you wanted to speak to us?"

"I heard back from London earlier about Anderson's replacement."

"Go on…"

"It's an army captain called Broad and he's in Amsterdam right now."

The words had a deadening effect on the pair of them. Natasja sucked in her cheeks, worry etched in her expression.

Vogt rubbed his face. "Tell me everything."

Sam did as instructed, taking them through the entire conversation with Emma and Hannah. Vogt interrupted him only when he described the events before Broad had come into the role, and the suspected suicide.

"Makes sense with everything we know, the timelines match. They obviously killed Anderson thinking they had a ready-made replacement, only to find that person not playing ball. What do you do then?"

Sam answered, "Get yourself someone who will."

"Precisely."

Finishing his tale, he looked at both of them, waiting to hear their thoughts. "So what do *we* do?"

"Well, my people would be able to find Broad within minutes," Vogt told them. "Foreign tourists need to provide identification at all the hotels here."

"He's a single male tourist in Amsterdam. We know where he'll be," joked Natasja.

Vogt ignored her. "We stand back for now. I'll have my people find out where he's staying and we can watch him until he makes a move. Then we bring in whoever he meets with as well. Might be the only chance we have of finding the rest of the Nile."

"We should presume the Nile will also be watching Broad," Sam added.

"Probably."

"Which means if we want to bring him in without raising suspicions, we'll have to be creative."

"After today's performance, it's the only opportunity we have now."

"What do you mean?" Sam asked, noticing the hostile glance from Vogt.

"You were supposed to get Bos and his paymasters to trust you. Instead, you piss them all off with a story that they would be able to disprove with one phone call. Rather than seeing you as a potential asset or even an ally, they now think you're playing games with them."

Perhaps Vogt had a point. "I was trying to trip them up."

"Then you were a bloody fool. You were supposed to have been trying to trip up Bos, not his paymasters." Vogt slid off the bed and rubbed his eyes. He looked tired. "Just come into the station tomorrow and wait until we hear about Broad moving. I'll come tell you you're needed at Interpol's head office and that I'm taking you over there. We can then see where the bastard goes. I'll speak with you both in the morning. If there's any trouble finding Broad this evening, I'll let you know. Taylor, wait here fifteen minutes before exiting the way you came in."

"Where are *you* going?"

Vogt looked at him pitifully. "I'm a senior law enforcement agent with quite a distinct profile. I'm pretty sure someone would notice a dwarf walking out of a brothel."

Not for the first time that evening, Sam didn't reply. Instead, he watched as Vogt went out of the rear door and walked further into the building. Natasja jumped up from the chair and climbed onto the bed.

"So, what shall we do while we wait?" she asked mischievously.

Shaking his head, Sam took a seat next to her. "It's been a long day."

She laughed. "It has. At least I didn't shoot you this time."

"True."

They sat for a moment in the red room, the mirrors around them reflecting every angle.

"I could ask Misty to come back in?"

"I'm okay, thanks. You're more than enough trouble for me at the moment."

"Don't knock it. She could teach you a few things."

"Hmm. I doubt that." He raised an eyebrow, and his blue eyes flashed as they took in the woman next to him.

They looked at each other and a silence fell between them. Sam studied her face and remembered that first night they had met. He had thought her beautiful then. In one desperate moment, he had thought hers was going to be the final face he would ever see. Many times during the months since, he had imagined it had been him pulling the trigger, not her. Yet after the past few days, and now that they were alone together, something felt different.

Sam had hated this woman. He had been glad when he'd heard she had been found dead. But now he leant forward, placed his hand round the back of her neck and kissed her. Natasja raised her own hands and dragged him sideways onto the covers.

She paused for a moment, pulling away slightly. "I should tell you I charge by the hour."

Sam smiled. "I couldn't afford you."

"Perhaps we will say this one's on the house."

TWENTY-ONE

HANS FRANSSEN PARKED his car on the street outside De Klerk's house. Night had already fallen but he was still early for the meeting. He debated staying in the car until nearer the agreed time, but decided against it. Best get it over with. Stepping out of the car, he walked the few metres up to the gated driveway and passed on through. The city centre greenery was striking. Even in a city like Amsterdam, De Klerk had chosen well. Franssen thought of his single tree growing in the hallway of his own apartment. The overpriced interior decorator had insisted it freshened the whole space. A horrendous waste of money. Wever would have told him to get a good woman to look after all that. But Wever was dead, killed by the younger Dudka brother, and now Franssen was left to deal with the brave new world.

What a world it was. A day of police visits, attempted assassinations, and now this. Another summons to a late-night conference with the Polish brothers, this time at De Klerk's own residence. *That* was a first. Until this evening all business had been completed on company property, surrounded by faceless guards. Franssen couldn't help it, fear crept unbidden into his mind. Crossing the gravel, he tried to concentrate on the job at hand. Reaching the door, he tried the electronic doorbell with its inbuilt camera, but nothing happened. He tried again, but no light or sound came out. In the end, he tried the old-fashioned option of knocking until someone came to the door.

"Having technology troubles?" Franssen asked the younger man as he greeted him.

De Klerk scowled. "The Dudkas insisted on no cameras."

The two men gave each other silent looks, which spoke more than any words either dared to say.

"Come on inside, we can at least have a drink before they get here."

Franssen followed his colleague into the large house, through the monochrome hallway and into the kitchen. A bottle stood open on the table. The guest wondered how much the host had already consumed without him.

"Whisky?"

"A small one. I'm driving, remember."

De Klerk grunted and went to get a second glass. Franssen noticed a slight fumble in his movements during the opening of the bottle. He took a seat at the table with his back to the entrance.

"So that fucking bitch came for you? Perhaps the Englishman was telling the truth?" De Klerk challenged him as he passed over a newly filled glass.

Franssen took a sip and pulled a face. "The Englishman was lying, my source confirmed it."

"Did your source tell you she was going to nearly kill you? How do you know they weren't lying to you?"

"If the Englishman was telling the truth, he would have shown us the evidence. My source was telling me the truth; there was no folder. He was trying to trick us to get something, anything, to help them. They're desperate."

"Hmm, but she's still out there… out there trying to kill us."

"She is, but I still think it was only coincidence that it all happened on the same day." Franssen held up the glass. "This is good, a single malt?"

"Yes, it's Irish. I find it smoother. But don't change the subject. We need to do something."

Franssen shook his head and swirled the amber liquid in its glass. "We don't need to do anything, my friend. We wait until the brothers come; it's for them to decide. Everything depends on the Galahad deal. We complete that and everything goes back to normal."

"So you think she's trying to stop it?"

"If not, why would she reappear after so long? The police certainly have no idea, but I'm now certain. Have you spoken to your contact?"

De Klerk shifted uncomfortably. "Yes, briefly, this afternoon. But save it till they arrive."

Franssen wondered where their heads were on everything. He dreaded to think what would happen to all of them if this fell through.

They sat in silence for a moment before a knock on the door signalled the arrival of the brothers. The two of them looked at each other for a moment before De Klerk left to welcome them in. Franssen sat still in his chair, his back to the doorway, listening to the approaching voices. Twisting in his seat, he looked round to see De Klerk leading both the elder Jakub and his younger brother Marcel into the brightly lit kitchen. Jakub smiled at Franssen as he entered the room and clapped him on the back.

"I see you started without us, my friends," he barked, looking at the opened bottle of whisky.

"Would you or Marcel like a glass?" asked De Klerk.

Jakub raised his hands and smiled warmly. "Not for me, thank you."

Marcel remained mute. Franssen eyed the pale-faced man carefully. Unlike his more jovial brother, Marcel was dressed in a black suit, an unbuttoned collar the only informal part of his attire. As he entered the room, he surveyed the whole area. Walking round the table, he took up a position next to the glass doors that led into the garden. After De Klerk had offered him the drink, he stopped showing any interest in the events around him. Instead, he stared out into the garden.

"But please have another yourself, and you, Hans. After the day you've had you may need the whole bottle."

"It turned out all right."

Jakub nodded, then took a seat at the end of the table. This left De Klerk to take the one with his back to the window and to the younger Dudka. He rubbed his face and looked at them all individually. The chubby face with its glasses studied the two Nile directors.

"Where do we begin, gentlemen? We have one of the most important deals of our careers on the table. Yet I'm sat here worrying about a woman we thought dead, and the Amsterdam police having finally been able to distinguish their arses from their elbows."

He paused, waiting for an answer. Receiving none, he continued.

"Let's start with the Galahads. I take it the contact has arrived in the city?"

The question was directed at De Klerk, who only nodded.

"And the rockets? Where are they right now?"

De Klerk swallowed and tried to speak, but the words initially became stuck in his throat. Franssen could see the strain all over the man's face.

"The ship is in the harbour and will be unloaded tomorrow."

"Which ship? I can arrange for a contact of mine to ensure it's unloaded first thing."

"I don't know."

"What do you mean, you don't know?"

"Captain Broad wouldn't say. He refuses to tell us anything else until he's been paid."

"So, we have to take his word for it? Does he not think we can't find out which ships have recently docked from England?"

De Klerk shook his head despondently. "He does but it won't help, he sent them on a ship that docked at numerous ports before

166

coming here. Plus, we don't know the container number, which means there are thousands of possibilities."

Jakub removed his glasses and rubbed his eyes wearily. "You should have let us come with you today. Marcel may have been able to help convince our Captain Broad to have been a bit more friendly."

De Klerk laughed nervously. "I doubt it. He already knows about Anderson and Harmison. Told me outright he knew we'd killed them both."

Jakub looked up at his younger brother, but Marcel was still ignoring the conversation. His attention was focused on the dark garden.

"There's worse."

The eldest Dudka looked back at De Klerk. "Worse?"

"Before he left England, he had to field questions from his superiors about the Galahads and if any were missing. His commanding officer was all over it and nearly found out about the missing shipment."

"So what? He had to deal with a stocktake?"

"He found out that the request came from Interpol here in Amsterdam. They tried to tell the British Government that someone was trying to sell them again. But Broad was able to cover it up. He shut it down, at least for now, but wants an extra ten per cent for his troubles."

Jakub Dudka sat back in his chair and placed his hands on the table. "It has to be Vogt."

"What?" asked De Klerk.

"The request from Interpol. It must have been from that poisonous little toad. They're still working together, him and Natasja. We found out that Wever and Vogt were working together when we were starting out, but it seems Natasja stayed on."

"Maybe, but there's two problems with that." Franssen now spoke and Jakub turned to stare at him. "First, my source in the police department has never mentioned them working together.

In fact, the police were as surprised as I was when she turned up."

"So Vogt's kept his relationship with her secret. Probably doesn't trust anyone else."

Franssen considered that and agreed with Jakub's assumption. "Okay, second, how do they know about the Galahad deal closing soon? We've been trying to get them for nearly a year?"

"I think I know." The voice was quiet, almost as if the speaker was fighting against it.

They all turned to stare at De Klerk.

"I found out something a few weeks ago."

"Go on," Jakub told him, his tone neutral.

"When arranging the deal, I used one of my old contacts, someone I've not spoken to for over a year. Well, he wasn't aware of the new arrangements and he…"

Franssen willed his friend to shut up, but it was too late.

"…he rang Natasja, thinking she was still working for us." He almost spat the final words out in a single rushed breath.

Franssen noticed Marcel had finally turned round to watch the conversation taking place at the table. He made eye contact with his brother, who grimaced and shook his head.

"Albert," Jakub muttered, using De Klerk's first name for the first time. He reached out to take the whisky bottle and refilled De Klerk's glass. "You should have told us; we could have helped you."

"I didn't know what to do," he admitted.

Franssen watched on, surprised as Jakub reached over and patted their host on the arm. "Forget it, we need to concentrate on the now. We need to figure out what to do about Broad."

De Klerk nodded. "I'm due to meet him again tomorrow."

"Where?"

"The Van Gogh Museum, on the second bench in the self-portrait room."

"When?"

"Two in the afternoon."

Franssen shuddered inwardly as De Klerk gave away his only cards.

"Okay, and he wants the money then?"

"Half, he wants half then, at which point he will tell us the location of the Galahads once they have been disembarked and have gone through customs. We then pay the rest on receipt. He wants it in euros."

Jakub smiled at De Klerk and stood up from the table. He looked round the expensive kitchen, its black granite worktops glittering in the spotlights. He turned to Franssen. "Has your source heard or seen if Vogt knows about Broad? That he's here in the city?"

"No, but like you said, Vogt's probably kept it quiet."

Jakub continued to look round the kitchen, opening the odd cupboard and looking inside. Franssen and De Klerk remained at the table, the latter still cradling his glass. Marcel remained standing, but now constantly watched his brother.

"In summary then, the deal's still on. If Vogt and/or Natasja knew about Broad, they would have taken him in already. Their actions today are of two desperate people running out of options."

Franssen considered the points, agreeing with Jakub's assessment. But then a pair of deep-blue eyes floated into his mind.

"What about the Englishman?"

"What about him?"

"If Natasja and Vogt are working together, we have to assume the death was staged by both of them. I've been told he came over to confirm the death at Vogt's request. But we now know that was never going to happen."

Jakub stopped his searching and came back to the table, standing over them all. "Fuck, I never thought of that. What's his game, then?"

Franssen didn't know. Earlier today, he had recognised that Sam Taylor was a different type of threat. But then he remembered back to the shooting. He could visualise Taylor firing at Natasja. He described it to Jakub, who looked equally confused.

"What's their game?" he asked no one in particular. "Vogt is working with Natasja to bring us down, but then he brings over Taylor to kill her?"

When no one answered, he continued. "We need to complete this deal. I have customers who will not accept another failure. Our enemies are trying to confuse us, to have us make mistakes. We cannot allow it. They have nothing, it's all subterfuge. Natasja, the Englishman, it's all that dwarf's attempt at breaking us. We still have Franssen's mole keeping us informed. We have the Galahads nearly in the city."

Franssen sensed the session was reaching its climax. He had never seen Jakub so wound up.

"What we need is time. Time to get this deal over the line. Then we can handle Vogt and Natasja. Even the Englishman, if we need to."

"How do we do that?" De Klerk asked him.

Jakub turned and smiled kindly at him. "We need a diversion; something to distract them while we get things over the line."

Franssen was distracted by a sharp intake of breath from across the table. Looking round curiously, he saw De Klerk arching backwards, a look of shock across his face. His eyes were stretched wide, the eyeballs almost popping out of their sockets. His face had gone deathly pale as he tried to reach up behind him, trying to clutch at something. Looking on in horror, Franssen watched as their host half stood from his chair, his body twisting in a horrible arch. Before he had even reached his full height, he stopped, tried to breathe, then a bright gush of blood came pouring from his mouth. He gave one last desperate grunt as the life left his body, before falling face first onto the table. The bottle of whisky was sent flying to the floor.

The hilt of a knife was left protruding from the now prone De Klerk. Above him, looking like nothing out of the ordinary had happened, stood Marcel. He looked down at the corpse with little interest as blood from the mouth began to spread across the table.

Franssen jumped up and away from the table. He stared desperately at the two brothers, expecting his own death. But Jakub raised the palms of his hands.

"Hans, it's okay, you are perfectly safe."

Franssen stood still, his heart pounding in his chest.

"I promise you, we mean you no harm," Jakub tried again, but Franssen kept his eyes on the younger Dudka. Marcel didn't seem to realise the effect his actions had had on Franssen.

Jakub shook his head. "Hans, please, it's all right. You are completely safe; we mean you no harm." He looked at Marcel. "Leave us, wait outside."

Pausing only to retrieve the knife, the younger brother ambled round the table. Franssen moved away from him as he made his way towards the exit.

Jakub waited for his brother to leave before walking towards the visibly shaken Franssen. He placed his hand on the taller man's elbow and directed him away from the body. "I'm sorry you had to see that, my friend. But we needed a distraction, as you know, and Albert had served his purpose. Tomorrow, Agent Vogt will have his team searching for the killer and thanks to the actions of Natasja earlier today, she will have to be the main suspect. Unless of course he decides to admit he's been working with her. So please, let's just move on."

Franssen, who thought he could never move on from what he had just witnessed, remained silent.

"We will need to leave soon, but I need you to do some things for me."

"Yes, of course."

"Good. First, we need the money. Can you arrange for it to be ready for transfer tomorrow?"

Franssen nodded.

"Then I want you to speak to your contact in the police. Have them find the body tomorrow morning. It'll keep them busy while we deal with Broad. You understand?"

Franssen did.

"You are a good man, Hans, the very best. We need you now more than ever."

Jakub reached round and gave the tall, thin Franssen a swift hug before tapping him on the cheek. Outside, they heard the sound of smashing glass as the younger brother broke the front door.

"Grab that second glass, Hans. Marcel is making it look like a break-in."

The head of the Nile gave the body of their now deceased host a final glance before leaving the still-shaken Franssen alone in the kitchen.

TWENTY-TWO

SAM LEFT Natasja in the brothel and made his way back onto the busy street. It was getting late now, the night passing them all by. Banking on the cool air helping to clear his mind, he decided to walk back to the hotel rather than flagging down a passing taxi.

As he had left her, she had given him a final lingering kiss before pulling back.

"Sam," she breathed, "thank you."

"Not sure you need to say thanks for what we just did. You pulled your weight, too."

"No, not for that. For believing me. You didn't have to take my word for… everything."

He looked at her. Over the past two days he'd felt a range of emotions for this woman. Yet now, he felt something new. He felt sorry for her. For the first time he saw the strain of the past year, the anger, the thirst for revenge mixed with a fear that had driven her into hiding.

Did he trust her? He wasn't really sure. He hoped that Hannah's search the next day might give him some sort of confirmation about her. She'd been involved in a highly powerful crime syndicate. She had been, and maybe still was, a criminal. The implication that she'd killed a British Army officer might be

173

receding, but there was still that doubt in his mind. Again, he wondered who the inside police officer that had been working for her prior to last year's events had been.

There were so many questions about her alone, he hadn't the mental strength to even try to consider who the current mole could be. Captain Broad looked to be their only hope. But he would have bet his life that the Nile was also telling itself that very same thing.

The next day dawned bright but cold. A crisp autumn morning had awoken the city to the new day. Sam woke early to find a text message from Bos, telling him to wait outside. There was also a picture message from Hannah, of Captain James Broad. It was a basic file photograph, showing a handsome face with dark-brown hair. Sam studied it for a moment before sending it off to Natasja to share with Vogt.

Sam rose slowly, took a hot shower and went down to breakfast. Two black coffees and a stack of pancakes later, he almost felt like he was ready to take on whatever the city would throw at him that day. Thirty minutes later, dressed back in the dark-green field jacket covering the now properly loaded Glock 17, he was outside awaiting his ride. His feet were once again dry in their boots after the hotel's radiators had worked their magic.

Standing there watching the traffic, he let his mind drift between two women: Ada Berger and Natasja van Rossum. What the hell was he going to do if they ever met? One thing was for damn sure, there'd be fireworks. Both were forces of nature that he would not want to cross willingly.

Sam's mental wanderings were broken by the arrival of Bos, pulling up in front of the hotel. A bright face greeted him as he fell into the passenger seat.

"Ready for another day of Dutch adventure?"

"God no, I've had enough of that for a lifetime."

"There's still plenty to go around. How was your evening? Do anything interesting?"

"Just went for a walk to clear my head. What did you get up to?"

"I should have told you yesterday, really. Peter's mother is in hospital. We went to see her."

"Is she bad?"

Bos frowned, then nodded. "Yes, it's cancer. Terminal, I'm sorry to say."

"Oh, I'm sorry."

"Thank you. It's why Peter's not come to see you yet. It's been a tough few days, especially with…" He paused, and for a moment he looked like he wanted to tell Sam something. Instead, he closed his mouth and continued driving.

Sam wondered what his friend had been about to say. 'Especially with the case? The woman?'

Bos changed the subject and filled the rest of the journey with generic talk of the English football season. Sam played along out of politeness. He was pleased when the short journey to the station ended and the pair of them were able to leave the car. It may have only been an inclination, but he felt his friendship with Bos was not the same as it had been. Either the change in rank, or perhaps his own subconscious responses to Vogt's suspicions, had made the pair less close. The thought saddened him as they entered through the glass doors into the reception area, where they were immediately set upon by Agent Vogt. Alongside him was Detective Hardenne.

"You two, don't get comfortable; you need to go with this one." Vogt thumbed towards Hardenne. "This young fool's had a tip-off from the control room about a disturbance at De Klerk's house."

Hardenne gave an agitated sigh. "I know one of the ladies who mans the phones. They just had a tip-off that something wasn't right at the De Klerk place. She knew we were working a case involving him, so messaged me."

Bos spoke up. "What type of disturbance?"

Hardenne answered. "We don't know, boss, just that the place looked broken into."

"Fine, get a car and we can go now," Bos told him.

The detective slipped off, glad to be away from the snippy Interpol agent.

Vogt turned his attention to Sam. "Taylor."

"Yes?"

"When you're done, you're coming with me."

"I am?" Sam feigned surprise.

"Yes, my superiors want to speak with you at The Hague. Soon as I hear when, I'll let you know."

The dwarf gave him a withering stare. Sam wanted to ask more about the change of plan, but instead turned from Vogt and followed Bos out of the station after Hardenne.

"Ever get the feeling Vogt doesn't like us?" Bos remarked, as they stood waiting for Hardenne to bring the car round. "Wonder what the disturbance is. You don't think our female friend was out late last night continuing her vendettas?"

Hardenne pulled up in a white, blue and orange police car and the pair of them climbed in. Sam took the back seat, which was cramped thanks to the tall men in the front. Sitting there in the back, he looked at the well-built Hardenne for a moment. He wore his hair close-shaved to his head and Sam couldn't help but be impressed by the thick neck muscles. The young officer had clearly spent the year in the station gym.

"When's that bastard leaving, boss?" asked Hardenne as he pulled into the fast-flowing traffic.

"Ignore him, my friend. It's not forever."

"Who does he think is, though? Honestly, he comes in here and kicks off over everything."

The two older men sat impassively listening to their colleague's rant.

"Seriously, I know it's wrong but I've never wanted to throw someone into the canal more."

"In England it's called dwarf-tossing," Sam retorted. "Anyway, Hardenne, how are you? Been up to much this year?"

"Not much to be honest, still the same really. Only now I'm doing as this guy tells me to."

"You were *always* doing what I told you," muttered Bos. "You know what this young officer's like, Sam. If he's not pumping iron and protein into himself, he's down in one of his cafés getting high."

"It's not illegal," Hardenne protested.

"Still not the best look for an up-and-coming officer, is it?"

Sam guessed this was a well-rehearsed argument between the pair.

"Where were you last night? Marley's? Or back at the Sailors' Pleasure?"

"Sailors last night," their driver admitted.

"Great, that's what we need. A member of the unit walking through the Red Light District in his evenings."

Sam flinched. "Out late then, Hardenne?"

"No! I was home before nine."

Sam tried to work out whether their paths could have crossed.

The car fell silent as they turned onto the leafy suburban street where De Klerk lived. Sam wasn't worried; he alone knew that Natasja had posed no real threat to the two traitorous directors.

"It's that one there with the gate and the Mercedes." Bos directed his subordinate to park up on the kerb outside.

Hardenne did as he was told and, pulling in, cut the engine. All three of them saw it then. The single broken windowpane. The door ever so slightly ajar.

"Fuck," Bos said.

"Yeah, I agree with you there," Sam added, his previous relaxed thoughts evaporating. "That's not good."

"Still got that Glock?" Bos asked him. "Good. Hardenne, stay here and call the station. Ask them to tell Vogt there appears to have been a break-in. Me and Sam will check it out. If you don't hear from us in three minutes, call for backup."

Sam reached down and pulled the pistol from its holster, the live ammunition back in place. "After you."

The pair of them climbed out into the fresh morning air. The built-up street blocked off the worst of the autumnal breeze. All around them, the trees were turning orange and red as their leaves hung loose. Sam followed Bos through the still unlocked gate and across the driveway. The large car, which he and Corsel had admired the day before, remained in the same position. Covering Bos from behind, his Glock clutched in two hands and pointed downwards, Sam approached the entrance.

"No glass," Sam commented as he stood on the front porch.

"Huh?"

"No glass out here; it means it was broken from the outside."

"Looks like someone definitely broke in."

"Or they wanted to make it look like they did."

Bos nodded, then called out into the house. There was no answer. He called again, but this time began to push the door open. As he did so, Sam could now see shards of broken glass covering the floor. The doorbell camera he had used the day before had been disconnected, with wires hanging out of the wall.

"Seems no one's home," Bos surmised.

"No one who's able to answer, anyway," said Sam, indicating down the corridor to where the kitchen door stood slightly open. Even in the light of day, they could see the glow of the kitchen lights seeping round the doorway.

They crept forward, neither speaking as they approached the kitchen. Bos went first. Holding his weapon in his right hand, he pushed the door open.

"Jesus."

Sam stepped past him to see slouched over the table, the prone body of De Klerk. His blood had pooled both on the table and around his feet.

"Best get on the phone to Vogt," Bos told him. "Our female friend has finally killed one of them."

TWENTY-THREE

SAM STEPPED past Bos and moved towards the table where the prostrate body of De Klerk lay still in its own blood. He moved slowly, careful not to disturb anything that could be tied to the killer. Stepping over an empty bottle of whisky, he tried to find a pulse in the thick neck. There was none, and already the body had lost most of its warmth. The skin, pale from the loss of blood, felt clammy. Looking down, he saw the puncture wound, the dark stains directing his eyes to the point of entry. From the tear in the shirt, Sam guessed a knife had been the weapon of choice.

"I'll tell Hardenne to ring the station," said Bos as he left the room.

Left alone, Sam studied the rest of the kitchen. There was no other obvious sign of a break-in. The double glass doors that led into the garden were both locked.

Moments later, Bos returned to the kitchen with Hardenne in tow.

"Jesus," Hardenne swore when he saw the body. "What happened?"

"Stabbed in the back," Sam told him calmly. "Have you called it in?"

Walking round the table to get a better view of the corpse, Hardenne gave the affirmative.

It wasn't long before they could hear sirens approaching. Sam left the other two to look round the rest of the house. He walked back out of the front of the house, stopping only to look at the broken glass in the door. Once outside in the fresh autumnal air, he proceeded to walk round the rest of the house. After the first round trip, he arrived back on the drive to see officers in their uniforms climbing out of their still-flashing vehicles. A small crowd had begun to form outside the gates and one of the arriving officers attempted to move people away.

Sam left them to it. Letting Bos deal with the practicalities of handling the crime scene, he walked back to the garden with its patio seating and took a chair in the morning sunshine. Inside, he could see the first shapes moving round, all eager to have a look at the dead man. He'd seen enough dead bodies not to want to be inside the house at that moment. Instead, in the calmness of the garden, he let his mind wander.

De Klerk's death had not come as a surprise. True, Sam hadn't exactly been expecting it. Yet the moment he had seen the broken door, the possibility that their host may not have been able to welcome them in had crossed his mind. At moments like this, he didn't really care who'd committed the crime. That would come later. Instead, as he watched the Dutch police officers organise themselves inside, he wondered why. Why kill De Klerk now?

The phone in his pocket vibrated and he answered it.

"Morning, Hannah."

"Hey Sam, having fun?"

Sam looked over to the kitchen and saw a camera flash as someone photographed the corpse. "Plenty, what can I do for you?"

"Are you able to talk?"

He looked round the empty garden. "Yes, why?"

"I've got something for you on Wever."

Sam sat up, his interest in the deceased former Nile leader piqued. "Go on."

"It's not everything, it's still pretty early and I'm waiting for a few more leads, but I've managed to get the coroner's report from his death."

"Broken neck from falling down the stairs?"

"Yes, how did you know?" She paused for a moment, but receiving no answer, carried on. "Well, it's like you said… Police found him at the bottom of his stairs one morning. He was still relatively warm and they don't think he'd been there that long. Eighty-three, lived alone, no next of kin. Pretty open and shut, to be honest. Nothing in the report that seemed out of the ordinary. Seems to have been a jeweller before he retired."

So at least some of Natasja's tale had been true. There had been a jeweller called Wever and he'd been found dead at the bottom of his stairs.

"Was the date I gave you correct? The same day as Anderson?"

"Indeed. Are you going to tell me why you've got me spending all this time searching a dead jeweller?"

"No, but you knew that before you asked. Have you got anything else on him for me?" There was something missing, Sam was sure of it.

Hannah sighed. "Fine, keep it to yourself. But no, there's nothing else at the moment. I'll keep digging for you."

"You're the best, Hannah, you know that?"

"Get off it, Sam, but honestly how are things over there? Emma's not happy that you're not sharing much with us."

"Tell her not to worry, everything is fine over here. I'm perfectly safe." Through the window, one of the officers could be seen stretching his fingers, showing what Sam guessed was the length of the knife wound. He paused for a moment, thinking about the police officer in the kitchen.

"Hannah."

"Yes?"

"Bear with me, but did the report say who the police officer was that found him?"

"Let me look."

Sam heard the tap of the keyboard.

"It was a Sergeant Corsel. Why, anything interesting?"

Was it anything interesting? Something had stuck in Sam's mind the day before as the pair of them had visited this very house.

"Maybe. I'll let you know."

Sam could feel Hannah's frustration at being kept out of the loop.

"Okay, tell you what. Find anything else you can on Wever and I'll tell you everything."

"No, you won't."

"Also, don't forget the Van Rossum woman, please."

"Another one of your women, Sam?"

"Only until you come along, Hannah."

She laughed and put the phone down.

Sam put the phone into his pocket and returned to leaning back in the chair. Inside the room, the officers were still at their grisly business. In his mind, a few more dots joined together. He wanted to speak to Vogt and he wondered where the grim-faced agent was. This was not what he wanted. After everything that had gone on over the past few days with Natasja, he now had to increase the pressure to find her.

Natasja's ability to move openly around the city, already difficult, had just become even harder. Every police officer in the city would have to be sent to find the woman who had faked her own death, attempted to kill one man and in the public eye was the prime suspect for an actual murder, while at the same time trying to use Broad to capture the Nile.

It was not long before Sam saw Vogt arrive. The short figure could be seen through the glass doors, taking in the scene, his face unreadable as it studied the dead man. He stopped for a moment and turned to look at Sam sitting outside in the warming sun. A few moments later, Sam watched him walk through into the garden.

"So then, Mr Taylor, they told me you've been out here with your own thoughts. Tell me what you're thinking."

"It wasn't a break-in."

"It wasn't?"

"No, and *we* both know it wasn't Natasja."

Vogt turned his head to make sure all the kitchen windows were closed. He came to stand by Sam on the flagged patio. Somewhere in one of the garden bushes, a bird chirped. The noise of people in the park drifted over the gate.

"Why wasn't it a break-in?"

"Ignore the broken glass, that was done afterwards. Though the camera was probably turned off beforehand."

"Proof?"

"He was stabbed in the back facing the front door where the supposed intruder broke in. You're telling me De Klerk sat and watched as his killer walked down the corridor, into the kitchen, round the table and stabbed him in the back?"

Vogt said nothing.

"The back door was locked as well. De Klerk knew whoever killed him. He turned off the camera and let them in. The broken door is purely for show."

"So who was it?"

"I don't know, probably the Nile. In fact, I have a suspicion it was the same person who killed Major Anderson."

Vogt reached into his pocket and pulled out one of his cigars.

"It's just a hunch."

Vogt gave a deep puff, forcing the flames into life.

"Based on?"

"I bet a good pathologist will be able to prove the same knife used here was also used in that hotel room last year."

Vogt paused for a moment, thinking on Sam's words. "You're probably right; at least then we'd know it wasn't Natasja."

Sam laughed drily. "You didn't suspect her?"

"No, but part of me wishes it was her. Would make life far easier. Instead, now I have to get every officer in the city looking for her. We have to keep going, see where Broad takes us. If we try telling the truth and bring in Natasja, it'll just drive the Nile underground."

"Agreed, let's stick to the plan. Let Broad lead us to the Nile. We at least know one thing. We have them spooked."

"We do?"

"In an ideal world they wouldn't have wanted to kill De Klerk in the middle of the Galahad deal. This is just a diversion, designed to draw more resource away to chase Natasja."

Vogt sighed, his shoulders sagging. "Broad's not left the hotel yet. I've had my people watching him since last night."

"Your people?"

"German Interpol, same people who helped with the ambulance."

They sat in silence for a moment, watching the events inside the kitchen. Sam saw Bos come to the window more than once to see what was happening out in the garden.

"Any more luck with proving your old friend Bos is working with them?"

Sam shook his head. "You're wrong about Bos; he's not the mole."

"You're blinded by friendship, Sam. We know there's a connection to Franssen. One which he's never shared, which you would have thought he would, considering the case."

"Perhaps he knew he'd become a suspect, just like what's happening now."

"An innocent man has nothing to hide."

"What about the rest of the team? Have you checked out Berger?"

"Yes."

"What about Hardenne? He's up to his neck in the café scene. Wouldn't be hard for someone to get to him."

"We checked Hardenne."

184

"And Corsel? Did you know he was the one who found Wever's body? Pretty easy for someone with an inside tip-off. Also, yesterday, I didn't quite catch it at the time. I had to think about it. When we were together, he said something strange, something he shouldn't know. He said how impressive the woman was, meaning Natasja. Managing to 'escape the Nile and the police'. How did he–"

"…know she had escaped the Nile?"

"Exactly. Only *we* know she's on the run from them. Everyone else here thinks she's still one of them."

Vogt puffed out a mouthful of grey smoke. Sam held his breath for the foul-smelling fumes to pass by.

"Quiet old Corsel, eh? Not sure I see it, to be honest. Hardenne, yes. I've had my eye on him for some time. But not Corsel. You know that's not enough to convict him, right?"

"I do. I'm also not convinced. There could be something else we've missed."

Vogt took a few steps past Sam and peered through the gate into the park. "Keep an eye on him, let's see what he gets up to. But whatever happens, don't let Bos off the hook. I want you watching him."

Sam sighed and gave in. "Where's Natasja today?"

"She's close, waiting for the tip-off from Broad's tail. As soon as we get word, we go meet her and get after him."

"Good, stick to the plan, see where he leads us and then take them all in?"

Vogt looked at the Englishman in surprise. "Not quite, we don't know who he's meeting. If it's only another middleman, we need to keep chasing. I want the goddamn big fish."

"Fine, but only if we know the Galahads are safe. If they look like they're falling into the wrong hands, we bring in everyone we have. Agreed?"

The Interpol man eyed him carefully.

Sam continued, "I know your endgame is to try and install

Natasja back at the head of the Nile, but don't fuck with me. Those rockets are what matters here."

"Taylor–" Vogt started, but Sam cut him off.

"Those rockets don't say 'made in Germany'. They were made in the United Kingdom and I can't let them get into the wrong hands."

"I thought your instructions were to find Anderson's killer?"

Sam was about to stand, anger etched across his face.

"Okay, Englishman, rockets come first. It's why we have a plan B."

Somewhere in the distant park, a dog howled. It acted to put a pause in the conversation as both men instinctively stopped to listen. Eventually, its unseen owner must have calmed it down and the pair returned to the topic of conversation.

"Do I want to know what plan B is?"

"You'll likely find out soon enough. If we can't see who Broad meets, it'll help ensure your rockets are safe and I can still get my big fish." The short agent grinned a cheery smile and pointed the cigar towards the kitchen. "Come on, look on the bright side. You can't say you're sad to see that bastard in there gone to hell."

Sam followed his gaze and looked back into the house. He could see white-overalled officers going about their business.

"No, I suppose not."

"It does make a problem for Natasja. Everyone will be after her now. It's a shame, as she does have rather a good alibi."

"She does?"

"She does," remarked Vogt, finishing the cigar and extinguishing the stub. He looked at it once before throwing it into the hedge. "At the probable time of murder, she was having intimate relations with an officer on the case."

TWENTY-FOUR

SAM LEANT on the brickwork of the house and watched the different crime-scene participants going about their work. It was a strange quirk of being a repatriation officer, that wherever he was in the world, he was always on the outside of any police force he found himself working with. His job was to ensure things were being done correctly, so he could report back to his superiors or the families back home that everything was being done to return their loved one. It didn't matter if they were dead, incarcerated or missing, they all had to come back. True, he would be able to work with the various forces, accompanying them on their visits. Even at times speaking to suspects, leading the interviews, being able to say what an investigating officer could not. But there was always a line he had to toe, beyond which he was not wanted. This was such a moment. The teams entering the house already knew their business. They didn't want an outsider looking over their shoulders.

Odd to think he had only gotten involved all those months ago to review the Anderson case. Now he had been dragged back into that strange no man's land of being an outsider on someone else's patch. Perhaps that's why he'd allowed himself to get involved with Vogt. It was something tangible he could do to help.

Inside his pocket, the phone began to vibrate. The notification on his smartwatch told him it was Natasja.

"He's moving. Vogt's men just phoned it in. Broad's in a taxi and looks to be heading to somewhere not far from here. They're following it now. Get Vogt and I'll meet you fifty metres down the street. White Skoda."

She hung up before Sam could respond. Sighing, he went to find Vogt. He found him in conversation with Bos in the front living room.

"I'll have the pathologist look at the knife patterns and see if there's any way we can connect them," Bos was telling the German.

Sam guessed Vogt had shared his hypothesis about it being the same killer with Bos.

"Remember Anderson's killer was left-handed," Sam interrupted them. "The pathologist's report was confident of that."

They turned to look at him as he entered the room.

"Time to go, Vogt. Your driver to take us to The Hague is here."

The grim face nodded in understanding. "Bos, I'll leave this to you. Do you need anything else before I go?"

"No, we're all good here. Plus I have Berger arriving at any moment."

Vogt left without another word and strode past Sam. Bos looked at him.

"You going with him?"

"I think so. Not sure I want to."

Bos laughed. "We need a proper catch-up. I want to know what you two were saying out in the garden. If Peter's okay, I'll take you for dinner tonight if you like?"

"I'll let you know when I'm back." Sam turned to leave, but as he did so he paused and turned to face his friend. "And Bos, I'm sorry if I've seemed distant this time, or difficult."

Bos studied him for a moment, then the usual friendly grin

burst onto his face. "Don't be stupid, you've had a lot on. The woman who tried to kill you is running around, for a start. That would drive anyone mad. To be honest, I'm not sure with what's happening with Peter and I can't say I've been the most engaging of hosts."

They stood there, both unsure what to say next.

"Taylor, get on with it," Vogt's voice called out.

They each pulled a face and went their different ways.

Ada Berger was just entering the house as Sam was leaving. She stopped in front of him and gave one of her most alluring smiles. "Going so soon?"

"Unfortunately, yes."

"Vogt told me to hurry you along."

Sam shrugged. "What can you do?"

Berger smiled. "Not much. Hope you didn't miss me too much last night."

"Of course I did. Hotel rooms are such lonely places."

"If you behave yourself with Vogt and put in a good word for me, I'll come see you again tonight."

What was the saying about buses, Sam thought as he agreed, then said his goodbyes before walking out.

Vogt was on the pavement by the time Sam joined him. They bent under the police tape and pushed through the small crowd which had formed, for which Sam was grateful as it blocked off any view from the murder house of who they were being picked up by. They found the white Skoda and got in. Taking the front seat, Vogt immediately asked for an update.

"He got a taxi straight from the hotel and is heading in this direction. Your guys think he's heading towards one of the museums."

"Makes sense, a good public place," said Vogt. "De Klerk could probably have walked to all of the major ones from his home. He never told Wever where he met his suppliers, but he could alternate between all of the major museums and never be out of walking distance."

"The Van Gogh, Stedelijk, Diamant, Moco, and the Rijksmuseum," Sam suggested.

"You know your tourist destinations, Sam," acknowledged Natasja. "But it could be any of them, or even perhaps one of the many cafés. Or worse, they may just drive straight on through."

They continued to drive, Natasja using her phone to follow the progress of the tail on Broad. As they grew closer to the moving dot, their assumption of the museum district proved more accurate. They were barely four hundred metres away when eventually the blue dot stopped moving outside the Van Gogh Museum.

"Quickly Natasja, get closer," Vogt growled as they made their way slowly through the traffic. In the distance, they watched a taxi pull up on the side of the road. A car Sam presumed had been the tail drove on by, its job completed.

Sam watched as Broad climbed out of the taxi and stood on the kerb. He could just make out the dark coat over a pair of jeans.

Vogt turned to Sam and passed him a small plastic case. "Here, put one of these in, channel four."

Sam took the case and opened it. "What's this for?"

"You're going inside to follow Broad."

"Alone?"

Vogt sighed. "I have rather a distinctive profile, remember? Dwarves don't make the best covert officers."

"But you're small enough to go unnoticed." Natasja chuckled.

Vogt glared at her.

"I can't say I'm happy about this."

Vogt laughed. "You wanted to bring him in."

Sam remembered the earlier conversation. "What about plan B?"

"She's plan B," said Vogt, thumbing towards Natasja.

"Time to get out. I'm running out of places to park."

Vogt looked back at him one final time. "You've got the photo? And my people will have taken a fresh one from the hotel as he left, so you will know what he's wearing."

"Sam, get the fuck out of this car," Natasja ordered as she pulled to a stop.

Sam remained seated, still in bemusement. Both of the front seat occupants turned to stare at him.

"Channel four, get out now," Vogt told him firmly.

Sam did as he was told and got out of the car into the cold air. To his left, the white Skoda pulled back out into the single-file traffic. In the middle of the road, a tram rolled on past. Just in front of him stood the museum. At first look, Sam couldn't believe they had chosen to house some of the greatest art in human history in such a bleak building. The square dark-brick building looked more like a sixties council building back home.

He opened the plastic case and pulled out a small ear-plug. Moving the dial to the tiny number four, he put it in his ear and waited. A static voice soon came over the airwaves.

"Sam, can you hear me?" Vogt's gruff tone echoed into his eardrum.

"Loud and clear."

"Good, Natasja's sending the photo to your phone."

The phone vibrated in his pocket and Sam withdrew it to see the figure of Broad exiting his hotel. Broad's face looked similar to the earlier mugshot from Hannah. A distinctive, handsome face under dark-brown hair.

"I've got it."

"Good, now get after him. We don't know when he's meeting with De Klerk's replacement."

Sam looked at his watch. It was twenty-five past. "We've got thirty-five minutes."

"How do you know?"

"People meet either on the hour or at half past; it's human nature. He's too late for half past so it's on the hour."

"Right, so get in there and find him."

Sam turned to stare at the disappointing-looking building. "Where's the entrance?"

"Down the street to your right."

He swivelled on his heel and saw most of the crowds around him walking down the side of the building. He followed, wandering past a concession stand, and started scanning people. Amongst the numerous tourists, Sam struggled to spot the lone Broad. Hurrying his pace slightly, he followed the street until it split out into an open concourse.

This was more like it. The square building stopped and across from it stood an oval glass structure. All around the concourse, people hummed. He heard a variety of languages as he scanned the area again. Groups of schoolchildren were being hurried along by weary teachers. A queue of people were shepherded into a roped-off area, having their bags and tickets checked before they entered the museum. Sam decided to start there, and began to walk round the assembled tourists. Eventually he saw him, standing just to the front, about to enter.

"He's at the front of the queue, about to walk in. I'm going to lose him again if I join at the back."

"Follow him straight in."

"How?"

"Improvise."

Sam swore, but did as he was told; as Broad left the queue to make his way through a set of glass doors into the museum, he followed him. He increased his speed as he drew closer to the door where a pair of ticket collectors stood waiting. Broad was just showing his ticket on his phone as Sam arrived.

"Have you got your ticket, please?" the doorman asked.

"I'm so sorry, my wife and kids are already in there. She has my phone with them on it. She just went in; let me shout her." Sam stepped forward and began shouting the first woman's name he could think of as loudly as he could. "Hannah? Hannah?"

Everyone around him began to stare as he called out even louder.

"I'm so sorry about this. I told her to wait. Hannah!"

The two guards began to look uncomfortable. Broad stood next to Sam, looking confused.

"Please sir, can you call her?"

"I can't. I told you, she has my phone! We dropped our keys and I needed to go back and look for them. Hannah!"

The museum staff looked on helplessly as Sam continued to shout through the doors.

"What the hell is going on?" What seemed like a manager had arrived on the scene.

The two doorkeepers tried to explain, but Sam cut them off.

"I'm really sorry, but my wife has gone in without me and I can't get in. I'd ring her, but she's got my phone."

The manager looked uncertainly at Sam, debating what to do. Behind him, the queue of visitors was growing. At the side of him stood the silent Broad, looking on.

"She's probably taken the girls to the toilet," Sam explained.

The woman in charge sighed and told her subordinates to let him in, then turned away. Another painful tourist, she had decided, as she went back to watching the clock tick down to the end of her shift.

Sam dashed forwards into the museum. He took the glass steps down into the open entrance hall. Moving to his right, he walked towards the toilets and waited for Broad to enter the museum. In the disruption, Sam had managed to get a good look at his target. The man was younger than Anderson and Sam had been surprised by the confidence he exuded. Whatever Broad was walking into, he was confident about its outcome.

"I'm in," he said to the hidden earpiece.

"Good, nice show."

"When in doubt, act the stressed parent and make as much noise as possible."

Vogt laughed over the airwaves. "I never took you as the paternal type."

"I'm not, but I've watched my sister's kids and nothing makes people more uncomfortable than a stressed parent."

"Won't Broad now recognise you when you're following him?"

"No, the average person forgets a stranger the moment they walk away from them. Plus, I'm keeping my distance."

Broad had headed towards a stand of maps. Taking one, he opened it up.

"He's also inside."

"Good, Natasja's parked up and will be outside in case we need plan B."

"Which is?"

"Single man in Amsterdam."

Sam shook his head and began to move forward behind Broad. "I don't want to know. What am I looking for?"

"Find out who he's speaking to and if possible, get a photo. Send it to us and I'll have my people outside ready to follow them."

"Right, and then you take them straight in?"

"Something like that."

They were crossing the foyer now and Sam kept his distance as Broad made his way to the elevator. He debated getting in with him, but once he saw Broad was the only inhabitant, he held back. Sam was just close enough to see his hand reach out and press for the top floor. Waiting for the doors to close and the digital floor numbers above to begin to ascend, he pressed for the next lift. Moments later it arrived and stepping in, he pressed for the top floor just as another passenger entered.

Sam was taken aback by the sight of his travel companion. A tall, pale and extremely thin man had entered. His pale face was gaunt, the features sunken as if on a corpse.

"Which floor?" he asked, regaining his composure.

The man merely indicated his approval of the current selection and stepped back to the other side of the space. Taking the opposite corner, Sam kept his eye on the startling man. He was dressed in a dark suit, which hung oddly on his slim frame. Sam guessed it had been bought directly from the rack as no tailor would have let his customer walk out with such a fitting. The stranger must have felt Sam's stare as he looked over his shoulder towards him. Dark-green eyes stared blankly down at him before turning back to watch the door. Sam shuddered and subconsciously reached to touch the concealed Glock under his jacket.

As the doors pinged open, Marcel Dudka walked out first and strode purposely into the exhibitions. He had been watching Broad from the moment he'd stepped out of the taxi. He'd watched the strange scene at the door where the Englishman had talked his way inside. Marcel had been too far away to hear the conversation, but he'd guessed this must have been the Englishman, Taylor. The way in which he had walked across the concourse had caught his eye. Then the moment he had not joined Broad in a near-empty elevator had confirmed it.

Marcel had been tempted to kill Taylor in the elevator there and then. It would have been quick. He could have had his knife across Taylor's throat in the blink of an eye. But Jakub had been clear that everything had to go smoothly. They needed the Galahads more than anyone could know. Jakub could talk a good game, better than most. But behind the warm smile, past even the cold Marcel, the Dudkas were just a small dot in a longer chain. He let out a grim smile as he walked to find his brother, already somewhere in the museum. There was always a bigger fish.

TWENTY-FIVE

ON THE FIFTH floor of the museum, Sam was glad to watch as his elevator companion strode away. He began to scan the floor for Captain James Broad.

"Where are you?" Vogt's voice buzzed in his ear.

"Top floor."

He quickly spotted Broad circling some of the exhibited artwork not far from the elevators. Watched from afar, the Ministry of Defence man seemed completely at ease, just one of the many thousands of tourists visiting one of the city's major attractions. Sam kept his distance, always positioning himself in the room adjacent to Broad's. As they began to wander round various works of art, he started to wonder where they would actually stop. There were benches and chairs dotted around each of the rooms, but Broad kept walking past them.

Sam checked his watch again. The digital screen now read five to. He was beginning to think he'd been wrong about the timings, when Broad suddenly stopped his aimless wandering. Instead, turning on his heel, he began to make his way to the stairs. Sam followed, keeping in step with his target.

"We're moving," he told the invisible Vogt.

"Good, keep going."

As Broad reached the top of the stairs, he paused for a moment then looked around him. Sam diverted sideways back into the wider exhibit. He paused for thirty seconds, counting each second in his head, hoping his target had moved on. Peering round, he saw the staircase was now empty. He ran to the balcony that overlooked the entire flight of stairs down to the atrium. No sign of Broad from there. Thinking quickly, he ran round the open space to be able to look down over all of the staircase. His heart leapt to his throat.

"Shit."

Sam was about to tell Vogt the bad news when he suddenly saw Broad making his way down the third-floor staircase.

Broad was now at the second floor. As he reached the first floor, he broke off out of the stairwell and into the exhibition. Sam sprinted to the staircase and began to take each flight of steps as if his life depended on it. By the time he'd reached the first floor, his heart was pounding in his chest. Walking out of the stairwell, he found himself on a floor covered in the great artist's works. Sam, being artistically blind to such things, had no idea what he was looking at. Instead, he pushed on into the museum's depths to find Broad.

"It's nearly the hour mark," the voice in his ear reminded him.

"He'll be late. Classic power move. Puts the other party on the back foot."

Sam nearly convinced himself with that argument as he searched for the elusive Broad, finally catching up with him in a gallery filled with portraits of the red-haired painter. A small sign told him the white-painted room was the self-portrait gallery. Pausing to pretend to look at one of the smaller framed pieces, Sam wondered if people would still resort to oil painting to create the latest selfies if camera phones didn't exist.

Glancing over his shoulder, he saw Broad had paused at the far end of the room and was peering into the next. All around him, people were making their way through the museum. Small groups mingled together and occasionally blocked his view. A number of school parties were in the gallery being shown round by an excitable tour guide. Sam couldn't tell who looked more bored, the teachers or the pupils.

Broad had finally made up his mind and began to move forward. Sam paused for a moment and spoke over the radio.

"He's about to make contact."

"Good luck."

Broad had now stepped out of view and into the next room. Sam eased his phone out of his pocket, ready to take a photo. Crossing the room, he heard the tour guide trying to explain in a poor French accent to the pupils how the artist used his brush to form the paint. Sam chuckled as he heard one of the pupils describe what their guide could do with said brush.

Reaching the doorway into the next gallery, Sam paused for a moment to assess the room. Like the previous gallery, the room was nearly full of people. It took him a moment to notice Broad sitting on a large bench in front of a large print of one of Van Gogh's famous self-portraits. The artist's eyes seemed to be glaring straight at Sam as he watched Broad. The captain was now facing towards Sam, but not focusing on him. Instead, Sam could see his lips moving. Directly behind him sat two men, both of whom had their backs turned away.

"He's meeting someone now, but I can't see who."

"Why?" Vogt hissed.

"Because the bastards are looking away from me. Just hang on."

Sam looked round the wider gallery and decided it was just crowded enough to walk across it unnoticed. Pacing forward, he slowly made his way further into the busy room. Broad was at the far end and it would take Sam a few moments to reach him. As Sam walked forward, a new group of schoolchildren was led into the gallery. Another set of bored faces stared at the bright oil paintings that had defined a genre.

Broad was still talking to the backs behind him. Sam thought he looked slightly frustrated. It would have been the first time he had heard that he was no longer dealing with De Klerk. Sam was about ten feet away from the bench now. Seeing the latest school tour was moving towards him, he decided to use it as cover to move round and get the photograph of whoever was sitting on the other side of Broad.

Instead, everything went wrong. The first Sam knew of it, was what felt like a low kick between his ankles. This was followed by a strong pair of hands forcing his shoulders forwards over whatever was between his legs. His attention completely on Broad, Sam had failed to see what had caused this sudden change in direction. Instead, he felt his entire body weight stagger forward then begin to fall. Yet rather than landing on the hard museum floor, he fell into the first line of the school party, his flailing hand grabbing the unsuspecting tour guide by the shirt as together, they fell into the first of the students.

Sam fell with his innocent victims into a heap on the museum floor. The phone in his hand was gone, lost in a mangle of bodies. Around him were the teenage screams of anguish from the unfortunate girls who had been caught in his ungainly tumble. Next to him, rising to his knees, the tour guide asked him what the hell he was doing. Sam raised a hand in apology and turned to look behind him to see who had caused him to fall. He had known from the hands on his back that it had been deliberate. The space behind him was empty. Whoever had done it had vanished into the crowded room.

"Bastard," he grunted.

"What?" Vogt's voice echoed in his ear.

"Nothing," Sam told him as he turned his attention back to where Broad had been sitting.

Sam climbed to his feet to be met by an angry-looking teacher. The woman mouthed a spurt of French at him.

"Je suis désolé d'avoir trébuché, veuillez m'excuser," he told her, apologising for his trip.

"I take it from your French you didn't get what we need?" said Vogt, in his ear.

"No." Sam sprinted to the exit.

"Fuck, get after him. Natasja," Vogt radioed.

"Yes?" Natasja's voice came over the airwaves.

"Plan B, look out for him leaving. We can now presume he's being watched."

Had the deal been done? Sam doubted that. The meeting had been too quick, too informal, for a final handover. They still had time. Reaching the stairs, he headed back down to the entrance hall hoping to spot Broad, all the time wondering what the mysterious plan B could be. He had to push through the crowds of visitors to try to catch up with the disappearing prey. As he reached the glass stairs that led back out into the city air, he saw Broad's dark coat.

"He's alone and coming out now, main entrance."

"Don't worry, I've got this," Natasja's calm voice told him.

Sam lost sight of Broad again while he finished climbing the staircase that led up from the lower-level atrium. Bursting out of the glass-domed building, he looked around for Broad. Seeing him walking to the left, Sam began to follow, wondering where Natasja would be. They were now walking out of the museum and into the wide open space of the Museumplein. A flat parkland field covered the area. To their right was a busy road with a tram stop in the middle. To the left, the imposing Rijksmuseum, where its tall towers overlooked food stalls busy with customers.

No sign of Natasja. Broad was now further into the Museumplein and Sam watched as he headed towards the Rijksmuseum. Deciding he had best continue to follow, he walked on. Broad was now level with the seating area of the different food stalls lined up along one side of the park. Sam could smell the various offerings of hot dogs, fries and waffles. Oh, to be a tourist in a city like Amsterdam, he thought again. Instead, he was stalking an international arms dealer.

Broad had now taken a different path, one which led to a fountain with its pumps shut off for the winter. As Broad came level with the first stone lip of the pool of water, Sam saw Natasja come into view, dressed in a long beige coat. Her hair waved golden in the afternoon sunlight. She clasped a handful of what looked like flyers.

Now also level with the pool, Sam took the opposite route round. He watched Natasja walk up to the unsuspecting Broad. From his position across the fountain, Sam saw both sets of mouths moving. Broad looked slightly uncomfortable as Natasja tried to give him one of her flyers. Stepping forward until her face was pressed against Broad's ear, she must have whispered something to him. As she stepped away, his face changed and he looked down to see she had slightly opened the long coat. Even from across the pool, Sam saw a flash of a long leg.

Broad's face now showed a sly grin and he nodded at her before taking a flyer. They looked to have finished, but just before Broad was about to walk away, she pressed herself against him once more. Her mouth went to his ear and she whispered a final parting before pulling away. Finishing their conversation, the pair went two different ways.

"Right, let's go, Vogt's men will follow him," Natasja's voice came into Sam's ear. "Follow me round the back of the basketball courts to my left."

Sam turned back the way he had come. Walking briskly, he found Natasja tying her long blonde hair back, apparently completely unfazed by what had just happened.

"Plan B, lonely single man in Amsterdam. He was only going to be doing one thing this evening. Visiting the Red Light District." She showed him her flyers. Sam saw they advertised a private strip club somewhere in the city.

"I gave him a flyer, told him I was working this evening and would give him a special time. Even told him to come for eight and ask for Kat."

"How do you know he'll come?"

"You don't know what I said to him," she teased.

"But why? What's the point?"

She shrugged. "It's what you asked for. We'll be able to bring him in. But this way we can do it without being seen by either the Nile or the authorities. He turns up expecting a good time and we persuade him to help us. If we pick him up now, we get the Galahads but lose the Nile."

Sam could see her point. After what had happened in the museum, it was clear both parties were after the same fish.

"Fuck, how do we know the Nile won't pick him up beforehand?"

"We don't, but they'll find it hard to get him during the day. Plus, we have to presume their deal is still on. They'll want him to play ball. If we're lucky, we can use Broad to lead us to their people. If we're unlucky, we make him tell us where your Galahads are. Either way, we win."

Vogt, listening over the microphone now, chimed in. "Whatever happens, those rockets will be safe."

Sam ran his hand through his hair nervously. Not for the first time, he felt like a passenger on this case.

Natasja seemed to notice his unease. "Come on, relax. I'll take you for some food before we go and get ready for Broad."

Sam looked at her. The hair now tied back, the coat now fastened. Once again, he let her lead him into the city.

Across the park, watching a pair of pigeons explore the grass, sat Jakub Dudka. The podgy elder brother's mind was working overtime as he waited. Eventually, Marcel came to join him.

"Is he being followed?" Jakub asked as his younger brother sat down next to him on the bench.

Marcel grunted.

"Good, at least something's working."

Marcel waited for his brother to continue.

"Broad wants paying in full before he discloses the location. I tried to tell him about what had happened to De Klerk, but even that didn't appear to bother him. He told me straight out he knew what happened to Anderson. I'm supposed to meet him tomorrow in the café at the Rijksmuseum."

Jakub again paused, waiting for his brother to respond.

"Thinks he can play us. He's probably worked out that he is our last resort."

The younger brother still did not speak.

"We cannot wait much longer, brother. They won't let us."

Marcel sniffed and scratched his nose.

Jakub grew frustrated. "What happened with the other tail? Who was it?"

Finally, Marcel spoke. "The Englishman. He followed Broad into the museum. But he was alone. He didn't see you."

Jakub swore. "At least it proves he and Vogt are working together. And they're not working with the wider police. Otherwise, we'd be locked up right now."

Marcel shrugged. "He didn't follow Broad out of the park. I don't think anyone else did. Some prostitute accosted him, but that was it."

"So, what now?"

The brothers fell silent as each considered their options.

As usual, Jakub spoke first. "We have to take him. There's no other option. We don't have any more time and they'll not wait any longer."

He paused for a moment to gauge Marcel's reaction.

"Can you arrange it? Bring him to the boathouse?"

Marcel reached round with his left arm to rub his right shoulder, the movement opening his jacket to reveal the long-bladed knife in his inner pocket.

"Tonight, he will no doubt leave the hotel to explore the city. We can get him on the way back from whatever hole he goes to."

Jakub smiled for the first time since leaving Broad. He always trusted Marcel. More than anyone else in the world, he knew he could rely on his brother.

TWENTY-SIX

SAM AND NATASJA returned to the white Skoda, parked just around the corner from the Museumplein. Vogt unfolded his arms and stretched out in his seat. The dark-blue pea jacket was still fastened across his chest. "So the Nile knows we're after Broad. This makes things more difficult." He looked at Natasja. "How did your interaction go?"

"He's hooked, he'll come to Esme's tonight and then we can take him."

"Are you sure?" Vogt asked.

"Positive. I gave him a promise he won't want to miss," she told him with a sly smile.

Vogt sighed and looked out of the window. "Well, it's all we've got. I just hope Broad's feeling lonely this evening." He looked at his watch. "Let's drive over and get set up. We can pick up dinner along the way."

Natasja restarted the car and set off back into the city's busy streets. Sam, a passenger in more ways than one, sat back and watched as the narrow houses flew past. He wondered how many visitors knew that the distinct narrow houses were all designed to avoid the extra taxes levied on the width of a building. The historic buildings had only arisen to become narrow and long to keep the taxman at bay.

Leaving the car on a side road, Sam followed his two companions back into the city's Red Light District. In the late-afternoon sunshine, the streets felt different to the night before. They wandered amongst more locals this time. Numerous cyclists flew past them as their riders went about their day.

"Who actually has right of way here? The cars, cyclists or pedestrians?" Sam asked in frustration as he dodged past another two-wheeler.

Natasja laughed at him. "You did just cross a cycle path."

"They're everywhere. How am I supposed to get across?"

"You need to be more respectful. There're more bikes in this city than people," Vogt told him.

"Way they ride, I'm not surprised. I feel targeted on two feet."

"I bet London's just a metropolitan paradise," Natasja muttered.

Eventually they arrived outside Esme's, a darkly lit establishment with a flight of stairs leading downwards. Bright-red neon lit up the entrance where three burly bouncers stood watching.

"Should I be surprised it's already open?" asked Sam.

"You shouldn't be. Keeps all of its customers satisfied whenever they need their kicks," Vogt told him.

Sam eyed the group of bouncers in the doorway. "More of your friends?" he asked Natasja.

"Of course."

Vogt didn't join them. "I'm going to get us some dinner. There's a burger bar just up the road. You two go in and get ready."

They watched as Vogt stalked his way through the crowds. The short figure was soon lost to them on the busy street.

"Come on, I'll get you a drink." Natasja grabbed Sam's arm and led him towards the entrance. She smiled at all three of the bouncers.

"Not seen you for a while. I was beginning to wonder where you'd got to," their leader greeted her, then stood on his toes to land a kiss on her cheek. Looking down at him, Sam saw a large round man whose neck seemed non-existent. The bald round head seemed to be stuck straight onto the huge shoulders.

"You know me, Boris. I always come back."

"I hear you booked the showroom this evening? Should I look out for more of your guests?"

"Just the one tonight, an Englishman. It won't be until later and he'll be asking to see Kat. When he does, can you let me know before you send him in?"

The round face lit up into a smile, showing bright-white teeth. "Ah, one of those evenings then."

Natasja smiled sweetly at him and ran her hand down his arm. "You know me."

"I'll see he gets a drink first, then have him brought in to you."

Natasja smiled and thanked the bouncer. "Oh, I forgot, there's also another person coming. He's called Vogt. You'll know him when you see him."

"I will?" the bouncer asked.

"He's on the shorter side. Even more so than you!" she teased. "But he's with us, so send him straight through to the room."

Boris scowled and looked Sam up and down. "And who's this one?"

"He's with me. Be nice, Boris."

Sam stared straight into the man's dark eyes, trying not to blink.

"You must also be English." He laughed and said something in Dutch to his companions. "Come on in, the pair of you."

Boris stepped back and the two of them walked down the stairs into the strip club.

"What did he just say to his friends?" Sam asked Natasja.

Natasja laughed. "He said he could tell you were English."

"How?"

"Because only an Englishman would come to a strip club not knowing where to look before he'd even got inside."

Sam bristled but said nothing. They reached the bottom of the stairs and were waved in by the bored-looking woman in the ticket booth. Pushing through a pair of double doors, they entered the heart of the club.

The whole space was darkly lit except for the numerous platforms dotted around. A range of tables, chairs, sofas and stools were placed all around them. There must have been nearly forty people already inside. Most were seated around the occupied platforms, where women in differing stages of nakedness performed. Loud music blaring from large speakers dominated his senses. Sam watched the nearest performer complete her routine. She finished in a stretch so low to the stage floor, she was able to take the outstretched euro notes between her teeth.

They walked towards the bar and Natasja leant over and spoke in the barman's ear. The man looked at her for a moment, then nodded to the right where another set of doors led off.

"This way. We can get in the room and I'll go to see the manager."

Passing out of the main room, they entered a long corridor with doors leading off to each side. Bright metal numbers were screwed onto each, counting upwards.

"Private booths," she told him. "You pay your money, you get your girl or boy."

They went past the closed doors until they reached the final room. A fire door stood next door to it. A bright-green exit sign stood glowing in the darkened corridor. Natasja twisted the handle and walked in. They entered a spacious room decorated in dark-brown furnishings. A long sofa covered two sides, while a fully stocked bar was fitted into a corner. In the middle stood what looked more like a bed than a stage. Soft leather covered the surface, while two poles were fixed to the side.

"Bit big for a private booth?" Sam asked Natasja, who had

headed to the bar. He watched on as she took off the long coat to reveal a short black dress. He could now see what had caught Broad's eye at the park.

"It's not a private booth, it's the party room. Or you may call it the orgy room."

Sam looked down uncomfortably at the long sofa.

"Don't worry, it gets a good clean. Gin and tonic?"

Sam nodded, took off his own coat and moved to the bar, taking a stool in front to watch Natasja preparing two glasses.

"Tough day, eh, soldier?" she asked, as she dropped ice cubes into a glass.

"Something like that." He looked round the room again. A long mirror ran all the way round, only stopping for the door. He didn't need to look up to know there was a mirrored ceiling.

"Chin up, things'll soon be picking up," she told him, pushing a filled glass over. "Or at least, *your* night will after this."

"Do you mean in here with Broad, or later with you?"

Natasja's eyes lit up as she smiled seductively and began to drink her gin.

Sam lifted his glass and drank the refreshing liquid. He wondered where Broad was at this moment. He wished he shared his partner's confidence that the Nile wouldn't pick him up first.

"I need to go and talk to the management, then find out where that bastard dwarf has got to. He's probably outside having a cigar with Boris. Stay here and don't play with anything."

Sam watched and admired the Dutchwoman as she left. The dress fitted her perfectly, revealing her long legs. As the doors shut, Sam pulled out his phone and turned on the screen. Two missed calls from Emma. Ringing the head of the repatriation office back, he heard the Irish brogue answer quickly at the other end.

"There was me thinking you'd gone rogue on us," Emma Read spoke over the speaker.

Sam swirled on his bar-stool until his back was against the

wooden surface. "Me? Go rogue in Amsterdam? What do you think I'm doing? Sat in some strip club enjoying myself?"

"Not on my time you're not."

"Of course not, but why the call?"

"Hannah's left for the day and asked me to relay this back to you. She found some more on Wever and Van Rossum."

"Go on."

"We had to go through the embassy for this, but everything Hannah told you previously was correct. The deceased Wever was a jeweller in his eighties who died last year falling down the stairs in his home. There's not much more to report on the cause of death, but Hannah did say you asked who found him. Why?"

Sam paused for a moment. The fact that it was Emma ringing him and not Hannah meant there was going to be more questions than answers.

"I wanted to speak to the officer in charge," Sam answered.

"Why?"

"I wanted to know if they were involved in this case," Sam answered honestly.

"Why? What's the link?"

Sam sighed. He knew he had to admit some of the smaller details if he wanted to get Emma to share whatever Hannah had found.

"There's a chance he might be linked to the Nile."

"How? By all reports, he was an old retired bachelor. Not your usual international criminal?"

"It's just a hunch, something we're looking into. What else have you got for me?"

"We looked into his next of kin for you. There was a son, Erik, but he passed away some years ago."

"What about Van Rossum? Did you find anything on her?"

"There's no one alive called Natasja van Rossum," Emma told him, her voice betraying her.

"Right. What else do you have for me, then? You wouldn't be ringing me if that was it."

"I'm waiting for you to tell me what you're up to, Sam."

"I don't know what you mean."

Emma's patience snapped, though she wasn't angry with her subordinate. They had worked together too many times for that. She knew how Sam worked.

"She's the woman who shot you, isn't she?"

He wondered how Emma could possibly have known.

"Maybe, I'm not sure."

"Really? You're not sure? Well, let me clear it up for you. This Wever you asked me to look up, and his son. Turns out he had a daughter who on her birth certificate used a different name. She was a Dominique van Rossum, but did have a mother called Natasja van Rossum, who died fifteen years ago. Strange that, isn't it?"

Sam ignored her, too busy in his own thoughts. So Natasja or Dominique was Wever's granddaughter. He should have guessed. Back in the windmill he'd felt something wasn't quite right with the story.

"Sam?" Emma asked.

"Yes?"

"What does it all mean? What are you doing over there?"

Sam considered his response.

"She didn't kill Anderson."

"How do you know?"

"I just do."

"But she still shot you and faked her own death."

"I know."

"And?"

"And what? She had a reason for it."

Emma laughed down the phone. "Don't we all. But seriously, you sound as if you've spoken to her."

"I have."

"Jesus, Sam, does Vogt know?"

"He's the one who brought it about."

"What? Even the fake death? Why?"

Sam stood up and walked round the room.

"It's a long story, Emma. But just know we are close to finding those Galahads. Broad's on his way to us right now and he'll lead us to them."

"To us? You're with her now?"

"Not right now, no. But trust me, she didn't kill Anderson."

"Don't tell me you're sleeping with her? Only you would end up in bed with the person who tried to kill you," Emma groaned.

Sam ignored her. "You told me to come here and find Anderson's killer. This is the best chance we have."

"I don't want to know what you're up to right now. I wish you *had* been in a strip club."

"I *am* in a strip club, did I not say? Well, it's a party room, to be exact."

Emma gave up trying to get any more from him. "Do you need anything else from me?"

"No, by this time tomorrow we should have the Galahads and if we don't have the Nile, I may as well come home."

"Just be careful, Sam. Make sure you do come home."

Sam closed the call and turned round just as Dominique van Rossum walked back in.

TWENTY-SEVEN

NATASJA WALKED in still in the tight black dress, completely at ease in the strange surroundings.

"Everything okay?" asked Sam as she walked towards him.

"Perfect. We have the room for as long as we want it. They've cleared the alleyway behind the fire door so we can park up one of Vogt's vans and get Broad away once we've finished. And Boris'll let us know when Broad arrives."

Natasja placed one hand on his thigh and reached with the other to pick up her forgotten glass. Raising the glass to her lips, she left the resting hand where it lay.

Sam turned to look up into her narrow face. "Where's Vogt?"

"He's directing his team down the alleyway. If everything goes to plan, we'll have Broad in a station before midnight, plus we'll have the location of the Galahads."

"Cheers to that." Sam placed his hand round the curve of her back, the silk of the dress soft between his fingers. For a moment he fought the urge to call her by her birth name, to tell her that he knew her secret.

Natasja moved forward and kissed him gently on his cheek. "You see, there's nothing to worry about, we'll get your rockets back. Plus if Broad knows what's good for him, he'll tell us all he knows about the new contact and where he's meeting them next. This time we'll be ready for them."

"That's if he hasn't already either sold them or been captured."

She pulled away and rubbed his chin. "You are too negative, Taylor."

"Old habits."

Natasja pulled a face, but was interrupted in her reply by the entrance of Vogt. The two of them quickly parted.

The Interpol agent stepped into the room and held up three paper bags. "The private rooms are next door. You're in the wrong room unless you want an audience?"

The three of them ate the dinner of burger and chips.

"Oh, I forgot to tell you," Vogt piped up. "One of my team outside told me they got some early results back from the knife wound on De Klerk. It's only an estimate based on the photos, but they say it could well be the same knife that did for Anderson."

"Great, that means we have a knifeman to worry about," muttered Sam.

"That a problem?"

"It's not my ideal scenario," he confessed. "I've had some bad experiences with knives."

"That statement would normally be followed up with an explanation," Natasja chided him.

Sam swallowed a chip. "I was stationed at a base in Scotland when we were called to one of the barracks. A squaddie had come back drunk from a night off base. Went on a rampage and stabbed half his platoon before they were able to restrain him. And not before he had killed three of them. The barracks looked like an abattoir, blood everywhere."

Natasja and Vogt had stopped eating and were listening quietly.

"I was on clean-up duty. I also had to attend the autopsy of the three who didn't survive. Had to spend hours standing over a doctor as he examined the wounds. Don't think I'll forget it. All the time I was there, the doctor didn't stop talking about the intrigues of knifework on the human body."

"Learn anything useful?"

"Not to get stabbed. Basically, our bodies are not suited to it. Once the blade gets through clothes and skin, the rest of us is pretty soft. Apparently, it's why a lot of people's defence after killing someone with a knife is that they didn't mean to kill them. They just didn't realise how little strength is needed."

Vogt nodded and pointed at Natasja. "It's why so many wives who murder their husbands have used a knife. Negates the man's strength."

"Exactly," said Sam. "After the attack, we were all sent on a knife defence course. I think it was run by some Canadian sergeant who spent the day telling us not to do a Hollywood."

"A Hollywood?" Natasja asked.

"Yes, letting the attacker hit you to get an advantage or to land your own attack. He told us very seriously that the actors don't feel pain and it wouldn't take long before the loss of blood finished us off."

"Don't worry about that. I've been taking notes for next time." Natasja winked.

"No way I'll be giving you a second chance. But don't knock the defence classes. Saved my life once when dealing with an American at Camp David in Afghanistan. Was able to disarm him without receiving a scratch."

Sam sat back, remembering the out-of-control ranger swinging the steel blade at him. He'd had to fight all his natural instincts to get out of the way to step into the lunge and break the man's swing. A twist of the man's wrist and a kick to the groin had finished it. His audience listened with interest.

"Let's hope Broad brings a knife to our gunfight," said Vogt.

"When's it ever that easy?"

All three of them laughed. The relaxed atmosphere betrayed their nerves.

Sam's watch vibrated and he looked down at the digital screen to see a message from Emma.

24 hours before I call you in

Ignoring the warning, he pulled his sleeve over the screen and looked away. He noticed Vogt watching him.

"Why d'you bother with things like that?"

"Like what?"

"The smartwatch. Doesn't it drive you mad?"

Sam looked down at the square screen with its green silicone strap. It was one of the latest models and he was rather fond of it.

"No, why would it? Everything in one place. I haven't carried a wallet around for years."

"I don't get it, having endless notifications for everything in life."

"Ignore him," advised Natasja. "He thinks the world's following him via the evil CEOs of big tech."

"No, I just don't think it's healthy to have it on you all the time. Take that one Sam's wearing, for example. Can it track you?"

"Yes."

"Exactly, and that means your work will always be with you. What you need is one of these."

Vogt reached over into his coat pocket and pulled out a large plastic phone.

"Perfection – long battery life, two modes, text and call." The German lovingly patted it.

"I thought you didn't have a phone!"

"I said I didn't *like* them. Not my fault if people think I've not got one."

"You don't help by encouraging the idea."

Vogt checked his watch. "He'll be arriving soon. Natasja's arranged for Broad to be brought into this room. Once inside, the pair of you will interrogate him and get the location of the Galahads, right?"

"Why just us two? Where'll you be?"

"He's a law enforcement officer. He won't be able to use the same techniques as us," Natasja asserted, clearly having been already informed.

"What do you expect us to do to him?" Sam asked, unsure if he liked this aspect of the plan.

"Improvise," Vogt told him bluntly. "I'll be outside the fire doors in the van. When you're done, bring him to me and we'll reconnect by the vehicle. Understand?"

"Then we get the rockets?" Sam asked firmly.

"Potentially. Let's just see what we get out of our friend first."

Sam didn't like that answer at all.

"Good. I'll leave you two and check on the van. Any issues, we've got the radio mics."

Vogt stood up from the lounge, stretching his stubby legs as he fastened his coat. "One last thing, you two."

"Yes?" they said together.

"Don't fuck up."

Sam waited until Vogt had left before turning to Natasja. "What are you planning to do?"

She ran her hands through her long blonde hair. "Guess it kind of depends on him, really. If he's cooperative, we won't have to worry."

"You always make me worry."

"Relax, this room is soundproof. No one'll hear us."

"That wasn't what worried me."

The brown eyes sparkled. "If you're squeamish, just look away. But hide behind the bar when he arrives. Wait till the door is closed, then step out with your gun. I'll do the talking, you just cover me. Agreed?"

Sam grunted and sat back by the bar. It wasn't long before there was a knock on the door and one of the bouncers came in to tell them Broad had arrived. They looked at each other a final time before Sam went and crouched behind the bar. He reached down to his belt and pulled out the cold metal of the pistol. The whole thing was mad. Ever since he'd arrived in the country, things had just been crazy and now here he was, hiding behind a bar in a strip club's orgy room. One hell of a story.

Minutes passed and he listened before the door to the room opened and someone could be heard entering.

Natasja's voice drifted over to him, welcoming Broad into the room. "Would you like a drink before we begin?" Sam heard her offer.

"Yes please, I'll have a beer."

The footsteps grew closer.

"Of course, handsome. You sit yourself right here."

Sam heard the scraping of a bar-stool.

"I didn't know if you'd be here," Broad said nervously as he took his seat.

"How could I miss out on such a gentleman?"

Crouching behind the bar, Sam watched as Natasja walked round to join him. Her long legs were right in front of his face, the dress high on the thigh.

"Are all the girls here as good-looking as you?"

Sam grinned to himself, listening to Broad trying to charm the beautiful Dutchwoman.

"Stop it," Natasja giggled, "you're making me blush."

Sam had to admit, she was pretty good at this.

"What beer would you like?" asked Natasja, now fully behind the counter.

"Heineken, please."

"One moment then, sweetheart." She bent down and joined Sam below Broad's eyeline.

Getting the hint, Sam stood and raised the Glock to point directly at Broad's face. "Sorry, we're all out of Heineken."

"Jesus Christ." The shaken Broad jumped up, sending the stool flying backwards.

"Not quite."

"Who the hell are you?" Broad's handsome face changed from surprise to anger.

"Not Jesus Christ."

"Where's the girl gone?"

Natasja stood up next to Sam. "I see you've met my friend."

"What the hell's going on here? Who are you people?"

"We'll come to that in a minute. For now, let's talk about you," Sam told him.

Natasja walked back round the counter. "Let's move to the sofa, Mr Broad."

"How do you know my name?"

Sam cocked the Glock to reinforce the message. "We haven't the time for pleasantries. Quicker you do as she says, quicker you can go."

Broad scowled. "I hope you two know what you're doing. I'm a British officer."

"Who sells rocket launchers on the side," Sam returned coldly.

A look of shock came over the man's face. He turned pale and looked at both of them. "I don't know what you mean."

"Did you enjoy the Van Gogh Museum today, Captain James Broad?" Natasja walked up to him and grabbed him by the jacket, forcing him forwards.

"Wait," Sam instructed them, and walked round from behind the counter. Broad was wearing a black denim jacket, which Sam quickly checked for a weapon. Satisfied that he was unarmed, he let Natasja lead Broad to the soft leather sofa. Keeping the gun pointed at him, Sam took a position in the middle of the room. Natasja, meanwhile, sat a few feet from the shaken captain.

"It's very simple, James," Natasja said softly. "You tell us where the rockets are and when you're next meeting your contact. Then we'll let you go, no questions asked."

"I don't know what you're talking about," Broad insisted.

Natasja sighed and rubbed her face. "Both you and I know what I'm talking about. You are a British officer on assignment to NATO. You have a delivery of Galahad rockets and their launchers somewhere in the city. Which you intend to sell to a group known as the Nile."

"Just who the hell are you?"

"We are like your friends in the museum. You have something we want and we're prepared to do anything to get it."

"You should let me go before I report you to the police."

"Go to the police? You of all people don't want to do that. Last chance, are you going to help us?"

Broad remained silent and stared stoically back at her.

"Fine, I don't have time for this." She stood up from the long sofa.

Both men watched as Natasja paused for a moment to pull the dress down slightly and walk towards where she had left her coat. Bending over, she searched the pockets for something.

Out of the corner of his eye, Sam saw Broad begin to move. "Sit down you bastard," he growled at him.

Natasja stopped what she was doing and stood upright. Turning, she kept her hands behind her back.

"Last chance, Captain. No one knowing where those rockets are is just as good for me right now."

Broad didn't speak.

"Fine. I've had my fill of English officers right now." Natasja pulled her hand from round her back, raised the suppressor-covered pistol directly at Broad, then fired.

TWENTY-EIGHT

A SUPPRESSOR WOULD NEVER COMPLETELY SILENCE A FIRED round and the acoustic after-effects were still ringing in the enclosed room. Natasja and Sam watched as Broad lay spread out on the red leather. For a moment, it looked as if their guest had been killed as they waited for a reaction to Natasja's shots. Instead, Broad finally took a deep breath and turned to face them, careful not to cut himself on the fragments of mirror which had fallen around him.

"Not sure the management'll approve of the new decorations," Sam commented on the broken mirror and two new bullet holes either side of Broad's head.

"Do you know how many mirrors they've had to replace in here over the years?" she asked him, waving the gun around.

"I'm beginning to wonder if you've been in this room more times than you care to admit."

"Oh, I have no problem admitting to it."

"Who are you?" The shaken voice of Broad interrupted them both.

Sam uncocked his own weapon and stepped closer to their captive. "People who can help you. Enough of the bullshit. We know who you are and why you're here. You are trying to – and I really hope for your sake you haven't already – sell a set of Galahads to some pretty nasty people. You met with them today. I'm guessing the person you met with was a new guy, yes?"

Broad reluctantly nodded.

"That's because they killed the last one, just like they killed the last two people in your shoes."

Still, Broad didn't speak.

"I don't know what game you're trying to play here, Captain, but it needs to stop. You're in serious danger and if you don't let us help, you could be dead before tomorrow evening."

"Bullshit, they won't hurt me. They need me more than ever now."

"You really think that?"

"They're desperate, trust me. Today they even sent the top guy, some Eastern European. I've got them right where I want them. They need me."

"If you're trying to play them, you're in even more danger than you think. But thank you, I think you've just confirmed that you have not already handed them over."

"Well then, now's your time. Make me an offer."

Natasja laughed harshly. "How about we just shoot your knees off, then hand you over?"

Sam rolled his eyes. "Captain Broad, I don't know what you think you've got yourself caught up in, but I promise you, you will not be leaving this room until you tell me what I need to know."

"Fuck off."

"Can I shoot him for real now?"

"Not yet."

A knock interrupted them and they both turned to see the huge bulk of Boris entering the room. He looked past them, first at the pale Broad and then at the broken mirrors.

He let out a wide smile, showing bright white teeth. "Seven years bad luck, Natasja."

"I'll live."

"But will he?" He indicated Broad.

"What do you mean?"

"Your friend here was followed into the club."

Broad looked up. "No I wasn't, I'd have noticed. Plus, who would be following me?"

Sam looked at him scornfully. "Your friends at the museum for one, and us."

"Three men, Polish, all came in after this one. One of them even asked at the bar after him."

"Are they still there now?" asked Natasja.

"Yeah. Nasty-looking bastards, the lot of them."

"Nile men, it has to be."

Sam turned back to Broad. "Last chance then, it's us or take your chances with them."

Broad glared up at them. "Bullshit, it's a trick."

Boris shrugged and began to leave. "Suit yourself. I'll keep them out of here until you're finished."

"No wait," Sam called after the retreating bouncer. Turning to Natasja, he asked, "You okay in here for five minutes?"

She eyed Broad before answering. "Yes, I'll put one in his arm for now to keep him quiet."

"If you must," Sam said with a sigh. "Boris, can you show me the tail?"

Broad stuttered something but they all ignored him.

Boris's large round face broke into a grin. In his deep voice he replied, "Sure, my pleasure."

Leaving Natasja in the party room with Broad, Sam followed the bouncer back into the main part of the club. The room was fuller now, with more guests surrounding the tables and stages.

Boris first pointed to the bar. "There's two over there, in the dark coats."

Sam looked over at two bald men facing away from him.

"The other one is over there, by the exit." Boris swept his arm to the other side of the room.

Sam could just about see a featureless face.

"How do you know they're Polish?"

"Because I am," Boris told him. "I'd know the accent anywhere."

"I'm going to need your help."

"I'd already guessed. What's the plan?"

"Take out all three and bring them to the party room," Sam told him confidently. The sheer size of Boris gave him absolute confidence in what he was planning.

"I take it you're not going to be asking them nicely to join us?"

"That a problem?"

"No."

Sam thought for a moment. "Have you got any cable ties or something to restrain them?"

Boris gawped at him in disbelief, then motioned to one of his team from across the room to come over. Once arrived, he spoke in the man's ear and pointed out the lone target sitting at the table. The new man smiled excitedly and went off.

"That's one down, so me and you can deal with our friends at the bar."

Sam watched as Boris's man joined with another and began to make their way to the intended target.

"You going to be all right with just the two of us?" Sam asked.

He immediately regretted it. Boris stopped walking and looked at him accusingly.

"Yes, you're right, more than enough of us."

Boris grinned and patted Sam's shoulder. "You'll be okay, little army man. Natasja told me you're an old pro at this."

"So how do you want to do this?"

Boris reached out and took a glass from a half-naked waitress. Until that moment Sam had been so focused on the three Nile men, he'd forgotten he was surrounded by naked women. The realisation distracted him for a moment, until Boris pushed the glass into his hand.

223

"Take this and pour it on one of them. I'll do the rest."

The Polish bouncer grabbed Sam by the arm and pushed him towards the bar. Walking forward, he began to assess the two Nile men. Neither looked that inviting to entice to violence. From behind, there was nothing to choose between them. In the end, he decided to go for the right-hand man. It would mean his own right hand would have room to swing when needed, whilst his opponent would be encumbered by his companion. That was, if *he* was right-handed. But what if he was left-handed? That made Sam think about Anderson's killer. Whoever that was had been left-handed. Perhaps it was one of these two men.

Sam tensed himself to move in. Without breaking his stride, he walked straight into the right-hand man's back. He poured the whole glass downwards, covering the entire torso.

"What the fuck?" The man jumped to his feet, followed by his companion.

"Hey, excuse me, be careful. I'm walking here," Sam retorted, feigning to be the injured party.

The actual injured party ran his hand down his back. "I didn't move. You ran into me."

Straight to it, decided Sam. "Bullshit, you bald fucking ape. You owe me a drink."

Sam's theory on taking on the right-hand man went through the window. The dry companion had remained silent until then. Instead of words, he let his fists do the talking. Sam saw the round hook coming his way and blocked it with his elbow. Then jabbed forward with his right into the man's face. The speed of the shot forced the Nile man back more than the weight behind the fist. It had, however, left Sam open to the original target, who pushed him backwards. Sam had to wave his arms to regain his balance, losing valuable seconds.

The dry Nile man pressed his attack forward, aiming a low punch to Sam's stomach. Barely reacting in time, Sam forced the blow downwards and continued his retreat. All around them, people moved to escape the fight. Finding himself with a moment to counter, he landed a low kick to a knee, followed with a glancing blow to the temple. But now, the dry man was back and throwing punches blindly in anger. Sam dodged once, twice, and then landed his knee in the man's groin. Both of his attackers were now injured and Sam used the moment to take a step back to assess his next move. As he did so, he backed into the huge bulk of Boris.

Sam was pushed nonchalantly out of the way as the bouncer walked forward, grabbed both of the Nile men by the scruff of the neck, and slammed them together in one movement. Even amongst the blaring music, Sam heard a sickening crunch as both men's lights were put out. Boris just stood there holding the unconscious men in his hands. He turned to Sam, let out one of his white-toothed grins, and walked away. Following, Sam watched as the two Nile men were dragged across the floor. The speed and force of the violence had taken him completely by surprise.

"Why didn't you just lead with that?" Sam asked, catching up.

"Couldn't just have a bouncer beating up a customer for no reason. Bad for business."

They entered the corridor of private booths. The other bouncers were already carrying the other Nile man into the party room. Even from a distance, Sam could see the trail of blood dripping down one side of the unconscious face.

"Didn't take them long," commented Sam.

"They didn't mess around like whatever you were doing just then. All those blocks and dodges. Just hit the bastard next time."

They entered the room and Boris threw the two men onto the ground in front of Broad. The Englishman seemed to cringe away from the Nile men as a look of recognition dawned on his face.

"They were in my hotel when I left."

"Now you believe us?" said Natasja grimly.

Broad shook his head and tried to regain whatever was left of his faltering belief. Sam wondered why he so stubbornly refused to accept the truth.

"Could be a coincidence. There's no proof they wanted to cause me harm."

"Check their pockets," Sam told the bouncers.

Two of Boris's men went forward and searched the unconscious men's pockets. They removed three pistols, wads of rolled-up euros and three iPhones.

"See if any open with face ID."

The two men shoved each of the phones into the nearest face until one unlocked. They looked at Sam for further instruction.

"Give it to him." He indicated Broad. "Check the messages and photos; tell me what you see."

Broad took the phone. His facial expression dropped with each flick of his thumb. "There's just photos of me?"

"Now check the messages."

Broad did as he was told and flicked through again.

"There's just one thread, but it's in Polish."

"Then pick any of the bouncers in here. Ask them to translate. Go on. I don't know any of them."

Broad threw the phone at Boris, who caught it and then read aloud.

> Follow Broad back to the hotel. Room 217. 3am.
> Bring him back here.

"Not the smartest trio, they should have deleted the messages," Sam commented. "But pay peanuts, get monkeys. Yet I somehow think they would have found room 217."

Natasja laughed from where she was sitting and they all turned to look at her.

"What? I've never heard that one about monkeys."

Sam stepped over the prostrate figures on the floor and knelt in front of Broad.

"I'm going to level with you. Like I said, we need to know where the Galahads are, and I can't let you leave this room until you tell me. If you do, I promise you will be in the safest place possible. Somewhere these people, who you've got messed up with, won't be able to get to you. Or you can stay here and I'll let that tank of a bouncer show me how to hit someone properly."

He stared straight into Broad's face. Everyone else in the room stood still, watching the pair of them. Broad's shoulders dropped down, followed by his head.

"What do you want to know?"

"Later, I want to know everything... but for now, where are the rockets?"

Broad paused and took a breath. The bright vision of a bank account filled with euros was evaporating, to be filled with an uncertain future. "The P&O depot. Container three four six. A blue Kaye's Limited container. There's a lock on it and the code is forty-eight, fifty-eight, twenty-two. Once inside, there's a final lock; its code is 1942."

Sam gave Natasja the briefest of glances. They'd done it. Whatever else happened, the Galahads would be returned.

Staring back at Broad, Sam asked, "And the contact? When do you meet them?"

"Supposed to be tomorrow in the café at the Rijksmuseum. Same time as today. Third table from the far wall."

Sam stood up and looked down at the defeated Broad. The man was broken, but Sam was unable to find pity. Broad had been willing to fill his own pocket at the expense of innocent lives.

He turned to Natasja. "We'd best let Vogt know."

She nodded and went out of the room.

Broad looked up at Sam. "What happens now?"

"I told you we'd keep you safe."

"How?"

"By putting you in the safest place in the city right now. An Interpol holding cell."

Broad stood up in a mixture of shock and anger. "You never said that. You didn't tell me you were going to have me arrested."

Sam turned to Boris. "I think we owe you a beer."

"If these men are half as bad as Natasja says, it's a pleasure. It's important to show not all Poles are like them."

The bouncers turned to leave as three plain-clothes Interpol agents came into the room, Natasja and Vogt just behind them.

Vogt looked ecstatic. "Good job, Sam, Natasja. Love your work. Captain Broad, I'm very pleased to tell you that you're under arrest."

TWENTY-NINE

THEY WATCHED the van drive away into the Amsterdam night. Broad had finally cracked as two agents brought out the handcuffs. Tears had fallen down his handsome face. Sam felt nothing for the former fellow officer. He'd seen countless criminals taken to face their fate. Some had been innocent and had been free within hours. But watching as Broad was forced into the waiting van, Sam knew James Broad would not be returning for duty any time soon.

"I've another van coming for the three sleepers in there."

Sam turned to see Vogt stood next to him. The Interpol agent had lit one of his cigars and the smell of the tobacco drifted into the cold night air.

"What'll you do with them?"

"Keep them inside for as long as we can, if only for an unlicensed firearm charge."

"There's no worries about them warning the Nile any time soon. They won't be awake by the time we've picked up the Galahads."

Vogt eyed Sam for a moment. "We're not going for the Galahads, Sam. Not yet, anyway."

Sam turned on the small man, his anger simmering. "Don't say it, Vogt."

"I'm sorry, Sam, but they can wait. We're the only people who know where they are."

"It's not worth the risk. We can get them now before the Nile even know."

Vogt shook his head sadly. "We can't risk them finding out and going to ground. They have eyes all over the city and if anyone sees a police team charging into a shipping yard, they'll find out. We need them to come to the Rijksmuseum tomorrow. Without it, this will have all been for nothing."

"Bullshit, Vogt, you just want the glory of finding the Nile regardless of who gets hurt."

Vogt took the cigar from his mouth and pointed it at Sam. "Don't start being an idiot on me, Taylor. If we shut down the Nile, we stop any future Galahads falling into their hands."

"You're playing a dangerous game and I don't want anything to do with it."

Natasja walked out into the alleyway. "Well, the party room's free if anyone's up for it?" She stopped as she looked at the two men. "What did I miss?"

"He's leaving the rockets where they are." Sam waved his arm towards Vogt. "Just in case the Nile decides to collect them later."

"Taylor, this is my case and it's my decision. Your feedback is noted, but for now we do nothing."

"Fuck you, Vogt. Take your case and shove it up your arse, you slimy little bastard."

Vogt looked hurt. Sam immediately regretted the final comment, but it was too late.

Vogt regained his composure. "Thank you for your time, Mr Taylor. I think your help here is no longer needed. May I suggest you return to your hotel and we'll contact you in the morning. That is, if we need your further assistance."

Sam went to reply, but Natasja grabbed his arm. "Leave it; we're all tired and it's been a long few days."

"Just go, Taylor. You can have your rockets tomorrow. You can leave the Nile – and Anderson's killer – to the rest of us. Perhaps we may even do *your* job and prove who the insider is while we're at it."

"Come on, I'll drive you back to the hotel," Natasja urged him, and then more firmly, "We're going now, Sam."

She pulled him away from Vogt, who had turned to look for the next Interpol van.

"You shouldn't have said that to him."

"He's playing with fire, Natasja. He has no idea if those rockets will be safe."

"But you shouldn't have said that."

"The little bastard bit?"

"Yes."

"He'll have been called it before, hundreds of times."

Natasja stopped pulling and turned to stare at him. "Yes, he will have been called it probably a thousand times, but never by someone he both likes and respects. Think about it, to be in his position and with his size? He'll have had the abuse for years. But not from someone like you. You're different, you know the difference between a person's worth and their looks. Yes, he's playing a dangerous game with the rockets, but he knows the risks. Unlike you, he has to see the bigger picture and once you leave with your Galahads he's still left to pick up the pieces. You can disagree with him as much as you want, but you should still respect him and where possible, support him."

Sam didn't reply. He felt ashamed.

"Come on, the car's round here," she told him and put her arm in his.

They walked through the crowded streets, the sense of elation over Broad long gone now.

"I didn't know Vogt actually likes me," Sam admitted.

"Well, he does. He sees in you a kindred spirit."

"Really, how?" Sam couldn't help but chuckle.

"You both care. Too many people just do the job or the case. But you two work for the people."

She caught him looking across at her. "Stop it, don't you dare say anything, I'm just telling you the truth."

"I'm still worried about leaving the rockets. Perhaps me and you can check on them tomorrow?"

"Too risky. They could follow you to them. Now Broad's gone, they'll be even more desperate. Even more dangerous."

Sam debated the options in his head and realised that without Vogt's support he would have to wait.

Natasja drove them back through the city. Sam felt bone-tired watching the bright city lights flying past. They parked the small Skoda round the corner from the hotel. Natasja climbed out and retrieved a bag from the boot. Then, without a word of discussion, both walked into the hotel together. They moved through the lobby, past the bar and into the elevator. Exiting onto Sam's floor, he led her into the hotel room. She threw the bag onto the bed and unzipped her black dress, allowing it to fall to the floor in one fluid motion. Sam, meanwhile, turned on the shower and waited for her to join him under the hot water.

Later, Sam was sitting in the armchair drinking a large gin and tonic. He listened to the drone of the hair dryer coming from the bathroom. The warm shower followed by the ice-cold gin had restored his spirits significantly and he waited for Natasja to come back into the bedroom.

Moments later she returned, a towel wrapped round her midriff. "Hope you saved one of those for me."

Sam pointed to the filled glass on the tabletop and Natasja took a large sip. "I think we'll need to order some more of these."

"I think we'll need to, Dominique."

She stopped drinking and stood still for a moment before regaining her composure. "Ah, then I *definitely* know we will need to order some more."

She went over to the phone and dialled room service. After she finished, she climbed onto the bed and sat upright at the far end. Her long tanned legs stretched out before her.

"So, what do you want me to say? That I'm sorry I'm the granddaughter of an international criminal? That I'm sorry I lied to you? What difference does it make?"

"I don't know, I guess that's up to you to tell me. I'm not the one hiding anything."

Sam shifted in his seat and waited for her to begin.

"Fine, you want to know? Albert Wever is my grandfather, my father ran away from him in his early twenties when he found out about the Nile. He didn't want anything to do with any of it. Wever, although hurt, let him go. He never tried to contact him. My parents met and when they married, they took the name Van Rossum to protect us. They knew that sooner or later, Wever would make enemies. They took my maternal grandmother's name so both parties would have something new to start the marriage with."

"So, your mother wasn't a Van Rossum?"

"No, she was Natasja Corsel before she married my father."

Sam sat upright. "As in… Detective Corsel?"

"So you don't know everything. Yes, he's my uncle, my mother's brother."

"I thought he might be the mole, earlier today."

"What made you think that?"

"Something he said about you escaping from the Nile. Aside from me, you and Vogt, no one else should know that. Everyone else thinks you're working for them."

"A swing and a miss. He isn't the mole."

"Then I found out he was the one who found Wever's body. Sorry, your grandfather's body."

"Another swing and a miss. You didn't listen to me in the windmill, Taylor. You're still not listening to me now. I told you I let our man on the inside know I'd found him. Corsel just did the rest."

The realisation hit Sam like a wave. How could he have been so stupid? "So he was your man on the inside during the old days?"

Natasja rolled round on the bed and rested her head on his lap. "Of course! He was the best-connected sergeant in the force. Knew everything and everyone. He only became a detective to help me and Vogt try to find the mole."

The sly bastard, Sam thought, remembering the shared car journey. "And the windmill? Is that his?"

"Yes."

"I should have known. He told me he wanted to retire to one."

"He's a good man."

Sam stroked her hair. "I know. Tell me what happened to your parents."

A slight shadow crossed over her face. "They died in a car crash when I was fourteen."

"I'm sorry."

"It happens. Wever took me in. Until then, I'd never even known about him. But then out of nowhere he came, a complete stranger. But he looked after me. Taught me everything I know. You could say he always knew I'd get into the family business. When I did eventually join, he was the one who suggested I change my name again. You know, as a final precaution."

"I'm sorry about what happened to him."

"He didn't deserve to die like that. I know they killed him, whoever Broad met with today. They killed him, same for De Klerk and Franssen, they are just as bad. He was many things, my grandfather, but he was a good man. A kind man who found himself caught up in something that grew far beyond his expectations."

They paused for a moment, each reflecting on their childhoods – Sam growing up in the north of England with his family; Natasja being raised by her grandfather to take over an international criminal business.

Sam broke the silence. "Do you know the police think the Nile is named that to be a rival to Amazon?"

"Yes, Vogt told me. Wever would have found that funny. It's all because his small jewellery shop from years ago was called The Source of the Nile."

"Vogt knows your real name, doesn't he?"

"Yes. And about Corsel."

"He's a bastard."

Natasja looked up at him. "Why?"

"I told him my suspicions about Corsel earlier and he pretended to agree with me."

"He just wanted you to rule him out for yourself. You forget he's a clever man."

"He's still not found out who the real mole is."

"Between the three of us, we will. Vogt knew what he was doing bringing you in."

Sam thought about Vogt and the guilt about their last conversation swept back over him. "What happens now, then?"

She twisted her head and looked up at him. "When?"

"Tomorrow. I don't think I'm on the team anymore. Well, on the inside team, anyway."

Natasja studied him with her large brown eyes and placed a hand on his cheek. "Tomorrow, you apologise and we go on chasing those bastards. Trust me, your rockets are safe and Vogt will need you again. I will need you again. Maybe even this evening."

He grabbed her hand and kissed it. "I don't think you need anyone."

"You'd be surprised. I'm actually very complicated."

"That's for damn sure. Are you staying the night?"

"I am."

"You'll need to be gone before Bos picks me up." Sam stopped and remembered he was supposed to have been seeing his friend that evening. But there had been no contact from his Dutch friend.

Nor, for that matter, had Berger been in touch. For a moment, he felt slightly put out that his friends had forgotten him. Then a knock on the door announced room service and Natasja sat up.

"You get the drinks. I'll get into bed." Catching her towel as she flung it at him, he watched as she disappeared under the sheets.

THIRTY

HAVING SPENT the best part of the day watching over the investigation into the murder of Albert de Klerk, with its constant trickle of the different forensic teams, photographers, and finally medical personnel, Johannes Bos was ready to go home and crash. Not that there was any chance of that. Peter had rung to say that his mother had grown worse during the day and that he would have to stay at the hospital that evening. Bos would join him, the plans with Sam Taylor would have to wait. Sam would understand.

There was one final job to do that day and he knew he was putting it off. One last person who he should go and see to give the full details of what had happened. If only for their own safety.

He looked across at Hardenne, who had been standing outside waiting for him. "I think we can clear up here now."

The young officer looked genuinely pleased. "Okay, I'll start letting the guys know. Uniform have said they'll have people here overnight for us."

"Good, let Corsel deal with that. He'll probably know them from his sergeant days. Did Berger come back at all?"

"No, she's not been seen since she was called back to the station."

"Right." He would have liked Berger's company for this, even just for the sarcasm.

"I'll leave you to it; don't stay too long." Bos waved nonchalantly as he walked over the recently deceased De Klerk's gravel drive.

The drive took less than thirty minutes and he pulled the car into a visitor spot just as the man he'd come to see walked into his street. Hans Franssen stopped when he saw the marked police car outside his front door. The tall lean-framed man looked carefully at the vehicle before deciding to continue onwards. Bos waited until Franssen was level with the car before getting out.

"Good afternoon," he called.

Franssen came to a halt and stared at him. "Detective Bos, it's nice to see you again. Can I help you?"

Bos gestured towards the front door of Franssen's apartment building. "We need to talk."

Bos waited for Franssen to let them in and followed him through to the elevator.

"I must say, Detective Bos, we have seen each other far more than I'm comfortable with over these past few days."

Bos didn't reply as the elevator doors opened out onto the top floor. Franssen led him into the apartment. Stepping through the door and onto the tiled hallway, the pair of them walked into the kitchen area.

"Can I offer you a drink?" Franssen asked as he walked round the stone-topped island. "I've been out all afternoon, so wouldn't say no to something stronger than coffee this time?" He put his hands into his pockets and pulled out a set of keys, his wallet and a handful of receipts, then dumped them on the countertop.

Bos looked down at the assortment of items.

"I'm okay, thank you."

"Suit yourself. It's been one of those days." Franssen eyed him suspiciously. "What are you doing here, Detective Bos?"

"I need to talk to you about Albert de Klerk. He's been found dead in his home this morning."

Franssen stopped what he was doing and looked up at the police detective. "So she got him?"

"We don't know that right now, but I came to offer you my condolences and to repeat my offer of protection."

Bos looked down again at the counter, at the scrap of paper that had caught his eye the first time. It looked to be a receipt.

Franssen shook with agitation. "For the last time, I do not want anything from you people. You've already nearly me got me killed and now it seems you actually allowed De Klerk to be killed. You and your people need to leave me the hell alone."

Bos stared back at the Nile man. The visit had purely been a matter of courtesy, but it might yet reveal something far more useful. He put his hand in his pocket and eased out his phone.

"I'm sorry you feel that way. I appreciate this must have come as a shock to you." He looked behind Franssen to see the kitchen sink fitted against the wall, away from the island counter.

"When it comes to that woman, nothing is a shock."

Bos's fingers checked the silent button was switched in place on the phone's side. "I understand. I'm sorry I bothered you." He lifted the phone up to his face and turned on the camera. "Christ, is that the time? I'm sorry, it's been a long day for me as well. I've been at the murder scene all day."

Franssen's face softened slightly. "I'm sorry to hear that."

"It happens, it comes with the territory. But I will take you up on the drink offer. Just a water would be great, please."

Franssen looked as if getting his guest a glass of water was the last thing he wanted to do right now, but the long-held social customs of politeness held firm. Bos watched as Franssen moved away from the table. While his back was turned, he reached over the scattered items on the worktop. Three photos later, Bos had his phone back in his pocket and a glass of cold water in his hand.

He downed the water in one gulp. "Thank you. I'd better be leaving you now."

Franssen raised an eyebrow. "If that's all then yes, I guess I should say thank you for coming to check on me."

"My pleasure. You know where we are if you need us."

"I certainly do."

Back outside on the street, Bos stopped and breathed deeply. He looked up at the now darkening sky. Inside his chest, his heart was pounding. For months he had known that someone in the force had been working for that man, providing him with everything he and the Nile had needed to evade them. He felt sick, his stomach twisting in knots as he tried to steady his mind. The truth, which they'd all known but had never faced, was now in his hand. He twisted to look up at the building one last time, and at the bastard within its walls.

Walking to the car, he pulled out his phone and searched for a contact number for the venue on the receipt. He had to be sure.

A voice answered and Bos spoke. "Hello, this is Detective Johannes Bos of the Amsterdam police force. I need to come in and visit you. I'd like to review any CCTV footage you may have from this afternoon."

Hours later, Bos was back in the cabin of the canal boat where they had found the woman all those days ago. The plush cabin proved surprisingly comfortable and was the ideal location for the meeting that was about to take place. The police cordon had been removed that day, but the locals were still reluctant to come near. Bos had had no problem acquiring the key to the flimsy doors that led down from the wooden deck.

Bos looked at his phone once more, at both the photos he'd taken and the video he'd downloaded. There was no more doubt about it; he could clearly see what had happened. It was nearly time and he pulled the automatic pistol from its holster. Checking it was loaded, he prayed he wouldn't have to use it. He could have gone straight to his superiors, or to Sam or even to Vogt, but he needed this last test. To look her in the eye and to know why.

The boat creaked as a pair of feet climbed onto the deck. Bos tensed and leant backwards against the sofa. He was seated directly below the steps that led down into the tight cabin. A hand slowly pulled open the small doors and a slim figure made its way down the ladder.

Bos twisted in his seat and pushed his pistol into the torso of the new arrival.

"Ouch, is that really necessary?" Ada Berger asked her boss.

"I don't know yet, but for now let's keep it there," Bos replied in a firm tone. He leant forward and pushed his hand into the right-hand side of her jacket and retrieved her sidearm. "Come in and shut the door."

She did as instructed and made her way down into the small boat's depths. Bos watched her closely as she moved. Her long red hair was loose around her neck, the pale face lit by the warm lights of the sitting area. She looked at him with her slightly mocking stare.

"Bos, what's all this about? Why the secrecy? Why the gun?"

He ignored the questions. "Take a seat at the table and sit down, please. Keep your hands where I can see them."

She looked as if she was going to laugh at him.

"Sit down, Ada," Bos ordered, and finally she did as instructed.

"Johannes, please, what are you doing?"

Bos stared at her coldly, his anger barely kept in check. Everything that had gone on over the past year had been because of this woman. Still keeping the gun trained on her chest, he threw over the phone.

"Look at it."

Ada took the phone between her soft fingers and studied the image on the screen.

"It's a coffee receipt. What about it?"

"Whose order is on the paper?"

"How the hell am I supposed to know?"

"It's for a skinny chocolate latte with a caramel shot, chocolate sprinkles and extra sugar."

She paused for a moment before replying. "So what? It could be anyone's. What does it matter?"

"It matters as I found it in Hans Franssen's house." He let the name hang in the air.

Ada Berger closed her eyes. "Right, and that automatically means I've been having nice little coffee chats with a suspected member of the Nile. Get off it Bos, you're losing it."

"That's what I hoped, Ada, that just because I'd had a long day I was overthinking it. That my deputy, my colleague, my *friend*, wasn't working for the man we'd been trying to lock up for over a year."

"I'm not!"

"You're a bad liar, Ada. Flick across the image."

She did as instructed and turned the image over to see a CCTV video appear. Pressing play, she watched as her afternoon rendezvous with Hans Franssen played out on the small screen. As it ended, the tall Franssen leant over and kissed her cheek before leaving the table. Bos studied her as she watched the footage, wondering if she would continue to deny it.

Ada put the phone on the table and looked up at Bos. "I don't know what you want me to say."

"The truth."

"Simple, money. There's no hidden motive or passion driving me here. I couldn't care less about the Nile or its customers. I just want to be able to go home and live a life I want. But it's pretty hard on our wages to do that, honestly."

"If that helps you sleep at night."

"Says the man married to a wealthy investment banker. Don't try to take the high road with me. You wanted to know why, that's your answer."

"Fair enough. Point taken."

"Why have you brought me here? Why not just have me arrested tomorrow in the office?"

"Because I needed to know it was true."

Berger heard the pain in Bos's voice and looked away. No one spoke, the betrayal of the past year lying between them like a chasm. The old boat creaked against its moorings.

"I'm sorry, Johannes." She used his first name for the first time.

"I highly doubt that."

"I am. I never wanted to hurt you, or anyone else for that matter."

"Last year, it was you who betrayed the raid, wasn't it?"

Berger hung her head.

"Say it."

"Yes, but I never wanted you or Sam to get hurt. You changed the plans by going in with the armed units. If both of you had stayed in the car, then–"

"Then Sam would never have been shot."

"Yes."

"I have no idea what you're going to say to him when he finds out."

Berger just stared at him, refusing to answer.

"Fine, I'll leave you to think on it."

"What happens now?"

The Head of the Organised Crime Unit stared at her with a mixture of disgust and pity. He'd spent months thinking about who in the force had betrayed them. He had even discussed it with the wretched woman. Now all he saw was a stranger.

Bos stood up, almost brushing the roof of the cabin. His friendly face with its long blond hair, now looking strained and sunken, shadows had formed under his eyes. "We go to the station right now. No one else knows about this at the moment, so we can keep it quiet until it's been decided what to do with you. I'll have to leave it to the commissioner and Vogt to decide."

Berger's face suddenly turned pale, losing all of its remaining colour. Her eyes widened in fear and she gasped, "No, don't!"

Bos had not been looking at her as he pocketed the phone. Only the tone of her voice made him look round at her curiously. When he saw she was not looking at him but at the doorway, he spun round on his heel. A figure dived at him from the top of the stairs and forced him down to the deck. The gun Bos had been holding flew from his grip. Berger could only watch on as Bos fought with Marcel Dudka in a desperate struggle. Bos's height was no use to him now as he lay there with the younger Dudka above him. In Marcel's left hand, Berger saw the bright silver blade hovering over Bos's chest.

Neither man called for her aid in their tussle, both were focused on forcing all their strength into the tug of war for the knife. The point of the blade briefly touched the cotton of Bos's shirt before he twisted his shoulders to somehow flip his opponent and the blade. Now on their sides, the two men clung to each other's hands, the blade pointing upwards, each trying to force an advantage. As Berger watched on, fear filled her mind. Steps above them on the deck brought her to her decision and she leapt down to join the physical battle below her.

Placing her hands on the hilt of the knife, she joined forces with one set of arms and pushed with all her might. The eyes of the man in front of her expanded in shock and then fear as the knife twisted towards him. Together, the two sets of arms pushed forwards through clothing, into flesh, grinding between ribs and into the heart muscle. For a moment, the wounded man fought on before his strength failed and between them, they forced the sharp blade down to the hilt.

Ada Berger flung herself backwards and climbed onto the sofa, her own heart still beating hard in her chest. Panting, she couldn't look away from the lifeless eyes that stared up at her, the last moments of life etched within.

Marcel Dudka stood up from beside Johannes Bos's lifeless body. He flexed his arms as he looked down at his victim. The pale face twisted to one side as he studied the scene. Crouching, he bent and twisted the knife to drag it free.

"Are you okay?" Hans Franssen's face appeared at the head of the stairs.

"Yes, I think so," Ada mumbled, still looking down at Bos.

Franssen made his way down the steps, pausing only to let

Marcel slide past. The younger brother had not even spoken. Instead, his work complete, he left them alone in the cabin.

Franssen studied the body for a moment, then took Ada's hand, moving her away. "You were right to call us when he suggested meeting. Did he say how he knew?"

Berger, still in shock, gestured backwards. "He had a photo of our receipt from today and CCTV from the café."

Franssen looked at her in shock, the thin face worried. "Where did he get that from?"

"By the tabletop the receipt was on, I would have guessed it was your kitchen."

The watery eyes blinked a moment. "The bastard must have got it when he came over today."

"I wouldn't worry, he's not told anyone else. He told me he wanted to be sure first."

"That indecision cost him his life."

Berger watched as Franssen bent down and removed the dead man's phone. He studied it for a moment in his slim fingers before, opening a window, he dropped it overboard.

"We need you to concentrate, Ada. The organisation is in trouble and we need your help."

The red-haired beauty did not reply, so Franssen continued. "Tomorrow, make sure the police find the body. It will put them under more pressure. By the sounds of it we've lost one of our suppliers this evening, so may need to do something a little drastic. Ada, did you hear me? We want you to make sure they find the body tomorrow."

Finally, Detective Ada Berger looked up from the body. She flicked her hair back and flexed her shoulders.

"Fine, but you can tell those masters of yours my price has just doubled."

THIRTY-ONE

SAM LAY with his eyes closed in the morning sun. Starting from his toes, he stretched and tried to bring life to his stiff joints. Finally reaching his neck, he turned in the bed to see Natasja lying next to him, watching him with a bemused smirk.

"You look terrible," she chided him.

"We can't all wake up looking pristine like you," he said, admiring her in the light that escaped from the curtains. Her full lips curved into a smile and she kissed him.

"It's all genetics. You either have it or you don't."

Sam raised his eyebrows and pushed her backwards, reached over her for his phone on the bedside.

Natasja tutted. "Is that what you do? You wake up to find a naked woman in your bed and you go for your phone, to what – ring your mother up?"

"My mother wouldn't approve of a girl like you," he told her as he swiped.

She hit him with a pillow before climbing out of bed. Sam watched her walk across the room before returning to the phone. He was surprised not to have had a message from Bos. Checking his smartwatch, the digital numbers told him they had slept past the time he'd usually have collected him. With everything that was going on with Peter, he decided to leave it. The only message he had received was from Berger, asking what time he'd be in the office that morning.

"Anything interesting?" Natasja asked as she pulled out a new set of clothes from her bag.

"No, looks like I'm not as popular as I used to be."

"Well, you have started hanging round with a bad crowd."

They ate a room service breakfast and still received no word from Bos or anyone else on the team. Sam was conscious of his parting words to Vogt. Perhaps the agent had meant what he'd said and he was in fact out in the cold. The morning wore on and Sam suggested to Natasja that she contact Vogt.

"It doesn't work like that. Well, unless there's a problem. Don't worry, he'll be in touch."

"It's not him I'm worried about." Sam had tried ringing Bos three times since breakfast. Each call had gone to voicemail. He wondered whether Peter's mum had passed away in the evening, leaving Bos off the grid. He didn't reply to Berger. Somehow, having Natasja next to him, it didn't seem right.

Eventually it was Natasja's phone that rang. She answered it and spoke quietly into the microphone. Sam watched, trying to read her facial expression. There was a slight flicker as her eyes widened in surprise, but then she regained her composure. Hanging up, she stood up and threw Sam the green field jacket.

"Come on, Vogt wants to see us." She said no more, instead waiting for Sam to tie his boots. He hung the Glock from his belt as Natasja picked up the Walther.

Natasja still didn't tell him where they were going, or why. Even as they made their way downstairs, she refused to go into it. Instead, she drove the pair of them away from the hotel and back into the city.

"Where are we going?" Sam finally asked as they entered the city's maze of streets.

"It's not far. I'll have to park up and you can walk round. It's probably not the best idea for me to be seen there. Especially since last time I was there, I was pretending to be dead."

Sam eyed her across the car. "Why are we going there of all places? Back to the boat?"

She shrugged. "Vogt'll be able to tell you."

"That's if he's still talking to me."

"He will be. Don't worry about that."

Natasja parked the Skoda down a side street. "It's just down the road we came off. Walk down there and you'll see the police cars."

"Police cars? What's going on?"

She looked at him and patted his arm. "You need to speak to Vogt."

Sam did as he was told and climbed out into the street. A thin drizzle was driven into his face by a stiff breeze as he turned around. It felt as if winter could not be far away as the cold air penetrated the thin field jacket. He shivered as he walked and stuffed his hands deep into his pockets. Walking round the corner, back onto the main road, he saw the first blue flash of a police car in the distance. Heading towards it, he tried to guess what could have happened.

Nearing the scene, Sam saw two uniformed officers keeping a small crowd back from the familiar blue canal boat. Looking past them, Sam could see people moving about trying to cover the rest of the scene. There was Ada Berger, deep in conversation on her phone. Sam's eye was drawn to the strange figure of Hardenne sitting on a bench within the police cordon. From where Sam stood at the back of the small crowd, he looked to be crying.

"Hey Sam," a voice hailed him.

Sam looked to see Corsel beckoning him from the other side of the police tape. Sam waved and began to push through the crowd.

"What's happening?" he asked as he reached the older detective.

Corsel looked at him in shock. "You don't know?"

"No, I've only just arrived. No one's spoken to me all morning."

Corsel looked uncomfortably at him and grabbed his arm, pulling him towards the boat.

"Where's Vogt and Bos?"

"Vogt's on the boat. I think it best if he tells you," Corsel mumbled. "I'm really sorry."

Sam stopped and pushed Corsel's hand from his arm. "What do you mean you're sorry?"

Corsel shrugged, he looked unusually dishevelled this morning. The rain had soaked his hair and was now dripping down his face.

"Where's Bos?" Sam asked him again, firmly.

When he received no answer he asked yet again, this time a strain of anger in his voice. "Where's Bos, Corsel?"

"He's inside." Vogt spoke from the deck.

Sam turned to look at him. "What do you mean, he's inside?"

"Sam, Bos is dead. He was found inside the boat this morning."

Sam felt as if he'd been shot again. The shock of Vogt's words may not have physically thrown him backwards, but inside he felt as if he'd been knocked off his feet. A knot grew within his stomach, which he had to swallow down. Around him, people had stopped what they were doing to watch. Hardenne, tears mixing with the rain, looked up. Berger stopped speaking on the phone to watch, too. But Sam had no perception of the people around him. Instead, he looked down at the Interpol officer and spoke in a low voice. "Show me."

Vogt turned on his heel and led Sam onboard the small vessel. The wood was slippery from the rain as his boots found their footing.

"In here." Vogt led him down into the cabin.

Stepping down into the cosy room, Sam looked down at his friend. The body, still in the grip of its final battle for life, lay on the floor. Its owner's face, once a beacon of friendship, now appeared drained of all that once made it unique. Sam's experienced eyes flew over the crime scene. The table, its chairs, the sofa and of course, the body. The red stain across the chest was the giveaway clue to his friend's final demise.

"He was found this morning; a neighbour tipped us off to say something wasn't right here. We arrived not long after. The crime-scene investigation team are just setting up outside before they begin. But I would say I've seen enough bodies to guess he's been dead since late last night." Vogt spoke softly, treading carefully with every word. "What do you think?"

"What do I think?" Sam scoffed. "What do I think."

"What happened? What does it mean? Is it like De Klerk? It's certainly similar – knife wound, tip-off on the morning of a major deal."

Sam knelt by his friend. The body covered nearly the entire floorspace. He agreed with Vogt's time of death. The pain of his fight for life was etched across Bos's face still. "So you think this is another one of the Nile's people being killed for our benefit?" Sam asked drily, the sarcasm barely hidden in his words.

"I'm not saying that."

"Good, because you'd be wrong. This is not like De Klerk. It is probably the same murderer, but this is not the same."

Vogt waited for Sam to continue.

"Look at the body. Bos fought his attacker. Whoever killed him had a hard time doing it. When the pathologist looks at him, he'll find bruises on his arms and hands. If he'd been working for them, it would have been the same as De Klerk. No messing around. If I had to guess, I think they wanted to see if they could find out where Broad had got to. But Bos managed to fight back."

"I'm not saying you're wrong, Sam, but it's a stretch."

"*Everything* has been a goddamn stretch. Has Peter been told yet?"

"No, the commissioner will go round soon."

"Good, then I'll leave you to it while I go and get my rockets."

"What?"

Sam stood up and pushed past him back to the deck. "You heard me. I've had enough of playing everyone else's game. I'm taking things into my own hands and you can either join me or get the hell out of my way."

They had made their way back into the open air and Sam's voice had attracted the attention of everyone on the street.

"Sam, I'm sorry about Bos, but think about it. Think about what we are trying to do here."

"It's too late, Vogt. I'm going and if I'm lucky, perhaps I'll run into someone from the Nile."

Sam stood on the deck and for the first time since hearing the news of his friend's death, he looked around him. A dozen faces turned to stare at him, faces all covered by the fine unrelenting rain. All looked despondent, defeated in their year-long pursuit of what seemed a mythical organisation. An organisation it seemed could reach out from the shadows and take one of their own. He saw Berger and walked over to her.

"I'm so sorry, Sam," she began, embracing him. "Bos? I can't understand."

Sam placed his hand on her back and patted it gently. "I know."

She stepped away and looked at him. The thick red hair was kept dry by the hood of her coat. "What do we do now? How do we even try?"

"We'll find them, Ada. But I've got to go and do something."

"You do?" she asked quizzically.

"I'll speak to you later."

She looked like she wanted to ask more questions but Sam, now pressed for time, had already walked away. He nodded at Corsel, remembering his relationship to Natasja, as he headed back the way he came.

"Sam, wait," Vogt commanded. "If you must do this, I'm coming with you."

Surprised, Sam turned to look at the small Interpol agent as he ran after him.

"I don't agree with you on this, but if you have to do it, at least let's do it right."

Sam nodded and continued heading back to where Natasja waited. The pair of them walked out of the cordon and through the crowd.

"I'll get a couple of vans to meet us there," Vogt said as he tried to keep up with Sam's pace. "We can try to get them away before anyone sees us. It'll still give us a chance to go to Broad's afternoon meeting."

Sam wasn't listening. His mind, usually so tuned in to his surroundings, was all over the place. A cold anger had taken him over and he barely acknowledged the breathless Vogt as he struggled to keep up.

In his haste to get back to the car, he failed to notice the two men tailing them. He also failed to register the white van parked on the side of the road, a black Land Rover alongside. The first he knew of any trouble was the appearance of three men stepping out onto the pavement. His instincts began to kick in and he tried to quicken his pace.

"For Christ's sake, Taylor, slow down," Vogt panted.

"Stay behind me," Sam instructed as the two parties closed in.

Vogt suddenly saw what Sam meant. "Shit."

The three approaching men split. One went towards Vogt and two for Sam. Beside him, Sam felt Vogt try to reach for his firearm, but it was too late. In broad daylight, in the middle of Amsterdam, the Nile had struck. The two men in front of Sam went to grab his arms. In response, Sam drove between the pair of them, twisting round to land a solid kick to the back of one's leg, followed by a quick jab to the kidneys. As the injured man went down, Sam felt anger swell within him. Days of frustration, followed by the pain of Bos's death, now let loose in this moment.

Beside him Vogt was being overpowered, but Sam was powerless to help as the second man attacked. He had chosen to lead with a full roundhouse punch, which Sam swerved to avoid. As the blow went past, Sam grabbed the outstretched arm and pulled it past him. He was now back to his original starting position and, still holding the off-balance attacker, he threw him into the nearest wall.

Now able to turn his attention to Vogt, he began to step forward when a screeching noise distracted him. Hands reached out towards him from the open van. Sam tried to step back but fell into one of the fallen attackers. Deciding attack was the best form of defence, he prepared to charge his way out, when from nowhere his vision blurred. The world in front of him wavered and then disappeared.

Vogt, his whole body locked in his attacker's firm grip, could only watch as the two men who had been following them finished beating Sam with the metal bar. The Englishman staggered once, twice, then fell into the arms of new attackers reaching from inside the van. They dragged him inside it before turning their attention back to Vogt. It only required one other person to overpower Vogt and within moments, he too was thrown inside.

An unseen voice gave an order in a language Vogt didn't recognise and the van lurched forward. Vogt, still in shock at the audacity of the attack, felt rough hands searching his pockets. They quickly found the phone and pistol. A pair of handcuffs were placed tightly on his wrists before he was thrown to the back of the van. Lying there, he watched as the unconscious Sam was searched. One of the guards handed his phone and Glock to the man in the passenger seat.

Another voice spoke and Vogt's heart jumped as he saw the flash of a knife. An arm grabbed the sleeve of Sam's coat and slashed the knife between his wrist and the green watch strap, slicing the skin. The soft silicone broke apart in an instant and the guard passed the watch over after the phones. For a moment, the van was filled with the noise of the city as a window was opened and the collection of electronics flung out of it.

THIRTY-TWO

SAM'S SENSES began to fire signals back into his brain. The first signal that fired was pain. The dull throbbing pain that pounded his head overtook all other available senses. Eventually, this was replaced by the uncontrollable urge to vomit, which triggered the rest of his faculties to come back into focus. He rolled over and vomited. The concussion sickness ripped at his insides as their contents spilled out.

Spitting the last remaining vestiges from his mouth, he opened his eyes. He found himself in a brightly lit storeroom. Dotted all around them were empty boxes and between them, slumped against the wall, was Vogt.

"Good to see you still alive."

"I don't feel it," Sam replied as he lay back on his side.

The taste of vomit burned at the back of his throat. His head was throbbing and he hesitantly placed a hand to feel for the damage. A large lump could be felt through his hair. Dried blood felt sticky to his touch, but he was glad not to feel any cracks in his skull.

"Still in one piece?" asked a concerned Vogt.

"I think so?" Sam answered as he slowly tried to raise himself. The only outlandish sensation beyond his head came from a wetness round his left hand. Looking down, he could see a deep cut starting from the top of his wrist and slanting downwards.

Sam swore. "The bastards took my watch." He studied the deep cut and flinched as he saw a flash of white where blade had reached bone.

"I know, and our phones."

Sam rose and sat upright to assess the place they were in.

"Where are we?"

"I don't know, but I'd bet a month's pay it belongs to our Nile friends."

Fighting back the clouds that were congregating within his mind, Sam asked, "What happened?"

"We were ambushed. As we left the crime scene, they were waiting. There were too many of them. It wasn't our fault."

Sam's mind tried to register Vogt's words. Suddenly, the events of the past day hit him like another blow to the head. Broad's capture, Natasja... and then Bos, sprawled lifeless on the deck. The concussion sickness returned and he leant to the side and retched.

Vogt watched on in silence as Sam wiped his mouth. "We need to do something about that wrist," he told him, pointing to Sam's left arm. "I tried to tear off some clothing, but..." He left the sentence unfinished, embarrassed to admit he hadn't been strong enough.

Sam looked round for something to tie his wrist up, but beyond the boxes around them, there was nothing. "My coat. I'll be able to take the sleeves off."

Slipping the green field jacket off his shoulders, he gave the material a hard pull at the sleeves, ripping the seams apart. After a few minutes of medical improvisation, Sam's cut was covered tightly.

"Guess they taught you that in the army?"

"Yes, but in the military police you spend more time putting them on others than yourself."

Vogt grinned grimly. "Nothing changes there."

"What about you? Are you hurt?"

"Nothing a cigar and a whisky won't solve."

It was Sam's turn to grin. "Would prefer a gin."

"When we get out of here, I'll buy you a bottle."

Sam looked round the room again. "So where's *here?* Did you see anything?"

Vogt shook his head and walked round their small prison. "Nope, the van they caught us with drove right in. It's a warehouse of some sort. They dragged me out and carried you up some stairs, through an office and into here."

"How long were we driving?"

"Difficult to say but it felt like half an hour to forty minutes."

"Bastards. Did they ask you anything?"

"Not yet, but I expect they'll be asking one question."

"Where are the bloody rockets."

Vogt grimaced. "Yes. I'm sorry, Sam."

Sam bit his tongue. This was not the time for recriminations.

"Did they get Natasja?"

"No."

"Then that's one thing."

"What can she do? She's alone in a city where both sides of the law are looking for her."

Sam rose painfully to his feet, the pain in his head making him unsteady. "I'd bet a lot more than either you or me could do."

Slowly, careful not to lose his footing, Sam walked over to the door. He tried the handle.

"Nothing ventured, nothing gained," he uttered as he walked back to join Vogt.

They both sat back on the floor, facing the locked doorway.

"So what's the play here?" Vogt asked.

"Time, that's all we can do. They desperately need the rockets and we would quite like to get out of here. We have to give Natasja as much time as we can though."

Vogt sighed and rubbed his arms. He'd not told Sam of the

pain throughout his body. He'd been dragged up the stairs by a guard and the bruising was beginning to ache.

Neither knew how long they waited. Sam tried counting in his head but the blow was still taking time to recover from. Eventually, a voice came through the door.

"We're coming in. Stand up at the back of the room with your hands in the air. If you move, you'll be shot."

The pair of them eyed each other, but did as they were told. Standing slowly, they raised their arms and waited. The door opened slowly at first, then flew open to reveal four guards waiting for them. Semi-automatics aimed into the room.

"If you're room service, you're a bit bloody late," Sam told them.

"Ah, the Englishman is alive," a voice called out from behind the guards. "Stand back and let him through. It's about time we met."

The guards moved back from the doorway to give both Sam and Vogt room to walk out. Stepping out into an office, Sam saw a large wooden table with a number of chairs laid out around it. Three men sat waiting for them. On the right sat the tall figure of Hans Franssen, the wispy grey hair combed backwards. He was still dressed in a full three-piece suit, but Sam was quick to notice there was a distinct lack of smartness in the once crisp outfit.

Next to Franssen were two men Sam didn't know. The one on the left he realised with disdain was the pale-faced man from the Van Gogh Museum lift. So it had been him who had tripped him up into the school party. The skull-like face looked at them with complete indifference. Sam felt in the pit of his stomach that this must have been the man who had killed Bos, De Klerk and Anderson. The man emanated death.

Between them both, sat the man whom Sam took to be the man in charge. The large overweight leader of the Nile sat back and smiled at the new arrivals. Placing the tips of his fingers together, he sat back in his chair, the alcohol-induced red face protruding a large smile of welcome.

"Good to see you on your feet again, Mr Taylor," the man in the middle greeted him. "Take a seat, the pair of you. I took the liberty of getting you some food brought over." He waved to two sets of packaged sandwiches, crisps and unopened bottles of water.

Knowing there was nothing to be gained from refusal, the pair of them sat opposite their captors. Sam mirrored their host, grabbed a bottle of water and leant back in his chair. Vogt took a sandwich and sat next to him.

The man in the middle smiled at them. "So, welcome to the Nile, gentlemen. I guess I should introduce myself. My name is Jakub Dudka and this fine fellow on my right is my brother, Marcel. You both know my associate, Hans Franssen."

Marcel Dudka didn't move a muscle as his brother spoke. Franssen, on the other hand, glared at the two officers. The four guards remained standing behind Sam.

"Thank you for your warm welcome. I'm Jack Parker and this is my partner, Barry O'Neill. It's not often we engineers from the sewage and waste works get such a warm welcome," Sam replied.

"Yeah, normally it's just the same old shit," Vogt added, between a mouthful of cheese and ham. "You should try the sandwich, Parker. It's good stuff."

"You know what, O'Neill, I think I will. There's a good old saying in the sewage and waste works. Eat when you can." Sam reached over and opened his sandwich.

Jakub Dudka watched on, an amused smile etched upon his face. "Honestly, I love the humour, an Englishman and a German making jokes. I could watch you all day. But I think not. Sam Taylor, English Foreign Office Repatriation Officer."

"British," Sam cut in. "I've pals from Scotland who'd not like that."

Jakub raised his eyebrows and continued. "Karl Vogt, Senior Interpol Agent."

"And future Olympic high jumper," Vogt interrupted him.

Sam laughed out loud, spitting a mouthful of water.

"Very good, but I don't think so." Jakub continued, "Shall we just cut the cards and get right to it?"

"I mean if you have to, but I'd like another sandwich if I can, please?" Sam asked.

This time, Jakub ignored him. "We all know why we are here. I need something, which you can provide me with. In situations like these, there are always two options. One, you do it my way and there may be a way out for you. Or you do it my brother's way and there is no way out."

Neither Sam nor Vogt answered. Instead, Sam spoke to the other Dudka brother.

"Oi you, chatty. Was it you who killed my friend?"

The dark-green eyes turned to stare at Sam. "Who was your friend?"

"You know who, you slimy bastard. Did you kill him?"

"Maybe, I don't keep track."

"Then I will when I get out of here."

Jakub firmly put his hand on the table. "Mr Taylor, please. The Galahads, shall we?"

"Shall we what?"

"Shall we discuss where they are? I think we can be adults about this. I know from my sources that you have Captain Broad, but you have not shared this with the Amsterdam police force. Which leads me to deduce that only you know where they are currently residing."

Vogt and Sam remained quiet.

"Fine, let's make this easier, shall we? I'll pay both of you the same amount I had agreed with Broad. One million each."

Vogt and Sam eyed each other.

"That's a big number," Sam admitted. "But I think if I'm selling my soul to the devil, I'd like a bit more for it. One point five."

Dudka didn't flinch. "Fine."

"That makes it interesting, but we'll need a few hours to discuss it," Vogt added.

"You have two minutes." Jakub tried to sound threatening, but when Vogt and Sam burst out laughing, he frowned. "You think this is funny?"

"You really are desperate for these rockets, aren't you? I take it you've really pissed somebody off this time."

"I don't think so, Mr Taylor."

"Come off it. You're scared, Mr Dudka. First, you start knocking off your own people, then you let a piece of shit like Broad push you around. Now you've just lied about being willing to pay us off. You're shitting yourself."

"I did not lie to you."

"Yes you did, there's no way you'd let either of us walk out of here. You're going to kill us even if we give you the Galahads all wrapped up for Christmas."

Jakub Dudka looked disapprovingly at the pair of them. "I see where this is going, gentlemen. You may be right about the end result, but there's still the choice of which path to take. So you'd prefer option two, then?"

Marcel Dudka rose to his feet and took off his jacket. At the other side of the table, Franssen's face turned distinctly pale. The younger Dudka walked round to stand behind Vogt and waited for his brother's instruction. At a nod from Jakub, the four guards rushed forward and grabbed the pair of them by the arms.

"Start on the little fella first please, Marcel."

"I won't tell you anything, you fat bastard."

Marcel leant forward and placed Vogt's hand on the table.

"I know you won't." Jakub gestured at Sam. "But he will. Begin."

Quick as a flash, Marcel Dudka's other hand came out and drove a knife square into the back of Vogt's hand. The Interpol agent let out a gasp of pain but was kept in his place by the two guards.

Sam tried to force himself free from his own restraints, but the two arms were going nowhere. "You evil bastard," he snarled at Marcel.

The Dudka brother just shrugged and twisted the hilt of the knife further into the back of Vogt's hand.

Vogt screamed.

THIRTY-THREE

MARCEL BEGAN to draw the knife slowly from its position and the two guards relaxed their grip on the small man's arms. Vogt grasped his bleeding hand in the other. A mark on the wooden table showed where the tip had gone clean through. Putting the pain to one side he glared at his tormentors, but did not speak. Marcel instead turned the chair round to face him. Picking Vogt up by the front of his jacket, he held him up to his face. The pale face smiled once, before slamming the forehead into the bridge of Vogt's already squashed nose.

The dull thud of the blow could be heard across the room. Sam still fought against his captors. Marcel, grinning at the broken nose, then threw the unfortunate Vogt across the room into a side table. The smaller man landed with a hard crash before falling to the ground. Still restrained, Sam could only watch as the younger Dudka ran forward and began to violently kick the now prone Vogt again and again. The action seemed to ignite an animalistic side within the pale man. Marcel seemed to have lost any control as he rained down the blows. Each kick drove the beating on and on, until Sam began to fear the worst. Vogt had fallen silent, no cries or screams came from the crunched-up body.

Marcel finally paused for a moment. Regaining his

composure, he grabbed the barely conscious Vogt upright by his hair. Twisting the face round towards Sam, Marcel pressed the blade of his knife against Vogt's cheek. A thin trail of blood began to appear as the blade made its way towards Vogt's broken nose.

"Enough," Sam shouted.

"Marcel." Jakub stopped his brother.

Marcel paused, the blade inches from Vogt's nose. The pale face looked up from his work to stare at his brother. The younger Dudka seemed almost disappointed to have had his enjoyment halted.

Jakub waved his hand at Sam. "It seems our friend has something to say."

"Sam, no," Vogt groaned. Marcel yanked the dwarf's head back and twisted his grip.

Jakub laughed, a low-pitched cough-like noise. Sam wanted to hit the red-faced bastard.

"You slimy prick."

Jakub laughed again. "If you're going to tell me to pick on someone my own size, I'd say you're not as original as I first thought."

"No, I was going to ask if your mother put you up for adoption together or individually."

Vogt spat a lump of blood from his mouth and chuckled until another kick from Marcel silenced him.

"Tell me where my rockets are or I'll have my brother cut your friend to pieces. Starting with his nose."

"Why are you starting with his nose?" asked Sam.

"Marcel!"

"Okay, stop, I'll tell you where to get the bloody Galahads. They're in a shipping container in the P&O depot. Container 347. It's next to a blue Kaye's Limited container. There's a lock on it and the code is forty-seven, fifty-seven, twenty-two, Once inside, there's a final lock. Its code is 1941."

Jakub eyed him carefully and without looking away, he told

his brother to release Vogt. The Interpol agent fell to the floor and stayed still.

"How do I know you're telling me the truth?"

"You don't, but I think Vogt looks better with his nose intact."

The two brothers locked eyes before Jakub looked at Franssen. "What do you think?"

Franssen seemed nervous. "I don't know, but it sounds very specific. Perhaps keep them locked back in there until we can check it out. If he's lying, let Marcel practise his sculpting."

Jakub scratched at what remained of his receding hairline. "Mr Taylor, if you are lying, you will regret it. I would say 'live to regret it', but that's not quite correct."

Vogt groaned from the floor. "Fuck me, and they say we Germans have no sense of humour."

Jakub had finally lost his patience and told the four guards to take them back to their makeshift cell. As he was pulled up, Sam grabbed one of the water bottles before allowing himself to be dragged away. Vogt had to be picked up by his minders.

The guards threw Vogt back to the ground before leaving the pair of them amongst the piles of boxes. Sam knelt beside the fallen Vogt and gently turned him over.

"I think that went well," the small German groaned.

"They do seem a nice group."

Vogt smiled through the pain and Sam helped him crawl to the nearest wall. Sitting him upright, Sam studied the smaller man. The beating had left his face covered in cuts and bruising, the nose broken.

Taking hold of the bleeding hand, he muttered, "Let me have a look at this for you."

The wound looked bad, far worse than anything Sam could fix. "I'm going to try to clean it, then bind you up. It's going to hurt, though."

Vogt grunted an inaudible reply.

Sam found his discarded coat with its missing sleeve. Ripping the remaining sleeve clean off, he went back to Vogt.

The hand was still dripping blood, which was soaking into Vogt's lap. Taking the hand back, Sam slowly poured water from the bottle.

Vogt hissed in pain.

"Sorry, but it's the best I can do right now."

"I know, just get on with it."

Sam used the main body of the coat to dry the hand, before wrapping the sleeve tightly round the open palm.

"There you go, a boxing glove for your next round." Sam wound the final knot tightly around the wound.

"Thanks, I think."

"What about everything else? Anything I can help with?"

Vogt shook his head. "I don't think anything's broken, apart from the nose, but he really did me over."

"I know. I'm sorry about that."

"Don't be, it's not your fault. The man's an animal."

"They're all pieces of shit."

Sam sat down next to Vogt, leaning against the wall facing the doorway.

"Think you'll be able to walk?"

"Ha! Planning an escape?"

"We may have to. When they find out we lied to them, they'll be back in to talk to us again and I don't think they'll be as patient as last time."

Vogt rubbed his cheeks. "I don't think I can. You'll have to leave me."

"I'm not leaving you, Vogt. We'll think of something."

The two sat in silence, both recovering in different ways from their interrogation. Sam thought about the two Dudkas, considering everything they had said and not said. He wondered who the unseen people that were actually pulling the strings could be. There was always a bigger fish in the world of crime. Sam shivered as he remembered the destructive force of Marcel as he beat the helpless Vogt.

"How far away is the P&O freight depot?" Sam asked Vogt.

"I don't know. I don't even know where we are. We could be right next to it."

Sam swore. The thought of the vengeful Dudkas was not pleasant.

"Natasja will look after the rockets."

"She will?"

Vogt turned his head, wincing in pain. "She will, she won't let them beat her."

"I hope you're right."

"She reminds me of someone I once met when I was working on the refugee smuggling case." Vogt leant back against the wall, a warm smile growing on his face. Sam waited for him to continue. "There was this little girl, she'd lost all her family either back home or during the sea crossing. But every time something happened, she survived. She survived to fight another day. It was almost as if that very will not to let it beat her drove her on."

"Where is she now?"

"Berlin, I believe. She's been adopted by a nice family. Last time I saw her, she was just about to leave the orphanage." Vogt smiled at the memory, but then stopped. "That was a bad case. I saw things there that no one should see."

"The traffickers?"

"Yes, I once found a house so full of refugees that they had to sleep on top of each other. There was just the one overflowing toilet to service countless families and that was in supposedly modern-day Europe. These people, they were just cattle to those in charge. They were hunted by gangs so inhumane that any sense of empathy was lost in the hunt for money."

"What did they do? Just traffic people into different countries?"

"If only. Once they got them into whichever country they chose, not the victim that is, but the traffickers, they made sure that the refugees never saw any government or asylum facility. Those poor bastards were locked away in sweatshops, slave labour factories and of course, the sex trade. You've seen all the videos and photos of the boats hitting Europe's southern shores? Greece, Italy, Spain, all of them. These bastards would be waiting for the boats to arrive, the ones the authorities didn't catch mid-voyage. Then straight into lorries and gone. Humans just vanished into a network of thieves and crooks."

"What happened?"

"We hunted them, followed the pipelines, broke the dealers. All the way to the top. I'm not ashamed to say many of those we came across did not make it to any sort of trial."

Sam looked on as Vogt stared down, a grim smile of satisfaction etched on his face.

"I only wish I remembered the faces of those we saved. Of the children we gave hope to. But all I can see every time I have nightmares are the faces of the men we hunted. The fact that they were the same as you and me and yet could do such things."

"But that's the thing, Vogt, they are not like you and me."

"No," Vogt interrupted. "They are *exactly* like you and me. That's the thing, Sam. Yes, we arrested the grunts, those people we'd call on the fringe of our so-called society. But we also found those people we would call respectable. The haulage firm director, the landlords providing the safehouses, the goddamn respectable businessman at the head of it all. With the fancy house, public image and of course, the beautiful family back home."

"What happened?" asked Sam, already guessing the answer.

"He's dead."

Sam eyed him suspiciously.

"Don't look at me like that; it wasn't me. I wish it had been. No, he hung himself in his cell. Couldn't face up to his actions."

Sam thought of the times he'd seen the world's inequalities. "But that's why there's men like us, Vogt. We get to right these wrongs."

"Ha, spare me, Sam. For every one we stop, there's three more we miss. It's never-ending. We're just crusaders fighting against the tide." He winced as he tried to move position.

"Stay still and rest up a little bit," Sam instructed.

Sam thought about what he had just heard. He agreed about the hopelessness of it all. Someone else would always replace a missing link in the chain. But he now understood a bit more about Vogt's own decisions about risking the Galahads to break the Nile. Not to the extent that he actually agreed with the Interpol agent's final decision. But he did have some sympathy for him.

"I wonder who told them that we'd not shared the information about Broad's capture with the Amsterdam police?" he asked.

"Probably the same person who's been working for them the entire time."

"Then we can finally agree it's not Bos."

Vogt eyed Sam carefully, not wanting to bring up the old argument. "Why?"

"They killed Bos last night. That means they know he wasn't involved in Broad's capture. Surely they'd have wanted their mole more than ever at this moment. What's the point of having one if they can't get the one piece of information they need?"

"Okay, I agree with you about Bos. For what it's worth, I agreed with you when we saw the body. He fought his killer. Unlike De Klerk, he was clearly on our side. I'm sorry."

"Don't worry about it. We'll find whoever it really is. Although you were a dick for letting me believe it was Corsel."

Vogt laughed properly for the first time since his beating, the action making him wince. "So Natasja told you the truth?"

"Don't you mean Dominque?"

"You're a resourceful man, Sam Taylor, I'll give you that. But I'm not sorry about Corsel. You needed to find the answer in your own way. Do you feel any differently about the girl now you know?"

"No," Sam answered truthfully. "She was hardly a saint beforehand. At least now I know she was just in the family business."

Vogt chuckled. "He was a good man, was Wever."

"When he wasn't selling guns."

"He was caught up in something bigger than himself. But I

mean it, he was a good man to Natasja. He loved her a great deal. You'd have liked him, a rogue who had an English sense of humour."

"Not sure if that's a compliment."

Sam stretched his arms, trying to make the awkwardness of his next words less difficult.

"Vogt, I'm sorry for what I said last night."

"Don't worry about it, forget it. Water under the bridge."

"I mean it."

"Just get me a good Cuban cigar when I'm out of here and then we're good."

Minutes passed and both began to wonder when the door would open again. Both knew the next time they saw Marcel Dudka, nothing good could come of it. Sam just hoped he would have a chance to give something back to either of the Dudkas.

A noise broke through the walls to the outside office. It sounded like a door being thrown open.

"Marcel's back," Vogt commented sourly.

"And he doesn't sound happy. Stay there. When it opens, I'll rush the door."

"You won't get near him, Sam. They'll just shoot you down."

"I have to try something."

They heard the door-handle begin to twist. Sam tensed himself, ready to pounce on the first person to enter. He hoped that it would be an out-of-control Marcel. That would give him the opportunity he needed. Instead, Hans Franssen stepped into the room. Sam began to move forward and punched Franssen square in the face. Anger pulsed through his veins as he twisted round to drive at whoever came through the door next. At the same time, Vogt could be heard desperately shouting, "Sam, no!"

THIRTY-FOUR

WEVER WOULD HAVE LAUGHED at her and called her out for having such feelings towards Sam. He had felt love, had even loved her. But he always told Natasja to guard against such feelings, to beware of them. Yet here she was, thinking about a man she knew would not stay. She had known the moment she had met him that Sam Taylor was not a man to stay in one place.

Time passed and she began to wonder what Vogt would have them doing. The murder of Johannes Bos had complicated matters, that much was for sure. She knew he'd still want to try for the meeting at the Rijksmuseum café. But surely even he would agree to recovering the Galahads now.

Natasja decided she needed to stretch her legs. Leaving the Skoda, she wandered over to the main street. A café was open for business across the road and she ran over to grab a coffee to warm her against the rain. It was as she was leaving, coffee in hand, that she spotted Sam and Vogt making their way from the canal boat. A tram bell rang in the distance as she dodged traffic to return to the side road.

Watching the pair of them, an unexpected movement caught her eye. She thought Sam must have tripped, until she saw another of the men make for Vogt. Dropping the coffee, she began to run. After only a few paces she stopped as she saw a van pull up alongside the group. For a moment, she thought Sam was going to be able to break through when she saw him stop, freeze and collapse. Arms from the van reached out and caught the lifeless body, carrying it inside. The unevenly matched Vogt was next to be carted away.

Natasja turned and sprinted for the Skoda. Forcing the gear stick into reverse and then into drive, she slipped into the traffic, a few cars behind the van.

Watching closely, she saw one of the front windows open as several objects were thrown into the cold water alongside them. The light went from red to green and the traffic moved forward. Keeping close, she began to follow the van, falling back further in a panic when she realised the black SUV directly behind her was part of the ambush team.

The van left the city centre and followed one of the main roads along the Amstel. She wondered whether she should ring Corsel and try to get the van stopped, but the pull of finding the Nile's lair was too much. No. She pushed the thought out of her head. They merged onto the main ring road of the city, heading east, then anticlockwise. Still she had no idea where they could be heading. The van only began to indicate to leave the main road as they crossed the Amsterdam to Rhine canal, one of the main waterways out of the city. Whoever had taken Sam and Vogt now left the ring road for Zeeburgereiland.

Keeping as far back as she could, Natasja followed the small convoy onto the main road and then onto the Steigereiland. Turning off from the main road, the two vehicles drove down a small residential area before having to wait to cross the single-lane bridge. The van lurched forward and began the last leg of its journey, heading back under the main ring road and out to the industrial boatyards that formed a small harbour just off the main canal.

Natasja followed behind, along the tree-lined road. As the two cars in front slowed down, she counted off which of the boatyards they'd stopped at. High metal fences covered the area and she had just enough time to see the worn-out hulls of boats surrounding a single building. Driving past, she craned her neck for a final glance, seeing a sign for the *de blauwe werf,* the blue boatyard, before driving away.

After nearly a year of searching, she had finally found the source of the Nile. Now for the hard part. The drive had at least helped focus her mind as to what to do next and she pulled into the first parking spot a few hundred metres from the boatyard. First, she pulled up the maps app on her phone and reviewed the satellite imagery of the building she had just driven past. There was the single main warehouse, which faced onto the jetty. From the angle of the photo, she could see the large doorways for the lorries and vans to gain access. Part of the building looked to be offices, but most of the area was taken up by the main warehouse. About fifty ancient boats must have surrounded the place. It would at least give her cover. But first, the Galahads.

Her uncle Corsel answered the phone almost immediately. "Not like you to ring me at work, Nat."

"I'm sorry, but we have a problem and I need your help."

"Shoot, I'm all ears."

"Do you trust me?"

Corsel chuckled down the line. "Bit late to ask me that. But yes, I do, go on."

"Go to the station, round up every uniformed officer you can find. Well, everyone you know you can trust, and go to the commissioner's office. Tell him you know where there's some illegal military grade rockets belonging to the British Government. But that you can't trust anyone, so you're taking everyone."

"Everyone?"

"Yes, the more people present, the harder it is for anyone to talk or to betray you."

"I'm sure there's logic in there somewhere. What do I do then?"

"You go to the location I'm about to send you. Retrieve the rockets and take them somewhere safe. They are called Galahad rocket launchers and they could take down a jumbo jet. Once you have them, ring the British consulate and ask to speak to the repatriation office. They will be able to explain."

"So Sam's involved?"

"Of course. Do you understand what I'm asking for?"

"Yes, I think so." He repeated the orders. "I take it you don't want Hardenne or Berger involved."

"No, definitely not. But whatever you do, go now. I don't know how much time you will have."

"What do you mean?"

"You may have company, so get in and then get out."

Corsel sighed down the phone. "Okay, Natasja. Anything else?"

Natasja paused for a moment. "Yes. I need you to ask your friend to lend me his boat again."

"What, Lukas?"

"Yes, tell him to meet me as soon as he can. I'll send you my location when I get there."

"Christ, Nat, this is madness. What are you doing?"

"Just trust me." She paused, then added, "Also, when you're done, you can tell the commissioner that the headquarters of the Nile is at the *de blauwe werf*. Tell him to send everything he's got, but not until three hours from now."

"Why?"

"Because it will give me time to save Vogt and Sam."

"What?" Corsel asked, but Natasja hung up the phone.

Two hours later, she was squeezing the throttle of the small Zodiac as it bounced through the wake of the huge canal barge making its way down the Rijnkanaal. The rain had increased in the last hour and Natasja was glad of its grey cover. A cold wind blew inland from the sea and the hundred-metre-wide canal offered little protection from the elements. She guided her bouncing craft to place the huge barge between her and the destination.

A long breakwater ran alongside the marina where *de blauwe werf* was situated and as the barge made its progress past the entrance, Natasja turned the Zodiac back on itself. Slightly slowing the boat, she let go of the throttle and allowed the craft to drift inwards. Aiming for the jetty, she guided the boat to the shore. If the satellite was accurate, the jetty was shared between three different boatyards. Which hopefully meant the security would be somewhat limited.

Natasja swore as she realised the boat didn't have enough momentum to carry her the whole way in. The throttle now seemed to be even louder than before and she quickly let go. Natasja tried to look through the grey rain to see if anyone was stationed on the jetty. The Walther was ready in her lap, extra clips on her belt just in case. But as the rubber inflatable bumped into the wooden planks of the jetty, the place seemed empty. Natasja paused for a moment, scanning her surroundings. A wooden platform ran along the front of the three boatyards. *De blauwe werf* was on the right-hand side and a single locked gate was all that blocked her way in.

Stepping onto the planks, she moved forward slowly, waiting for a challenge she hadn't yet registered. Reaching the metal gate, she looked through the bars. She could see the dark outline of the warehouse in the distance. Between her and the warehouse stood at least five lines of dry-docked boats. Natasja looked down and grabbed the thick padlock that kept the gate fastened. Looking up for a final check, she almost screamed as a face appeared at the other side of the fence.

"Who the fuck are you?"

Natasja didn't even think, she raised the Walther and fired two shots. The suppressor reduced some of the noise, but it still seemed to break through the driving rain. Waiting to see if anyone had noticed, she looked down at the padlock.

"Fuck it." She fired at the padlock, instantly breaking it.

Pulling at the chain, she opened the gate and stepped through. Checking the now deceased guard, she was pleased to find an automatic rifle slung over one shoulder. At least she knew it was the right place. Sliding past each of the boats in turn, she reached the final wooden hull on its stand. Peering round the flaking paint of the boat, she studied the warehouse in front of her. Shutters covered three entrances. She guessed that there must have been at least one entrance on the left-hand side of the building for the offices. That left the rear and the right with, at minimum, one door on each. Deciding to go for the right-hand side, she began to hop between each boat. Reaching the final one, she froze as two of the shutters in front of her began to open.

Two vans drove out, their wheels screeching as the drivers sped off out of the yard, the black SUV following close behind. Whatever had caused the quick getaway, it seemed to have taken most of the yard's personnel.

Natasja now made the short sprint from the final row of boats to the warehouse. Feeling her way along the side of the building, she soon found what she was after. A simple side door gave her the access she needed. Entering the main warehouse, she found herself staring at the back of a pair of sports yachts. She'd seen too many of these to be impressed. Stolen from the Italian boatyards and transported here, each would soon be the plaything of a South American cartel.

Moving away, she slid round the side of the nearest boat. All around her were the stacks of crates marked with the various stock that made up the Nile. For a moment, it almost felt like home. Memories of times with her grandfather came flooding back. She scanned the room, trying to decide on her next move. As her eyes cast around, she noticed the black metal cages at one side of the room. Even from this distance amongst the green, blue and red jewellery boxes she saw the purple leather ones. From her hiding spot, she couldn't quite see the distinct Source of the Nile logo, but she knew it was there. The very pieces her grandfather had made all those years ago. The thought of these people having them made her stomach sick, but she pushed herself forward.

Crouching by one of the smaller crates, she tried to think what to do. Twisting behind her, she looked at the office built above the main warehouse. A set of steps led up to it, where through the glass window she could see three men were stationed. Two of them were young men she didn't know, but the third made her stomach lurch. Hans Franssen was sitting at the table. Even if those guards weren't guarding Sam and Vogt, she would enjoy a conversation with Franssen.

Natasja rose and as she did, her eye caught the wording on the crate in front of her. A box full of French-made anti-personnel mines. Considering it rude not to at least take a few with her, she paused and reached forward. Twisting the locks, she picked up three of the dark-green discs and carried them with her to the steps. Leaving them on the floor behind her, she climbed up as quietly as she could. Checking the Walther was cocked, she pushed open the door. All of the room's occupants looked up in shock as she entered. The two guards were the first to raise their guns. Natasja didn't even blink as she shot both of them.

"Oh my God, Natasja," Franssen screamed as he jumped from the table.

"Shut it, you prick. Where are they?"

Franssen nodded to a door at the back of the room.

"Where were the vans going?"

"To get the Galahads."

"Were these the only two left behind?"

Franssen nodded again, his face a mask of fear.

"Good, now open the door."

THIRTY-FIVE

SAM STARED as Natasja calmly walked into the storage room. She looked at the fallen Franssen, still recovering from Sam's blow.

"Well, I'm glad I made him go first."

Sam hugged her. "I don't think I've ever been happier to see you."

"From a man who's also found me naked in his bed before, I'm not sure how to take that."

"Enough, you two. Natasja, where are the Galahads?" Vogt called up from the floor.

They both turned and Natasja saw the broken Vogt. His face was a mess of blood and bruising, and his hand wound had already bled through Sam's coat.

"Jesus, Karl. What have they done to you?"

It was the first time Sam had heard anyone call Vogt by his first name.

"I'll mend, but where are the rockets?"

"Safe with Corsel and half the Amsterdam police force. He rang me to say they had them."

"Thank God." Vogt sighed. "Now please get me out of here."

Sam looked at her. "Where are the rest of the guards?"

"I don't know; he says they were all that's left." She indicated the fallen Franssen, who was now stirring. "Where were they all heading?"

"I told them to head to the depot, but gave them the wrong container number."

"That was not the smartest move."

"What, why?"

She looked at him. "These guys have people everywhere. One phone call could tell them the police have arrived and that the rockets have already gone. They could be on their way back at any moment."

"Shit, come on then, let's go. Suppose you have an escape plan?"

"I always do."

"Vogt's not going to be able to walk, so I'll carry him." Sam paused to look at Vogt for his approval. Vogt gave a curt nod. "What about him?" Sam asked, indicating Franssen.

"He's coming with us," Vogt told them, and no one objected.

Vogt placed his arm around Sam's neck and groaned as he was hoisted up.

Natasja jabbed at Franssen, forcing him to his feet. The older man looked distinctly shaken. He blinked profusely as he looked to each of them in turn. For a moment, he looked as if he might be about to say something, but gave up.

Leaving the storage room, Natasja bent down to retrieve the two guards' automatic rifles, which she slung over her shoulder.

"These are proper AR-15 assault rifles. I know the seller, nice man, lovely family."

Natasja led them through the office, Franssen limping between her and Sam. They were about halfway down the metal stairs when a loud bang came from the other side of the warehouse. The doors to the offices flew open and out came both Dudkas, surrounded by their guards. Both faces looked furious even before they had clocked the escapees.

Jakub was the first to notice. He raised a chubby finger and shouted across the warehouse. "Natasja! What have you done with my rockets?"

Natasja replied by unslinging one of the rifles and firing a quick burst over the warehouse, driving the newcomers to find cover.

"Quick, down the stairs," Sam ordered, forcing the cowering Franssen forwards.

Reaching the warehouse floor, all of them dived for cover from the hail of bullets fired by Dudka's men.

"Where's the exit?" Sam asked Natasja, still holding Vogt.

"Over there, down that aisle." She indicated towards a gap in the crates, but as Sam peered round, he was met by a stream of bullets.

"No, it's not down there." He crawled backwards and gently placed Vogt against the wall before returning to Natasja. "Give me one of those," he told her, pointing to the spare rifle.

"You know how to use a big gun like that?" she asked, as Sam checked the clip.

"Point it at the bad guy, don't close your eyes and squeeze the trigger," Sam told her, moving the firing rate to burst. The lightweight rifle felt strange in his hands. He'd not held such a weapon since being in the army. The gas-fed machinery in his hands was not designed to be in a civilian environment.

Sam slid across the floor and peered round to see movement in front of him. The sound of bullets hissed through the air around him. He fired two short squeezes of the trigger at a guard, breaking cover. Out of the corner of his eye, he saw Franssen had taken to hiding behind two large crates.

"What's the plan now, then?" he asked over the noise.

"I'm thinking on it," Natasja replied, then stopped. "Wait here."

She turned and ran back to the foot of the stairs, returning with the landmines she'd placed there earlier. "Time to put them to good use. Can you arm them?"

She threw one over to him. Sam looked at the device, a nasty weapon whose plastic trigger made it damned near impossible to detect. But one that could come in handy right now. He gently armed the first of the bombs by removing the safety pins and twisted the trigger mechanism into place.

"What do you want me to do now?" he asked her.

"Throw it at them!" she told him as she fired back.

Lying on his side, Sam attempted to slide the bomb down between the crates as if he was throwing a curling stone. It landed just short of the first set of guards making their way down the main aisle.

"Throw another one and look for Dudka."

Bemused, Sam armed the second device and attempted the same procedure, this time sending the device further down the warehouse floor. With the final one, he paused for a moment and looked to see if he could see either of the Dudkas. Spotting Jakub, he threw the final device along the floor. It came to a stop next to his hiding place.

For a moment, the firing stopped and a voice spoke out in Polish, causing the guards around them to laugh.

Then the same voice in English shouted over to them. "You know the trick with those is that you're supposed to hide them, or do you think I'll step on one for you?" Jakub Dudka taunted them.

Sam looked at Natasja. "He has a point."

She rolled her eyes at him. "Do you remember what I said when I first met you?"

"Please don't shoot?"

"No, I said I thought you had more imagination than that." As she spoke, Natasja wheeled round, took careful aim and fired at the landmine at Jakub Dudka's feet.

If Natasja had told Sam he was throwing three large explosives into an area where even more explosives were, he would not have agreed to have armed them, let alone throw them. The impact of

Natasja's rifle bullets penetrated the thin shells of the mine, causing it to explode. On its own, this would have at most only killed the elder Dudka. But this explosion triggered the two dormant mines, which then triggered whatever had been stored in the nearest crates, until a fireball expanded through the warehouse.

Sam was thrown backwards, landing underneath the metal stairs that led to the office in which they'd been kept. All around him, the shockwaves were building, pounding his eardrums. It felt as if the entire world was exploding in a vision of smoke and flame. The sound of the explosions echoed around him as the heat of the blast swept over him, even with the protection of the stairs.

Eventually, the sensations of the blast began to fade until all that was left was the realisation that he was somehow alive. Slowly, he began to uncurl his limbs from the tight embrace of fear. Looking up, he tried to make sense of the scene that was now in front of him. All around were bits of debris of what was once a fully stocked warehouse. Flames licked skywards into a huge hole in what was left of the roof. The two yachts were nothing but crushed, smouldering wrecks.

Reaching up, he used the metal stairs to drag himself to his feet. Somewhere beyond the constant ringing in his ears, he began to hear different noises. The roar of flames, the crashing of the falling roof, and the moans of the wounded. In the epicentre of the explosion, its survivors staggered around, lost in a daze. Sam remembered his friends and looked around him. His feet stepped on the broken pieces of wood, glass, and whatever else had once been whole. He tried to shout out but his throat, dry from the heat and dust, failed to work.

He looked and saw Franssen laid on the floor. His once perfect suit was covered in dust, singed by flame, his neck broken at an odd angle. Sam did not bother to check for a pulse. Where were Natasja and Vogt?

A new sound broke through the ringing in his ears and he

turned to see a figure rising in the distance. Marcel Dudka climbed to his feet and looked at the destruction all around him. Sam watched as the pale-faced murderer, now half covered in blood, studied his surroundings. He waited patiently until at last Marcel saw him, fury flashing across his green eyes.

For a moment they stood and stared at each other amidst the destruction. Behind Marcel, Sam watched as one of the guards helped carry an injured companion from the wreckage. None of them seemed interested in helping their master. Without a word, Marcel began to walk forward, drawing the long sharp knife from his waist. The metal flashed from the flames that flickered around them. Sam stood his ground and waited.

Marcel began to increase his pace and as the two men came together, he swung the knife in a vicious arch aimed right at Sam's eyes. Sam ducked and twisted, his attention fixed on the bright blade. The remaining Dudka brother tried a backswing, but found only air. Sam had moved forward, one hand aiming for the wrist holding the knife and the other for Marcel's face. Almost instantaneously, Sam caught Marcel's wrist as his enemy clasped his own. For a moment they struggled amongst the wreckage.

Sam stared into the bloodstained face, hatred firing his adrenaline. He tried to twist his way free, but Marcel clung tight. Instead, he led with a headbutt, which crushed into the Nile man's face, but seemed to have no effect. The bloody face just smiled back. Sam tried again, but it had the same effect. Now the pair of them pushed away and studied each other. The knife seemed extraordinarily bright in the smoke-filled space.

Marcel threw the knife from side to side as he moved forward again. Leaving it in his right hand, he prepared a hard straight jab. But Sam was ready for the feint. Knowing his enemy favoured his left hand, he waited. As the blow came in, Sam watched the knife almost fly into the other hand, which was already heading towards him. Stepping into the blow, Sam brought his elbow up into Marcel's face.

The blow should have broken the man's jaw, but Sam's elbow

just glanced off, leaving barely a bruise. Marcel countered with a low kick that forced Sam backwards. Sam lost his footing and fell to the ground. Landing hard, he rolled to his right, expecting Marcel to have followed up his attack. But when none came, he turned to see Natasja had joined the fight.

The Dutchwoman swung part of a broken crate at Marcel. Each swing was a vicious attempt at hurting the man who had killed her grandfather. But her anger was her downfall. Sam could only watch as Marcel waited for his opportunity and the knife slashed at her. Natasja staggered, dropped the wood, and clutched her stomach. Sam saw the blood seeping through her fingers. She fell to her knees.

Marcel, seeing his victory, moved in for the kill. Sam, now upright, once more ran forward and caught the outstretched arm as it was beginning its downward arch. Again, they struggled, both men focused on the blade. This time it was Marcel's turn to stumble as he tried to gain a foothold. Looking down, he found the small form of Vogt desperately clinging to his foot with his one good hand. With the other foot, he tried to kick the dwarf from his ankle as he tried to fight off Sam's grip.

Suddenly, Sam lost his grip on Marcel's wrist and the knife came down, cutting a deep gash down his thigh. Sam had to twist away as the upward cut also made its mark and sliced another deep gash up to his hip, jarring off the bone. Staggering, he somehow kept his footing as Marcel paused. This gave him a moment to reassess his surroundings. To his left he saw Natasja still on the floor, while directly in front, Marcel struggled to free himself from Vogt's grip. Sam breathed heavily, the pain from his leg now shooting upwards. Trying to put weight on it only caused more burning pain, making it impossible to walk on. Blood crept down his trousers, the red liquid warm on his skin.

It would be only moments before Marcel would finish Vogt. Sam took a deep breath, gritted his teeth and ran into Marcel. The combined weight of Sam's charge added to Vogt's grip on his feet and sent the Nile man tumbling to the ground. Immediately, Sam grappled with Marcel over the knife, while below them Vogt still desperately tried to hold the Pole's leg.

The knife was now hovering between the two men as each tried to twist the other's arm. Sam gritted his teeth and tried to force the blade away from his face. Instead, he found himself giving way, as the tip of the blade turned. Marcel Dudka smiled through the blood that covered his face and stained his teeth. Sam tried to source any remaining strength and pushed his hands forward. The blade paused in mid-air, both sets of hands clinging on. Out of nowhere, a third pair of hands joined the fray, then a fourth as Vogt and Natasja grabbed Sam's wrists.

Now the green eyes in front of him widened in shock, then fear, as the point of the blade began to turn inexorably downwards. The three of them pushed together and the blade found the soft skin of Marcel Dudka's neck. Within moments, the sharpened tip pierced the skin and was making its way into the sinew of his neck. None of them let up the pressure until they felt the blade grate against neck bone. Marcel spasmed once beneath them, and then fell still, the pale face having lost any of its remaining colour.

Panting, the three of them fell back amongst the wreckage of the Nile's empire. For a moment no one spoke, as they caught their breath.

"Natasja," Sam breathed heavily, "are you okay?"

He sat up to see her holding her stomach. Panic caught him and he rolled towards her.

"I'm okay, it's not deep. It barely cut through the muscle. My rock-hard abs finally paid off."

Sam breathed a sigh of relief. Somewhere, a siren could be heard in the distance. Around them, the flames that had consumed the wreckage were beginning to fade. The cold rainwater was beginning to find its way through the broken roof and more sirens were approaching, closer now so that blue light could be seen flashing against the rising smoke.

Vogt crawled towards them and climbed to his knees. The

grim face looked around him, at the criminal organisation he had hunted for so long. Then he turned his gaze to the people who had helped him achieve his goal. At Sam, as he tried to stem the blood pouring from his leg. To Natasja, still holding her stomach. Then without warning he barked out a laugh and waved his hand. "Whoever gets the most stitches is buying the drinks."

EPILOGUE

TWENTY-FOUR HOURS LATER, Sam was outside the Amsterdam commissioner's office. The featureless corridor felt a far cry from the chaotic scenes left by the explosions. The white walls were spotless in the autumnal sunlight. Sitting in the small leather chairs in the simple waiting area, Sam ran his fingers down his injured leg. The Dutch medical teams had made short work of both himself and Natasja. The stitches now holding his skin together felt itchy under their dressings. Vogt, on the other hand, had been kept in as the medical teams tried to coax his broken body back together.

A grin formed on his face as he remembered the conversation with Emma Read back in London. She had of course been very happy that Anderson's killer was no more, and that the missing Galahads were on their way back. The phone call from the Ministry of Defence had been a particular highlight. It wasn't every day she received an apology from a general. When she heard about Sam's injuries, she had sighed down the phone.

"Go on, say it," Sam prompted her.

"Two weeks, Sam, another two weeks of recovery leave, then I want you back. Don't even think about having another sick day for at least a year. And for God's sake, stop visiting Amsterdam!"

Perhaps Sam could spend some actual tourist time in the country. But before that, he had one more unpleasant task to do. The knowledge of what was to come made him cold. Yet it had to be done, so here he was waiting for the highest-ranking policing official in the city to finish up.

Only a day before, it had been in this very room that Corsel had arrived with over twenty of his fellow officers, to demand that the commissioner follow them to an unknown destination, blue lights flashing across town to secure the container. It had been a close-run race. They had learnt from one of the captured guards that the Dudkas had been on their way there before they were warned by one of their contacts near the P&O depot that their destination was already swarming with police.

Now, the smoking wreck of the Dudkas' operation was all that remained. Both Dudkas were dead. Marcel's body had been recovered, while Jakub's remains would have to be collected up.

Voices within the office could be heard starting the process of saying goodbye and Sam braced himself for what was to come. Sam stood as the office door opened and he went to greet Bos's husband. Peter was tall like Bos, but with short dark hair, cut close to his head. The tanned face looked strained and worn out, the pain of the last few days taking its toll. Sam remembered Bos telling him that Peter's family was Greek; the Mediterranean genes were clear to see.

Peter's face brightened as he saw Sam. "Hello Sam, thanks for coming."

They looked at each other for a moment before Sam reached out and gave his old friend a hug. "I'm so sorry, Peter."

"I know, Sam. Me too."

Parting, Peter gave him a quick look up and down. "Christ, you look terrible."

"You should see the other guy."

"Yes, I heard. Thank you for that."

"My pleasure."

They walked together down the corridor, pausing by an open window that looked over another of the many canals.

"How's your mum doing?"

"She won't have much longer to suffer. I'm thankful she's too far gone to understand what's happened to Johannes."

"I'm so sorry."

"Stop saying sorry, Sam. It's okay to say it's just a load of shit."

Sam smiled and patted Peter on the back. "Fair point. What're your plans for today? Anything I can help with?"

Peter eyed him. "My friend, you need to rest, not to worry about me."

Sam looked at his old friend fondly. "Bos was incredibly lucky to have had you, Peter."

Peter looked at his watch, the action making Sam conscious of his own missing watch and the surgical tape covering the sliced flesh.

"I'm sorry, Sam, I'm going to have to go. I'd offer to try to see you before you go, but with everything going on…"

"Don't mention it, Peter. Honestly, make sure you look after yourself, okay?"

Peter smiled and gave Sam a final embrace. "Oh fuck, I nearly forgot."

He reached into his pocket and pulled out his phone. "Johannes asked me to send you this if I didn't hear from him again. It was the last message he sent me. Typical that his final message was about work." He handed Sam the phone. "I'm sorry I couldn't send it earlier, but I didn't have your number."

"I wouldn't worry. My phone's at the bottom of a canal anyway."

Taking the phone, Sam tapped the screen.

Peter looked over Sam's shoulder. "Why the hell would he send you a receipt?"

The large red-brick hotel was one of Amsterdam's most impressive. The nineteenth-century hotel overlooked the Munt, where the river Amstel met with the Rokin canal, its waters alive with tourist boats buzzing along its surface. Watching from one of the large square windows, Sam looked on at the comings and goings of the city. The autumnal sun shone on the entire scene, adding a hazy tint to everything. Perhaps he was warming to the city, thought Sam, as he stretched out his legs under the table. Wincing from the sharp pain in his leg, he decided the thought was premature.

"I think I'll have a red wine this time," his dining companion announced.

He stared at the beautiful woman opposite him. The late sunshine seemed to reflect from the waters outside to cast a bronze light upon her face.

"Well, it's a gin for me. I think if we're eating in a Michelin-starred restaurant, I'll make it a double."

Ada Berger grinned at him. "Cheers to that."

The waitress came over and took their order.

"Now *this* is a good date, Mr Taylor."

"Well, I thought we had to celebrate the end of the Nile in style. I'd not seen you in the office. I thought you'd gone on holiday."

"I needed to get away, after what happened to Bos."

"Of course. It must have been hard for you."

"For all of us."

The waitress came back with a tray of drinks and the pair of them watched as she placed three glasses on the table. She handed Sam his gin, then placed the beer and champagne on the table.

Berger looked up at the waitress in confusion. "I'm sorry, I think you have the wrong order. This isn't my drink."

"No, it's mine," a female voice called out from behind her.

Berger turned in confusion, then shock, as she saw Natasja and Vogt walking across the restaurant towards them. The newcomers took the two empty chairs at the table and turned to look at Berger.

"What's this?" she asked Sam.

Reaching into his pocket, Sam pulled out a folded piece of paper. Berger took it. Seeing the printout of the CCTV screenshot, she quietly put it down.

She looked up at Sam. "How did you–"

"Get this? Seems Bos didn't trust you quite as much as you thought he did."

Her hand on the table began to tremble.

Vogt leant over and picked up the beer. "I wouldn't take it, personally, Ada. I just see it as cleaning up the trash after the party's finished."

"Sam, I didn't mean for Bos to get hurt."

"But he did, Ada, and that's on you. Now if you don't mind, we've got rather a nice dinner to have."

"And you have a ride outside waiting for you." Vogt pointed to where Corsel stood with two uniformed officers.

Berger looked from Sam, to Vogt and then to Natasja.

"Don't look at me, I'm just the other woman in all this," Natasja told her.

Slowly, Ada Berger rose from the table, the paper dropping from her trembling hands. As she reached her full height, she took a moment to compose herself. The faltering sunlight lit up her deep red hair. Her face seemed to harden as she came to accept what was happening. She turned to walk towards the waiting officers, then stopped. "It was never anything personal between us," she said, looking at Sam.

Sam shrugged. "No, you're right, it was just physical."

She said no more as she moved away from the table. They all watched as she was taken into custody, the final piece of the Nile puzzle put in place.

Natasja finally spoke as the officers left the room. "I'm just checking. You don't think me and you are anything but physical, right?"

Sam eyed her, grinning. "Christ no, I would say you're too physical for me."

"Can we just have a normal dinner without you two at it?" Vogt asked, picking up Berger's menu.

―――――

Later, as night had fallen, Sam leaned against the iron railing bridge that stood outside the hotel over the Munt. Below him, the cold waters of the city drifted past as they had done for hundreds of years. Next to him Vogt puffed at a cigar, his face still shades of blue from his beating, the nose re-broken back into position. They watched as their companion made her way over to them, the mysterious beauty who had run the police and criminal world ragged. Reaching them, she wrapped her arm round Sam's waist.

They walked along the bridge for a time, discussing the case.

"There's one thing I keep forgetting to ask you, Vogt," said Sam.

The small German looked at him, an eyebrow raised.

"The Dudkas, do you know who they were working for? Or who they were selling to?"

Vogt pulled on the cigar and then tapped the ash on a bollard. "I do, as it goes – a really bad bunch. They're based out of Paris at the moment and call themselves Le Central. Basically, a big-time operation with people everywhere and involved in anything you can think of. A real bunch of arseholes."

Sam stopped walking. "I've heard of them. They were the people behind my drugs bust in France during the summer."

"Yes, that will have been them. We've been chasing them for years. They were the ones behind the Nile takeover. I had hoped one of the Dudkas may have been more talkative."

The three of them walked on, Sam's mind now thinking of Le Central and if he would come across them again one day. Eventually, they reached the crossroads where they would have to split.

Vogt looked at them. "Have you got it?" he asked Natasja.

"Yes. The box is a bit singed from the fire, but the insides are totally fine."

"Good, then hurry up and give it to him so I can go home."

Sam looked at Natasja. "What are you two talking about?"

Natasja reached into her bag and pulled out a small green leather box, the gold Rolex lettering reflecting the streetlights. "Well, you lost your fancy smartwatch so me and Vogt felt it was a good opportunity to go back to the old-school way of things."

Sam took the gift and opened the case to see the metal watch, its black face encircled by a green surround. It was beautiful, an example of the finest Swiss watch craft.

"Natasja, Vogt, I'm sorry, I can't take this, it's too much."

"Nonsense, it didn't cost us anything. Our friends at the Nile donated it. Well, I swiped it from the evidence lock-up, along with all of Wever's old pieces for Natasja. I'm just sorry to say it only tells the time."

"It's perfect, thank you." Sam ran his thumb over the sapphire facing.

Natasja punched his arm. "It's a diving watch, which means that when the next woman shoots you then throws you into the water, it'll still be ticking at three hundred metres."

Vogt barked his loud laugh. "I'll leave you two to it. Sam, it's been a pleasure." He reached out a hand and Sam took it.

"Likewise."

"What will you do now?"

Sam looked round at the waiting Natasja and the beautiful city around them. He smiled for a moment before answering. "I think there's a converted windmill not far from here that I may stay at for a while. You know, to rest up and try the tourist life for a change."

AUTHOR'S NOTE

I'm never a fan of an author's note but wanted to take a moment to thank all of the people that made this dream become a reality. It must be rare that you can honestly say you've achieved a lifetime's ambition.

My first thank you has to go to my agent, Anna. She's the first person in the publishing world who truly believed in me and was willing to join the adventure. That feeling of having someone you've never met get excited about your work is something everyone should feel at least once. Next, to the incredible team at Bloodhound: Betsy, Fred, Tara, Hannah and especially my editor, Rachel. Thank you for welcoming me to the pack and being willing to take a chance on a new author. You have all given me an opportunity to do something I've dreamed of doing since childhood.

Next, I'd like to thank my early readers, the people who were kind enough to read the first iterations of Sam, warts and all! Alison, Robert, Kenneth, Brian, Jane (+Thomas), Mum and Dad. You will always be Sam's first readers, wherever this journey takes us.

Then, to my family. Without you I'd never have had the experiences in life I needed to create these characters. Each of you

293

has had an influence on me that words can never describe. Finally, to my girls, Kim, Ella and Megan – thank you for inspiring me every day, and of course for putting up with me.

With that there is only you left, the reader. Thank you for getting this far! I can promise you there are still plenty of villains out there across the globe still to be stopped. Sam Taylor will return.

ABOUT THE AUTHOR

Ben Baldwin is the quintessential Yorkshire man lost down south. Having grown up in the foothills of the Pennies, right in the heart of the Last of the Summer Wine country, he can now be found in Buckinghamshire. Living with his girls, his wife Kimberley, and their two children Ella and Megan.

If he's not writing, working or chasing the kids, he can be found exploring the Buckinghamshire countryside on his bike or hacking holes into it while playing golf.

A management consultant in the professional world, he would be first to admit it is only to fund their adventures in the family motorhome 'Henry.'

His journey into writing has been called 'a hobby that got out of hand' by his wife and the Sam Taylor series is his first foray into the literary world.

He can be contacted at www.ben-baldwin.co.uk.

A NOTE FROM THE PUBLISHER

We hate typos. All of our books have been rigorously edited and proofread, but sometimes mistakes do slip through. If you have spotted a typo, please do let us know and we can get it amended within hours.

info@bloodhoundbooks.com

Printed in Great Britain
by Amazon

52112369R00173